TRIPpING

TRIPpING

HEATHER WALDORF

Red Deer Press
A Fitzhenry & Whiteside Company
www.reddeerpress.com

Credits
Edited by Peter Carver
Cover image and design: Jacquie Morris & Delta Embree, Liverpool , NS
Text design by Tanya Montini
Printed and bound in Canada for Red Deer Press

Acknowledgments
Financial support provided by the Canada Council, and the Government of Canada
through the Book Publishing Industry Development Program (BPIDP).

Canada Council   Conseil des Arts
for the Arts   du Canada

Library and Archives Canada Cataloguing in Publication
Waldorf, Heather, 1966-
Tripping / Heather Waldorf.
ISBN 978-0-88995-426-7
I. Title.
PS8645.A458T75 2008   jC813'.6   C2008-903795-2
Publisher Cataloging-in-Publication Data (U.S)
Waldorf, Heather.
Tripping / Heather Waldorf.
[196] p. : cm.
Summary: Escaping a dull summer Rainey Williamson joins a school-sponsored eight-week
road trip across Canada. Up for the challenge Rainey who has worn an artificial leg since birth,
discovers that her long estranged mother is alive and well in British Columbia,
directly on the road trip route, and wants to see her.
ISBN: 978-0-88995-426-7 (pbk.)
1. Mothers and daughters – Juvenile fiction. 2. Canada – Juvenile fiction. I. Title.
[Fic] dc22   PZ7.W3536Tr 2008

To PG, for making it to
French Beach and back, too.

A million thanks to Peter and the other fine folks at Red Deer Press for going out on a limb with this one.

We find that after years of struggle
we do not take a trip; a trip takes us.

– John Steinbeck

CHAPTER ONE

The night before I embarked on my "Wild West Summer," I split up with Carlos Aroca. Of course, he didn't know about the breakup any more than he knew we were once a hot item. Sad but true, our torrid six-month romance had been just a figment of my imagination. An optimistic delusion. A lavish dinner-for-one buffet, satisfying my appetite for adventure and craving for a little affection.

In my mind—which would have been put to better use doing crosswords—Carlos and I had taken long hikes along Toronto's windy lakeshore. Joined the Parks Department's spring rafting trip. Made out like porn stars at the... well, never mind. The reality is that Carlos was just a guy I worked with at Pineview Children's Center on Thursday afternoons and Saturday mornings last spring. I taught crafts and pottery to six- and seven-year-olds. He coached the peewee swim team. I'd run into him at the pop machine at breaks and we'd chat, mostly about our crazy/funny/obnoxious charges. I was new in town, and Carlos was the first person to take the time to learn my name, ask about my hometown, and crack a few jokes.

He's flirting with you, I convinced myself. Maybe city life wouldn't be so bad after all.

Ha.

Here's some advice for any of you foolish enough to find yourself—like me—paddling solo through the Tunnel of Unrequited Love: Don't ever base an entire relationship on a shared workplace and a mutual addiction to 7UP.

"Rainey, are you packed?"

Later that same night, Lynda, my stepmother, poked her wavy red-haired head into the living room and caught me snuggling on the couch with Simon, the best-looking guy I know. Simon's unrestrained affection for me never wavers, making him the perfect male companion. He's a Golden Retriever—a clumsy, fun-loving, eighty-five-pound lap dog—and I'd surely miss his bad breath and sloppy wet kisses when I left for the West Coast in the morning.

"Rainey?" Lynda repeated, her entire willowy six-foot-one now present and accounted for.

Rainey was my grandmother's maiden name. Dolores Rainey. She died before I was born. My father, Greg, wanted to honor his mother by giving me her name, but my mother, Sara, in a short-lived moment of concern about my future, argued that naming a baby "Dolores" was fringing on child abuse. Had she never considered before settling on "Rainey" that, despite the "e," I'd be teased with every precipitation-related quip under the sun—no pun intended? "How's the weather, Rainey?" I've been asked every cloudy day since kindergarten.

I guess, when you consider all the other things I've been teased about, my name is small potatoes.

"Earth to Rainey?"

Back to Lynda. It was ten-thirty that Thursday evening, but she was just leaving for work. Lynda is an obstetrician. Getting called to the hospital at odd hours was the norm.

"I'm expecting some complications tonight," she said apologetically.

"Too bad babies can't be delivered by FedEx."

Lynda tossed her head back and laughed loudly, a *snort-snort-snort* more suited to some fat old prize pig. She had the annoying habit of mistaking my sarcasm for humor. "I probably won't make it home by morning to see you off," she added.

"No matter," I said, kneading Simon's floppy, silky-smooth ears. "Greg will drive me to the bus." My father is a computer consultant. He works mostly from home and is used to bending his schedule to drive me places. What choice did he have? Greg had been a single father from the time I was six months old and my mother left for parts unknown, until he married Lynda last summer.

"I'll miss you, Rainey." Lynda bent down and gave me a hug. I let her, but only because I knew it would be the last time I'd have to deal with her huggy ways for at least two months. Lynda gave hugs the way my grandfather used to pass gas—enthusiastically, often, and usually without warning. But at least she wasn't a wicked storybook step-monster. Lynda knew when she married Greg that I was, despite my *not subtle* rejection of most everything about her, a love-it-or-leave-it part of the arrangement. Besides, she has a dependent, too. Simon is *her* dog, and while I guess he is officially my dad's step-pet, he was the closest thing to a sibling I'd ever had.

"If you toss me my leg, Simon and I will walk you to the car," I said, extracting myself from her grasp and pointing to the floor across the room where I'd left it.

Lynda fetched the prosthesis and passed it to me like she would a crystal vase; she knew that my new, custom-designed Flexileg—it wasn't even a whole leg, just a below-the-knee model—cost more than her used Honda Civic. Greg had even tried talking me out of taking it on my trip, terrified that it would get wrecked in some outdoor mishap. But it was the most shock-absorbing, high-performance prosthetic leg available at the time, and I didn't want to spend my summer struggling with the mechanical glitches my old mid-grade leg was famous for.

"Promise me," Greg had begged, "that you won't trudge through any mud, or wear it in any boats." I didn't doubt that if I let my Flexileg sink to the bottom of a lake he would have zero problems sinking me along with it. While most of the kids leaving on the Western Outdoor Expedition (WESTEX) trip the next morning would be worried about bringing enough sunscreen and spending money, I also had to remember a can of WD-40 to keep my metal parts from squeaking.

I popped on the leg, bounded off the couch, and raced Simon to the door. Simon won. But only by a nose. And only because his nose is longer than mine. And because I tripped over my luggage piled in the hall.

Okay, so I'm a bit of a klutz. Big deal. I've always been able to stand up for myself. On my own two feet so to speak. Just ask Derek Rossman.

When we were seven, he got mad at me when I beat him at an obstacle race in gym class. He called me "Wimpy Gimpy Girl." I promptly pulled off the simple cosmetic limb I wore at the time and bashed him over the head with it.

My elementary school had a zero tolerance policy for students brandishing weapons; I was suspended from second grade for a week. My father doled out his own punishment by taking my prosthesis away for the duration. If we went out, Greg let me use crutches, but mostly I had to crawl or hop around the house on one foot. I couldn't ride my bike or run around outdoors. Instead of my usual bedtime stories, I got lectures on how my artificial leg was not a toy or instrument of war, and suggestions about dealing with future conflict situations using what Greg called "compassionate verbal strategies."

The day I was allowed back in school, I took my prosthesis off for show-and-tell and let everyone gawk at my stump. I passed the leg around the class and invited questions.

Jenira Kennedy spit her soggy braid out of her mouth long enough to ask, "Why is your leg like that?"

"I was born this way," I said. "It's called 'amniotic band syndrome.'" Mrs. Norris seemed impressed that I could pronounce such a long and important-sounding word, so I spelled it for her, too. She added it to our second-grade vocab list. *Take that, gifted class down the hall,* I thought.

"Does the leg hurt?" Mark Freeberg asked.

"Not unless it doesn't fit right." *Or unless I bash someone with it,* I giggled to myself.

Jimmy McGregor, whose father was a local bank manager, asked, "How much did it cost?"

"Mega-bucks. As much as a house," I said, which was a lie, but not as much of one as you might think.

When the recess bell rang, I slipped the leg back on and skipped over to a sheepish-looking Derek Rossman. I recited what Greg had told *me*: that just because my name was Rainey was no reason for me to have a stormy temper. I apologized for clobbering him, for making him cry, and for the three stitches in his forehead. I added that in the future it would be best for him not to mess with a partially bionic woman. Derek asked if he could call me "Robo-chick" instead. I told him "Rainey" would do just fine. Eight years later, he became my first boyfriend.

Despite many rants beginning and ending with "over my dead body," I'd become a city girl the summer I turned sixteen. There'd been no talking Greg out of packing us up and moving us from small-town Mollglen in eastern Ontario to Toronto to be with Dr. Lynda Hillcrest, a woman he'd met at—I'm so embarrassed to admit this—a *Star Trek* convention. Seeing my father smitten by anything that didn't involve computers—or *Star Trek*—was something I'd never get used to. "What is it about Lynda that makes her worth uprooting your life—*and mine*—for?" I'd demanded to know.

Greg just grinned like a dopey, lovesick goat and said it was simply a case of Lynda being "compatible software."

"She certainly has your hard drive purring," I'd muttered before stomping down the hall to my bedroom. And believe me, no one can STOMP quite like a pissed-off teenage girl with an artificial leg.

Those first few months in the city, I could have written an alphabet book about all the things I hated about Toronto: A was for aromatic—*not!*—air pollution; B was for broken-down buses; C was for the crowds of coyotes that lived just down the street in High Park... and so on.

Pissed off at Lynda, *and* my father, *and* Derek—the jerk broke up with me before I could even *suggest* making a go at long-distance dating—and too small-town naïve to even know *how* to get into shoplifting, or the drug-laced party scene, or whatever else Toronto kids did to blow off steam, I filled my new city life with seemingly constructive distractions: art lessons, intramural sports, applying for the WESTEX trip, the part-time job at Pineview Children's Center.

And Carlos.

I had no idea what I was getting myself into.

CHAPTER TWO

I hooked Simon's leash to his collar and followed Lynda down the short driveway to her Civic. Her plates read DRSTORK, a gift from Greg last Christmas.

Lynda opened the car door, turned to me, and gave me another hug, quicker than the first but with a rib-cracking squeeze, one that meant business. When she let go, I was half-expecting her to launch into a parent-like spiel about wearing enough sunscreen, and eating enough veggies, and not wasting all my spending money the first week. But all she said was, "Have a fun summer, Rainey."

I stepped back so Lynda could get into her car. "You, too," I replied quickly, not meaning it. I knew all about the "fun" summer she and Greg were planning while I was away. It was no secret that Lynda was trying to get pregnant—she talked about sex the way other people talked about the weather—despite my suggesting to Greg that any child of theirs might be born with Spock ears, the biological consequence of their dominant *Star Trek* genes.

(He seemed rather pleased at the thought. Figures.)

Lynda shut the door and turned the ignition key in one smooth move. She powered down the window. "Almost forgot. I left a package on your bed, Rainey. Just some extras I picked up at the drugstore this afternoon. And I made cookies for the ride tomorrow—the oatmeal butterscotch-chip ones you like."

Lynda, Lynda, Lynda. She was so nice to me all the time it made me want to puke. Had she forgotten the way I'd thrown Greg's "compassionate verbal strategies" to the wind when I learned that she and my father were getting married? Loudly, and with plenty of expletives, I'd blamed her for everything. For my dad's frequent weekend absences during the months they were long-distance dating. For my lousy algebra mark the spring they got engaged. For my breakup with Derek a week before the wedding. Even for the bad weather on that sad summer day when I was forced to say goodbye to my old house, my familiar school, and my best friend Jemma. All so *Lynda*—in cahoots with my father—could U-Haul my life to the city.

I never considered that Lynda might bring any positive changes to my life. But, damn, those oatmeal butterscotch-chip cookies. Greg and I ate mostly take-out pizza and frozen toss-in-the-oven dinners before Lynda breezed into our lives—and our kitchen—stocking our cupboards and refrigerator with "wholesome ingredients," waving her magic spatula/ladle/mixing spoon, and presto... casseroles, soups, salads, desserts to drool over.

On weekend mornings, when she wasn't at the hospital, Lynda made huge brunches: fruit-smothered waffles, exotic omelets, nutty muffins, fresh-squeezed juice. She even grew veggies and spices year-round in a little greenhouse behind the garage. Despite my busy life and athletic tendencies, I figured it was only a matter of time before Lynda's more-addictive-than-heroin "chocolate orgasm" brownies set up shop on my hips.

With a final wave, Lynda set off down the road to deliver a baby, and Simon and I started slowly up the sidewalk—me lost in thought, and Simon taking time to sniff the fire hydrants and tree trunks along the block. It was only June, but the Toronto air was muggy, the night sky covered in a gray haze. I couldn't wait to breathe clean air again, to count the stars at night.

"Will you miss me this summer?" I asked Simon as we turned left at the corner. He turned his big brown eyes up at me and flashed me his goofy dog grin. His tongue flopped out the side of his mouth. I scratched behind his ears and slipped him a mini-Milkbone from my pocket. "I wish I could take you on the WESTEX trip with me."

The WESTEX program was an annual, school-sponsored, eight-week study/camping trip that left Toronto the third week of June each year, headed slowly west to Vancouver Island, and returned mid-August. The trip, if you could believe the hype, placed emphasis on its "cooperative living model" and "experiential approach to learning," and was worth three senior

high-school credits: Canadian History, Canadian Geography, and
Outdoor Education. Six students were selected, one each from
six high schools in west-central Toronto. Applicants had to be
at least sixteen, finished eleventh grade, and sport oodles of
what the glossy WESTEX brochure called "academic excellence
and leadership potential."

I wasn't the first choice for my school; I was, after all, the new
kid. Despite leading a successful petition for more gym time for
female sports, volunteering to paint a Multicultural Week mural on
the cafeteria wall, and a three-night stint as Rachel Lynde's under-
study in the spring production of *Anne of Green Gables,* I'd only
landed third spot on the WESTEX list. I'd already resigned myself
to spending the long, smoggy summer making wire bracelets
and pinecone mobiles with the kids at Pineview, when I found
out that WESTEX's *first* choice—student council vice president,
drummer, gymnast, and winner of the provincial math
Olympics—accepted a last-minute opportunity to go to Europe
with her grandparents. Her runner-up—captain of the varsity
soccer team, president of the senior chess club, *and* a part-time
underwear model—bailed three days later when he was offered a
big-bucks summer job at Lakeside Yacht Club.

When Greg found out I'd bucked the odds and was selected
to join WESTEX, he gushed that it was a great opportunity, a
chance for me to explore the country, to meet new friends, and
to "snap out of my funk," whatever the hell he meant by that.

He was less enthusiastic about the fee, which he coughed up like a hairball, but agreed that it sounded like a good investment. He also seemed unusually interested in the British Columbia component of the trip. Where we'd be staying. For how long. At the time, I assumed his curiosity was fueled by some personal desire to learn more about a province he'd never visited.

But you know what they say about making assumptions.

CHAPTER THREE

When Simon and I wandered home, Greg was pulling up to the curb in his Batmobile. My father's old black Chevy was rigged with as much electronic equipment as a space shuttle. When I'd taken my driver's test, the examiner had spent so much time ogling Greg's high-tech stereo system that he didn't notice that I came within a hair of knocking down a stop sign. For better or worse, I passed with flying colors.

"Lynda's at the hospital?" he asked, noticing her car wasn't in its usual spot. Greg *always* asked, even though he should have been used to Lynda's late night disappearances by now. It's not like she was my vanishing—no, *vanished*—mother. Case in point: Lynda always came back. At least, so far.

Simon and I trailed him into the house. "How was your game?" I asked. Greg had taken up squash the previous month. Lynda had given him a year-long YMCA membership as a birthday present.

"Maybe she'll get you a hair transplant *next year*," I'd giggled at the time. My father wasn't at all sensitive about the paunch he'd grown since discovering the joys of Lynda's cooking: even back in Mollglen, he'd talked about wanting to work out more. He was, however, horrified that his once-thick sandy hair had started receding faster than the polar ice cap.

Frowning, Greg tossed his gym bag in the closet. "Squash isn't my thing. Maybe I'll try the running track next time."

"Maybe aqua-fit is more your thing," I giggled.

Greg mussed my hair, then trudged off to the kitchen to grab a consolation beer. Simon and I bounded off up the stairs to my third-floor lair to double-check that I hadn't forgotten to pack something important.

Home Bittersweet Home, I thought as I rounded the final landing. The three-story Victorian in Bloor West Village had been in Lynda's family since before World War II. She and Greg bought it from her parents before the wedding and had it remodeled top to toe. My step-grandparents were retired English professors. Claiming they'd seen enough slushy Toronto winters and university alumni dinners to last three lifetimes, they packed up and moved to a retirement ranch in Texas a week after Greg and Lynda tied the knot.

I was so pissed when Lynda and Greg "assigned" me the attic bedroom. Lynda seemed to think I'd be thrilled and honored— NOT!—about occupying the room she'd loved as a teenager.

"Are there spiders in that attic?" I'd demanded to know on

move-in day. "*Bats?*" Greg and I had lived in a bungalow back in Mollglen. My experience with attic rooms was limited to horror stories I'd read about or seen on TV. I stared skeptically up the stairs.

"The ghosts pretty much keep them away," Lynda laughed. Wasn't she a riot?

I'd persisted. "Isn't the attic where you hide relatives that you don't want anyone to know about?"

"We promise not to poison you with arsenic-laced doughnuts." Okay, so she'd read *Flowers in the Attic,* too.

I'd almost pulled out the stops. Lied about how it would be *so* difficult for me to trudge up and down all those steep stairs. But instead, with a theatrical sigh, I agreed to try it.

"That's a relief, Cinderella," Lynda said, grinning. "Because I've seen the downtown youth shelters." When provoked, Lynda gave as good as she got. Who could begrudge her that?

And I suspect she knew that no sane teenager—even a hard-hearted bitch of a step-daughter like me—could resist that spider-free/bat-free, freshly-painted attic space once they'd seen it. It had two skylights, a walk-in closet, my big bed from home, a huge desk, bookshelves galore, a TV/DVD combo, a mini-fridge stocked with Snapple, and a tiny bathroom with a fish-print shower curtain and a cupboard full of Body Shop shower gel.

If Lynda's efforts were a ploy to crack the ice between us before it became perma-frost, it worked like a charm. At least for ten minutes or so, until, winking, she confided, "I used to sneak my friends up the fire escape."

See, because of *her,* I no longer had any friends.

Now, Simon jumped on my bed and rolled belly-up for his nightly love fest. Giving his tangled underside a good scratch with one hand, I checked out the package Lynda had left for me with the other. As usual, she'd gone all out. There was waterproof sunscreen, Band-Aids, a few magazines, stamps for postcards, a thick, high-quality sketchbook and a set of professional water-color pencils and blending brushes that I knew cost at least eighty bucks and were definitely not from the drugstore (leave it to Lynda to figure out just the supplies that would be most practical for a camping trip without compromising my compulsions to blend and mix colors, and to make a special trip downtown to Curry's and pass it off like it was no big deal), spare flashlight batteries, three disposable cameras, the homemade cookies (would it hurt if I ate a few now?), gum, condoms...

SHE BOUGHT ME WHAT?

"Rainey?"

Simon and I both jumped at Greg's voice. So much for the creaky stairs serving as an early warning system. I quickly shoved everything back into the shopping bag. "Hi," I squeaked.

"Lynda buy you those?" he asked.

No point pretending it was the stamps or **sunscreen** he was talking about. I nodded, hoping I looked **sufficiently** bewildered.

"I don't know what she was thinking."

Seriously, what *had* Lynda been thinking? If she assumed Derek and I had been sleeping together back in Mollglen, she'd have assumed wrong. And Carlos... well, enough about him. Even the fire escape hadn't seen much use. The few friends from school I'd had over one day to work on a group presentation had come in the front door and never made it past the kitchen where Lynda had left her life-sized plastic "his and hers" reproductive organs out on the table. She'd been using the models to prepare for a talk she was giving at some obstetrical conference. Some families read cereal boxes or the sports page at breakfast. Greg and I got graphic lessons about sex, fertility, childbirth, and usually a whole lot more.

It was enough to give you gas.

"She was probably thinking about the twins she delivered to a fourteen-year-old last week." Greg snickered, but his wary eyes told me he wasn't quite sure what Lynda had been thinking, either. "And who knows," he added, "what effect all that fresh air might have on you? All work and no play and all that..." He plunked down on the bed next to me. Simon, feeling crowded, jumped down and padded across the room to stretch out on the bathroom tiles.

If I'd found the words, I'd have assured Greg that there would be no guys—I repeat, no guys—in the picture that summer. I planned to spend the summer a) learning about Canada, and

b) figuring out what to do with my life. Period. Because university applications needed to be submitted in the fall and I *still* didn't know what field I wanted to study. I'd seen enough physiotherapists, prosthetic engineers, and plastic reproductive organs to know that medicine wasn't my thing. Greg's high-tech obsession bored me. Listening to a picture-book illustrator that came to my school on Career Day gave me goose bumps (always good with pencils and brushes, I'd been sketching and painting as long as I could remember), but Greg was quick to stick a pin in my budding artistic ambitions. "Art is a nice hobby, Rainey," he said. "But, career-wise, it's not practical, and probably not lucrative. I'd hate to see you paint yourself into a corner." So, bottom line, I hoped that the WESTEX trip would point me to the trailhead of my practical/lucrative future. I intended to put my all into the program—to leave Toronto with a clear mind, a light heart, and definitely no boy baggage.

You know those bumper stickers? *The road to hell is paved with good intentions.* I assumed those sentiments didn't apply to the Trans-Canada.

Ha.

CHAPTER FOUR

"You seem a little out of sorts. Nervous about the trip?" Greg asked.

"I'm just tired. Last-day-of-class crazies at Pineview. Kids strung out on Sunny D and gummy worms. The usual."

It wasn't a lie. It just wasn't the whole truth. I was pretty sure that Greg didn't want to hear about my imaginary breakup with Carlos, anyway.

"You'll have plenty of time to rest once you're on the road," he assured me.

Newsflash: I spent eight weeks at Camp Wenibawabie every summer from kindergarten until the end of junior high. "Resting" on a camp bus makes you a target for everything from bubblegum in your hair to magic-marker mustaches that take weeks to fade. WESTEX wasn't going to be Camp Wenibawabie, but I knew that high-school trips had a similar level of treachery. Because we were older only meant the pranks could be more sophisticated. More humiliating. More deadly, even.

Greg took a deep breath. I waited for his traditional night-before-parting "I'll miss you" speech, as familiar, well-worn, and comfortable as an old sweat sock. So I was shocked when he said, "Rainey, I have something to tell you."

Cripes, the last time he started a conversation with "Rainey, I have something to tell you" was when he told me he was marrying Lynda and moving us to Toronto. The time before that was when he told me Grandma and Grandpa Jenkins had died in a car accident.

Anxiety etched Greg's face. It was bad news again, obviously.

When I couldn't take the suspense any longer, I groaned, "Okay, Greg, what gives?"

I'd been calling my father by his first name since I was three years old and found out he had a name besides Daddy. Some of his friends thought it was disrespectful, but Greg and I both knew he was more than your average "Daddy;" he was Captain Kirk and Mr. Mom rolled into one.

"Are you and Lynda getting divorced? Do you have cancer? I can handle it. Tell me."

He took another deep breath and blurted out, "Your mother is in Squamish."

I was prepared for anything. Anything but THAT.

The attic tilted to the left and began spinning. "*Squeamish?* Like how I feel about vomit and spiders?"

I'd heard Greg right the first time; I was just buying time. Waiting for the Tilt-a-Whirl to stop.

"*Squamish*. A town in southern B.C. About an hour north of Vancouver. According to your itinerary, one of the places you'll be staying is at Margaret Lake Park. It's down the road. Only fifteen minutes by car. From Squamish."

"So?" I blurted.

Greg frowned. "So... it's information that I thought you should have. What you do with it is up to you. You're sixteen years old, Rainey. I'm not going to force you to visit Sara if you don't want to."

"You actually think I *should?*" Greg rarely spoke about my mother, especially after Lynda came on the scene. But I knew how hard he'd tried to track Sara down—to tell her about the car accident that killed her parents, my Grandma and Grandpa Jenkins—three years ago. He'd been unsuccessful.

Greg patted my hand. "I thought maybe you'd like to."

I yanked my hand back. "How long have you known about this?" I grew up without a mother, ergo, I came to accept that I didn't have one. I knew Sara Jenkins gave birth to me, and that she was out there somewhere, but since that somewhere wasn't with me, I'd written her off. I told myself that she was like my left leg; that I couldn't miss what I'd never really had.

"Sara called me last November," Greg admitted. "She saw your Flexileg promo in a magazine at her doctor's office."

Last fall, the manufacturers of my swanky new prosthesis did a series of print ads showing teenage amputees from across the country doing everything from jazz dancing to downhill skiing. My ad featured me in-line skating at High Park. It was published in a bunch of health journals and medical supply catalogues.

"*You've known since November!*" I shrieked. The leftover noodles I'd eaten for dinner started slithering around in my intestines. "Why didn't... wait a minute... how did she even know it was me?" Okay, so the prosthesis was a tip-off, but I was hardly the only female single-leg amputee in Canada. The last time Sara had seen me, I weighed sixteen pounds, had sparse blonde ringlets on my head, no teeth, and saggy Pampers.

"You look like her, Rainey. You know that."

My father was right; I'd seen the photos. I glanced over at my reflection in the mirror above my dresser. As a teenager, Sara was as tall as me (I used to think I *towered* at five foot nine until I met Lynda for the first time). And like me, she'd had light brown eyes, a ski-jump nose, and thick, shoulder-length hair the dull beige of dirty dishwater. (Except I was a honey blonde that spring. Greg and Lynda thought it was hilarious that I dyed my mop to match Simon's, even taking a swatch of his fur to the pharmacy with me to match the shade as closely as possible. Call me crazy, but face it, girls, that dog had hair that would put Goldilocks to shame. Greg jokingly—or not—suggested I enter one of those "I look like my dog" photo contests.) Bottom line, I wasn't cover-girl gorgeous, not by a long shot, but I was okay-looking. Nothing to puke at. At least from the knees up.

"How did Sara know we moved to Toronto?" I asked.

"She Googled me and found my business phone number on line."

"Just like that?"

"People who aren't actually trying to *hide* are remarkably easy to track down these days."

It took Sara maybe fifteen minutes to locate my father? This after Greg, a flipping computer genius, had spent fifteen *years* trying to find my mother.

"Sara asked about your grandparents. I told her about the accident," he added.

Greg's own father died when he was a toddler. His mother passed away when he was eighteen, just a few weeks shy of his high school graduation. My father was left with no living relatives and ownership of the house he'd grown up in. When the Jenkins family moved in next door a few months later, bringing with them their seventeen-year-old daughter, Sara, Greg fell in love with all three of them.

Grandma and Grandpa Jenkins babysat me during the day when I was small so Greg could get his business off the ground. They went to all my elementary school concerts. They took me to Florida each March break. And they died on a patch of black ice on the 401 when I was thirteen, never knowing what had happened to my mother. After years of attempts to track Sara down failed, they assumed she'd changed her name. Or left the country. Or both.

Or... worse.

"*I can't believe you've known since last November!*" I screeched again. "Why didn't you *tell* me last November?!"

Greg eyed me warily. "I wanted to wait until you were more settled here. You already had a full plate adjusting to the move, Lynda, a new school, a part-time job. But, well... now this trip has come up."

I pounded my fist into the duvet cover. "You could have at least told me *before* I accepted the WESTEX offer!"

Greg didn't respond. He didn't need to. I knew why he'd put off telling me. He was afraid I'd freak out and quit the trip. Now it was too late. If I backed out now without a medical certificate, he wouldn't get his money back.

"Sara wants to meet you," he said slowly.

I threw myself back on the bed and talked to the ceiling. "We've met. She was present at my birth, was she not?"

"You know what I mean, Rainey. She hasn't seen you since you were a baby."

I sat back up quickly. "Whose damn fault is that?"

"Hers," Greg said, picking at a hang nail. "All hers. There's no debating that. But it's been sixteen years." He looked up at me and frowned. "Don't glare at me like that, Rainey; I'm not defending her. I'll *never* forget what she put me and your grand-parents through, not to mention depriving you of a mother growing up. But I'm relieved to know Sara's alive and okay. I'm not angry with her anymore."

Well, that made one of us. "She left because of me, didn't she?"

It was Greg's turn to throw himself back on the bed in frustration. "Rainey... we've been through this a million times..."

Yeah, yeah. So Greg always claimed he didn't know why Sara left that cold January morning when I was six months old, taking nothing with her but a backpack full of clothes and the three hundred and twelve dollar emergency fund that Greg kept in a coffee can in the freezer. She'd left a note, which Greg had kept, and which I found by accident one day in seventh grade when I was snooping through his desk for a paperclip. It said, "*I won't be back. Please don't follow me. I just can't take it anymore.*" "It" was anybody's guess.

My palms were cold and clammy despite the dry attic heat. "Didn't you even ask her?"

"No," Greg replied flatly. "I didn't."

"Well, why does she want to meet me now? After all this time?"

"She wants to get to know you, I imagine." Greg propped himself up on one elbow. "Maybe seeing that Flexileg ad made her realize how long it's been. How much she gave up."

"Whatever." So what if Sara was finally ready to make peace with her past; was I ready to make peace with *mine?* The plan was to spend the summer deciding my *future.* Greg was right when he said I already had enough complications in my life.

He dug into his back pocket and handed me a scrap of paper. An unfamiliar address and phone number were scrawled across the top in Greg's familiar script.

"Sara runs a used bookstore and craft boutique," he said. "I called her last night—"

"You what!"

"—and told her you'd be in B.C. towards the end of July. She seemed very excited at the prospect of seeing you, Rainey—"

"How could you!"

"—if you give her a call when you get to Margaret Lake Park, maybe you could set up a time to... visit."

"And if I don't?"

Greg sighed. "Then she'll leave you be."

"She won't stalk me?"

"No. It's completely up to *you* whether or not to visit Sara. She acknowledges that you don't know her and have no reason to respect her past actions. If you don't feel ready to see her this summer, you can always try again when you're older. Sara's promised to keep me posted on changes of address."

Like my mother's promises meant anything to me? I stared at the paper and blinked hard. "Greg, what's she been doing all these years? I mean, *besides* running a bookstore?"

"I don't know, Rainey. I didn't ask about that either. It's not that I don't care, but... I have a new life now. That's the sort of thing you could ask her about yourself if you were curious."

Not *that* curious. "Greg? What did you see in Sara?"

"She was beautiful," Greg replied, his lips twitching like he was trying to hold back a grin—or a sob. He sat up and massaged the kinks out of his elbow. "And I was lonely."

"That's *all?*"

"I was eighteen years old, Rainey. What else mattered?" Greg shrugged and started picking at a hole in his sock like his life depended on it. Every once in a while I realized just how badly she'd hurt him, my so-called mother. So I tried for a little levity. "Do you remember the time when I thought Sara was from outer space?"

Greg flicked a few strands of sock fluff onto the attic floor and flashed me an embarrassed grin. When I was nine, I'd overheard him tell a nosy business client who inquired about the whereabouts of my mother that I was the by-product of an x-rated alien abduction. I'd seen Greg's *Star Trek* Web site. I'd watched all Greg's old sci-fi movies: *Close Encounters of the Third Kind, Starman, Cocoon.* I should have been old enough to know better, but I let this news thrill and terrify me.

Until Greg got called to my school, this time to explain a writing assignment I'd titled, "My Mom Drives a Spaceship."

He zoned in on the paper still clenched in my fist. "So, you'll think about it?"

Like I'd be able to think about anything else now? "Sure," I mumbled. "But no promises."

"Deal." Greg draped his arm around my shoulder and gave it a squeeze before heading to the stairs. "I'll see you in the morning, Rainey. Please don't worry about this. I want you to have a wonderful summer. *Really.*"

DON'T WORRY ABOUT IT? What was he thinking? He'd had *eight months* to process that my mother, his lost love Sara, was alive and well and living the high life (high altitude life, anyway) out on the West Coast. Now, I had just a few weeks to decide whether I wanted to meet the woman who had given birth to me and had broken my father's and my grandparents' hearts.

Greg trudged down the stairs to his second-floor office. A few minutes later, the *Eagles Greatest Hits* drifted up the stairs. My father's comfort music. A sure sign he was a little more stressed about all this Sara business than he let on.

I took a long shower and then lay on my bed, staring out the skylight into the gray night as the final strains of "Desperado" mingled with Simon's peaceful snores. It was times like that when I wished I had a good friend in Toronto. Someone to confide in. Someone who could offer up objective advice. When he was awake, Simon was a good listener, but his nature was too forgiving, his view of the world too sunny. He'd never had a problem that couldn't be solved with Milkbones or a flea collar.

I briefly considered getting up to phone Jemma long distance. But my EX-best-friend and I hadn't spoken since early last September when, just two weeks after leaving Mollglen,

I called to wish her a happy birthday. Jemma had started blubbering immediately. Before ten minutes was up, she'd confessed to dating, kissing, and actually *doing it* with Derek all within four—4!—days of my moving to Toronto. Sniffing, she said they'd both been upset by my leaving. That Derek was sorry he broke up with me. That their misery had brought them together. That their love—blubber, blubber—was a sad but beautiful thing.

Once again dismissing Greg's "compassionate verbal strategies," I called Jemma nothing short of a cheap slut.

Maybe I'll send her a postcard this summer, I thought.

Ha!

Besides, I knew that even if I'd had a whole posse of friends to advise me, deciding whether or not to visit my mother was something I needed to do on my own.

CHAPTER FIVE

Greg always says that there are no true coincidences, that every-thing happens for a reason, even if those "reasons" aren't always easy, or even possible, to understand. I personally thought he lacked the heart to sum up my amputation, my mother's desertion, and a score of more typical childhood tribulations under the all-encompassing heading: *Shit Happens.*

Because what possible "reasons" might have had a hand in selecting me for the WESTEX trip? *Were* there "reasons" or was it just a fluke that Sara had seen the Flexileg ad? And what were her "reasons" for choosing *now,* when Greg had married, and I was practically an adult, to revisit her maternal instincts?

Supernatural forces are NOT conspiring to derail my summer plans, I chanted in my head as I loaded my luggage into the Batmobile the next morning.

So imagine my surprise—and *horror*—when Greg and I pulled in at the school parking lot and I got a look at the small group of students with whom I was to spend the next eight weeks.

What the hell was Carlos doing there at the WESTEX *departure spot!* It was barely seven AM; it wasn't like he could have just dropped by to watch a basketball game. Carlos wasn't even eligible to be a WESTEX participant; he'd already graduated from Saint Whoever's down on Bloor Street. He was headed to the Phys. Ed. Department at York University in September, he'd told me weeks ago, before he'd abruptly decided I was unworthy of his time and stopped talking to me.

Carlos struggled to unsnag the zipper of a gym bag. I watched him a few seconds, until he looked up and saw me. His face contorted like someone trying to swallow a pinecone. "Hey," he choked out.

"Hey, yourself," I replied back, working to breathe, forcing my attention back to the car where my father was tossing my gear out of the Batmobile's trunk onto the asphalt.

"You're traveling in *that?*" Greg asked, gesturing with his head towards a big, old, puke-green passenger van parked nearby. A group of kids I assumed were my fellow WESTEX participants were piling sleeping bags and backpacks into a small cargo trailer hitched on back.

"Beats hitchhiking," I replied, hoisting my fifty-pound backpack onto my shoulder—and almost tipping over backwards as reality gave me an ugly hip check.

THAT's why Carlos is here, I thought, inhaling sharply. Holy bleeping shit on a stick.

That twelve-seater was his. It had to be. Months ago, Carlos told me he'd bought a van from a friend. Put in a new engine. Bought new tires. Installed new seat belts. He'd used the van all spring to chauffeur the Pineview Peewee swim team to and from meets all over south-central Ontario. During our pop-machine conversations, he always described his weekend plans in terms of what he'd be doing to—or *with*—his van. He called it his "butt-ugly pride and joy." If Carlos had a girlfriend, he'd never mentioned her.

I turned to grab his attention again. I needed confirmation. "You're going to be our driver?"

"Yup."

"But... I thought... aren't *you* working at Pineview this summer?" I asked.

"Nope."

But Carlos loved working at the children's center. It was his "calling," he'd told me during one of our long-ago pop-machine chats, to be a gym teacher, a coach.

"Why aren't you working at Pineview this summer?" Carlos gave a hard tug on the stubborn gym bag zipper and cursed as it gave way, snagging his pinky.

"This came up last minute," I replied.

"Yeah. For me, too. I needed to get away for a while." And without another word to me, he slung his gym bag over his shoulder, stuck his bleeding finger in his mouth, and slunk away.

I said goodbye to Greg, transferred my luggage to the cargo trailer, and introduced myself to a few of the other kids milling around—all while keeping one ear open to a conversation Carlos had struck up a few feet away with a tall guy in a Habs jersey and an old Expos baseball cap. When Habs-dude asked Carlos how he had landed the WESTEX job, my ears perked up like a German Shepherd's.

"My older sister, Carina, went on this trip three years ago," Carlos replied. "She keeps in touch with Brooke McLean, one of the leaders. A few weeks back, the original driver broke a leg and had to back out. Carina suggested I apply as his replacement. I'm also a certified lifeguard, so the school board figures—"

"Hey, Rainey!" Greg yelled out the car window, ripping my attention away from Carlos and Habs-dude.

Why was Greg back? Please, no more last-minute revelations.

"You forgot..." He pointed a thumb over his shoulder into the back seat.

I rushed over to the car and yanked my old wooden crutches out the open rear window. They were to use if my stump got sore or irritated, or if the Flexileg got damaged or lost ("But it won't, Greg! I promise!").

I blew my father another kiss goodbye, and with a honk of the Batmobile's horn, he was gone, for good this time.

Hello, summer!

"WESTEX will look good on your teacher's college applications,"

Habs-dude was saying to Carlos now.

"But working at Pineview would have looked just as good on your applications!" I felt like yelling.

I just didn't get it. Carlos didn't even strike me as an outdoorsy guy. Certainly not one who would apply for the WESTEX job, even if it *had* come looking for him.

I needed to know what was going on.

"No, you don't," Greg would have said, if he'd known. "You only *want* to know what's going on. Focus on what you need first." Greg was always going on about wants and needs, usually at the mall when I *needed* to buy school books and what I *wanted* to buy were CDs and art supplies.

What did I need now? Easy. I *needed* to learn enough about Canada to earn my WESTEX credits. I *needed* to take a serious look at my after-graduation options. And I *needed* to figure out what to do about my mother.

I did *not* need a boyfriend. Especially not Carlos.

"Crutches?" he sneered as I wedged them into what tiny space remained in the back of the van. "Planning to sprain an ankle?"

"Spare firewood," I replied, deadpan. I was wearing long pants that morning, but Carlos would find out soon enough why I'd brought crutches. The fact that we'd spent all those cold-weather months chatting at the pop machine, and neither my prosthesis—nor my WESTEX application—had come up made me wonder how much about *him* I didn't know. If Carlos was a thousand-piece jigsaw puzzle, I had about seventeen pieces, and the rest I'd made up to suit myself.

Stupid, stupid, stupid.

It went like this: Back in March, way before WESTEX even became an option for me, a lonely summer in the city loomed large. I thought, *Rainey, why don't you try to turn those pop-machine chats with Carlos up a notch? Just a notch. A teensy, tiny notch. After all, this is a new millennium; it's not a criminal offense in Canada for a girl to ask a guy out. Maybe there's life after being dumped by Derek, the scum-sucking, best-friend-stealing loser, after all.*

So I asked Carlos out. Not on a *date,* just as a friend, to a one-day Youth in Sports symposium I'd heard about at school. I thought it sounded like something Carlos might be interested in. I figured if we spent some time together outside of work, got to know each other a little better, did lunch, I'd be able to determine if there was enough chemistry to try for more.

I repeat: Stupid, stupid, stupid.

Instead of accepting my invitation—or gracefully declining, which would have been disappointing but not devastating—Carlos got all red-faced and blustery as he stammered out that age-old, over-used *"I have to help a friend move that day"* excuse. With a mumbled "sorry" and a shrug of his shoulders, he made a fast exit.

I tried telling myself that I'd just caught Carlos at a bad

time. And for a few days afterwards—okay, I lie, until right up until my so-called "breakup" with him the previous evening— the wary optimist in me waited for a heartfelt apology from Carlos, or at least a short explanation for his weirdness. A chance to kiss and make up.

But no apology or explanation ever came. Definitely no kisses. Just more avoidance and brief nods in passing. Uncomfortable silences as we fed quarters into the vending machines. Nothing like having a heart full of romantic hopes burst apart like a swollen appendix every single day for weeks.

Being invited to join WESTEX was my big opportunity to put Carlos in particular—and boyfriends in general—aside for the greater good. To cleanse my emotional wounds, apply some psychological Polysporin, and get on with it.

But now what?

C_HAPTER SIX

Sudden downpour.

Dan Shipman, the WESTEX headmaster, herded us inside the school and stuck *Hello. My name is...* stickers on everyone, despite the fact we were only six participants, two leaders, and Carlos, who had to stay outdoors to secure a tarp over the cargo trailer.

"Did you bring this wet weather, *Rainey?*" Dan asked me when we were all seated in a circle on plastic chairs in the otherwise empty gym. His loud guffaw echoed up to the rafters.

"No, Mr. *Shipman*," I replied. "Did you bring a life raft?"

He snickered. "Please, everyone, just call me Dan."

Dan looked to be around my father's age. He was short and round with a big face, a full beard, and oval ears that stuck out from a mess of wiry dark hair. He wore a tan golf shirt and brown shorts revealing thick, hairy legs.

Habs-dude leaned over and whispered—loudly—in my ear, his breath smelling of peanut butter and jelly. "Dan the Man looks like a grizzly bear."

Dan raised a bushy eyebrow at Habs-dude. "I'll take that as a compliment," he said, then directed his attention to the full group. "Before we head out today," he started, "I just want to welcome you all and give you a chance to meet each other. As you know, my name's—"

"Yogi!" Habs-dude shouted, removing his ball cap, tossing it up into the air, and then catching it back on his head.

"—Dan. And though I've taught Canadian history and geography for many years, this is my first year with the WESTEX program. In many ways, we'll all be learning together..."

"Recipe for disaster," a black girl with a bald head remarked from across the circle. It was too soon to know if she was serious.

Time for a few icebreakers.

"If you could be any kind of animal, what would you be, and why?" Dan asked the group.

Habs-dude's name was Alain. He'd spent his first thirteen years on a farm in New Brunswick. Now, he was on break between spring hockey clinics and his first fall practice in late August. If he didn't get drafted by the NHL, he wanted to be a sports photographer. "And if I could be any animal, I'd be a bear... so I could sleep for five months of the year."

What was it with Alain and bears?

"How about you, Rainey?" Dan asked.

"I'd be a centipede," I said. "So I'd always have a spare leg to stand on." Nobody got it—yet.

Gradually, Dan's questions grew more serious. "Why did you apply for WESTEX?" he posed to the circle.

Homer, who'd moved with his parents from China to Toronto when he was an infant, a self-proclaimed "science fair geek" and future neurosurgeon, said he'd never lived anywhere but in high-rise apartment buildings and thought it was time to "get down to earth."

"What do you hope to achieve this summer?" Dan asked next.

Isabella, the youngest of eight female siblings, was an actress/singer wannabe. She "hoped" to experience Canada up close so she'd never forget her roots once she became a star. "I'm *kiiiiidding*," she said, tossing her silky, chestnut mane over her shoulder and gazing around at our decidedly unimpressed faces. But the fire in her eyes said something else, that Isabella would slit her grandmother's throat for a chance to be Hollywood's next IT-girl.

Dan moved on to the next question. A doozy. "What are your greatest fears about the program?"

It was way too soon for me to go there. Besides, just listing the things that I feared about visiting—or not visiting—my mother could take all day. So I made up some smart-assed fear of overdosing on S'mores and passed the torch to Meena, the black girl with the shaved head, an aspiring veterinarian. She frowned up at the sheets of rain pelting the gym's Plexiglas windows and said, simply, "I don't like thunderstorms."

Frank was sixteen, but looked twelve. He sported bright orange hair, was a good foot shorter than me, and skinnier than an Olsen twin. Hold up a match on fire and that was Frank. Career-wise, he was planning to make his first million selling enviro-friendly cleaning supplies. He was off to a good start; he'd earned his entire WESTEX fee selling Happy Earth rug shampoo door-to-door. When pressed about his fears, he shuddered. "My so-called friends duct-taped me to a chair last night and forced me to watch *The Blair Witch Project* on DVD. Their twisted idea of a going-away present..."

"And now you're afraid of... ?" Dan prompted.

"Everything."

Next up, Brooke, our WESTEX co-leader and resident guidance counselor, laid out the ground rules. A tank of a woman with a no-nonsense salt-and-pepper buzz cut, Brooke sported the perma-smirk of a woman who thinks she's seen it all. (And maybe she had; she'd been along on every WESTEX trip since the program started eight years ago.) Brooke spoke with a heavy east coast accent. She was originally from St. John's, she'd informed us with pride, lifting up her shirtsleeve to display a small tattoo of Newfoundland on her right shoulder. "You," she said, pointing a stubby index finger at Alain. "Call me Screech, *even once,* and you'll be on pot-scrubbing duty for the rest of the summer."

Alain laughed. "Can we call you Cod Lips instead?"

Dan guffawed. Brooke's sharp blue eyes bore into him, as cold as two icicles, then addressed the full group. "Rule Number One: Safety is our first priority. Seatbelts must be worn in the van. Life vests must be worn in all boats. During free time, you must travel in pairs or small groups. Always let Dan or myself know where you are going and for how long."

"Do we have to check off a daily BM chart, too?" Alain wondered—out loud, of course.

Brooke ignored him. "When away from our designated campground, please ensure that the cell phones you were required to bring are charged and that Dan's cell phone number is programmed into your speed dial. An adapter is available for you to charge your phones off the van battery as necessary."

"What? We can't send up smoke signals?" Homer asked.

"Don't be so sure," she replied. "There may be times, particularly once we arrive in the mountains, when your cell phones will be out of range."

"What *goooood* is technology if it can't save your ass in an emergency?" Isabella interjected, frowning at a chip in her red-painted fingernails.

"Many problems can be avoided just by acting in accordance with park safety regulations," Brooke replied. "Obey poison ivy warnings. Stick to the marked trails. Don't eat poison berries. And follow wildlife encounter guidelines to the letter, particularly those concerning bears and cougars."

"And Bigfoot?" Alain laughed.

Frank: "*NOT funny!*"

"Rule Two," she continued. "No drinking, drugs, stealing, or violence. Period. To be caught engaging in these activities will result in your immediate expulsion and the loss of your credits. There are no tuition refunds."

Dan grinned at our solemn faces. "WESTEX isn't a 'Hoods in the Woods' program, you know."

"Not yet, anyway," Homer said, shrugging good-naturedly.

Brooke ahemed. "Rule Three: Teamwork is essential. WESTEX is not a game or a competition. It's not *Survivor*. We can expel you for breaking the rules, but we *can't* vote someone out just because they are annoying or not pulling their weight. Dan and I expect you to sort interpersonal problems out amongst yourselves. We will act as mediators/arbitrators *only* if team attempts to resolve issues fail, or if the same conflicts surface repeatedly."

I thought of Greg's "compassionate verbal strategies." Maybe that was *his* care package. A summer's worth of positive conflict management techniques. Too bad I'd never had much luck with them in the past.

"Rule Four," Brooke stated. "Just as tempers will flare on occasions, so will hormones. Dan and I will not attempt to interfere with relationships which may develop along the way—so long as they do not interfere with the rigorous outdoor curriculum, academic expectations, or the effectiveness and morale of the team. With all that said, males and females must maintain separate tent arrangements at all times."

"Tents?" Frank piped up.

"Ah, who needs tents, anyway? Here's to sleeping under the stars!" Alain shouted.

Frank shook his head. "No, no. I meant... we're sleeping in *tents?* There are no... cabins?"

"And *finally*," Brooke continued, stifling a cough. "We had some problems last summer with practical jokes."

Dan leaned forward in his chair. "You guys ever tried the one where you dip a sleeping person's hand in a bowl of—"

Brooke's wicked sneer cut him off mid-sentence. Then, oddly, she burst into giggles. "I love that one."

CHAPTER S_EVEN

Ten minutes later, the rain stopped and sunlight burst through the clouds. Everyone quickly clambered into the van, eager to get the WESTEX show on the road—literally.

Surprise! The Carlos-mobile had no air conditioning. Even with the front windows down and the rear vents open wide, we were all dripping with sweat even before the van turned northbound onto Highway 400. My stump itched like crazy, but it seemed the wrong time to remove my Flexileg, so I sat tight, visualized winter, and tilted my head back to catch what little breeze blew my way.

"Unlike the early settlers who headed west in covered wagons, WESTEX heads west in an Easy-Bake Oven," Homer said, stripping off his shirt.

Isabella was sprawled beside me on the bench seat nearest the back of the van.

"Who knew we'd be traveling in the luxury of a *sauuuuuna?*" she groaned, fanning herself with the latest *Vogue*. Isabella's way of drawing out key words—a dramatic effect she'd picked from some low-rent voice coach, no doubt—was already getting on my nerves.

"At least the seats recline," I replied, ironically. Our backrest was broken. Every time Carlos drove over a bump or pothole, the back of the bench would bend back a few inches before righting itself with a loud *SNAP!* Whiplash City. When Isabella told him about it during a quick bathroom stop near Barrie, Carlos flashed her a stellar grin and said: *Hey, no problem,* he'd tighten it up over lunch.

I seethed. Why was Carlos his usual outgoing, friendly self with everyone but me? I couldn't help glaring at the back of his ball-capped head as he chatted with Brooke up front. If he could feel my negative vibes, he didn't let on.

"The driver's *cuuuuuute,*" Isabella squealed in my ear. It was so loud inside the van with the wind from the open windows, the other raucous conversations, and the old Blues Traveler CD someone had cranked up on the stereo, I wasn't worried about Carlos overhearing.

"You already have a boyfriend." Isabella had spent the previous thirty minutes telling me about her "true love," Sammy. He'd left the previous week to teach sailing at an upscale summer camp in Quebec.

"I can still look," she argued. "Besides, it's not like I want Carlos for myself. He's *sooooo* not my type."

What did Isabella know that I didn't?

"Carlos is *waaaaay* too Mr. Nice Guy," she continued. "Look at the way he laughs at Alain's dumb-ass jokes. Or the way he nods at everything Brooke says up there. Dan could tell Carlos that the *mooooon* was made of mozzarella and he'd buy in. He looks like one of those little bobble-head dashboard dogs."

Mr. Nice Guy? Well... Carlos was NICE-looking in a tall, brown-haired, blue-eyed, clear-complexioned way, but he wasn't distractingly handsome. He had a NICE buff body without the hyper-inflated chest and limbs that screamed steroids. Before he went weird on me, I thought Carlos had a NICE personality. Had it been appeasement on his part? Why would he have wanted to appease *me*? I was just a homesick kid fresh from Mollglen who'd latched onto the first NICE guy who seemed to share some of my interests.

Isabella ranted on. "Seriously. What kind of *smooooooth*-talking city boy spends the summer between high school and university chauffeuring a bunch of twelfth graders across the country on a camping trip?"

"The kind with a passenger van?" I suggested.

Isabella imitated a game-show buzzer. "*Wrooooong.* The kind who is running away from something."

"Or some*one*?"

"Or some*one*," she agreed. If that someone was me, Carlos had messed up pretty badly.

"I haven't got time for guys this summer." Maybe I needed to pick up one of those tight elastic bracelets so I could snap it hard against my wrist every time my thoughts wandered away from my Official Summer Plans. Wouldn't meeting the WESTEX objectives, making decisions about my lucrative/practical career future, *and* worrying about visiting—or not visiting—my mother, be enough "fun," as Lynda called it, for one summer?

Isabella tossed me an incredulous glance, and flipped her hair over her shoulder. Long, silky strands whipped me across the face. "I give it a week."

CHAPTER EIGHT

Our first stop was at Orillia, a town ninety minutes north of Toronto.

Carlos killed the van's engine at a municipal park by the shores of Lake Couchiching. We piled out quickly, glad to be sprung from the steambath on wheels.

"Last one in is a rotten egg salad sandwich!" Alain yelled, ripping off his T-shirt, and stripping down to his boxers. He dashed across the grass to the beach, then belly-flopped into the water. Think *Baywatch* meets *The Simpsons*.

Isabella pointed us in the direction of the female change house. "Well, *giiiiirls*, let's be civilized and get our suits on."

The small building reeked of damp cement and disinfectant. Isabella wasted no time plucking a bright pink bikini from her day pack.

"Great bathing suit, Isabella," I remarked, extracting my own boring-blue one-piece from my bag.

"Thanks. You guys can call me Izzie. *Aaaaall* my friends do."

"I can't wear pink bathing suits, Izzie," I said.

"Why's that?" Meena asked, already half into her striped green swim suit.

No point putting off the inevitable. I snapped open the legs of my warm-up pants and popped off my prosthesis. "Because I'd look like a pink flamingo."

"So cool!" Meena shrieked. "My cousin is a prosthetic engineer in Hamilton. He designs arms. I went to work with him last Career Day. Is your leg a single-axis or multi-axis? SACH or SAFE? Dynamic Response?"

Cripes, Meena knew more about artificial limbs than I did.

Izzie stared a second, then recovered quickly. Any girl whose physical imperfections made Izzie look like a movie star by comparison was Izzie's kind of friend, I imagined. "When did you, like, lose your..."

"Leg?" I said. "Before I was born. My first ultrasound was normal; I've seen the tape. By the second, a band of amniotic fiber had wrapped itself around my left leg mid-calf and severed it off."

She scrunched her nose up. "What happened to the..."

"Severed part? I'm not sure. All this happened when I was barely the size of a dill pickle. It probably came out with all the other gunk when I was born. Or," I laughed, "maybe my mother's *still* walking around with my foot in her uterus."

"That is *sooooo....*"

"Gross?" I suggested. "Yeah, I know."

The three us hurriedly finished pulling on our suits and

headed for the beachfront. Frank had already joined Alain in the water; they were racing toward a buoy about fifty meters offshore. Brooke was setting up lunch at a nearby picnic table. Homer and Dan were on the wharf, laughing with Carlos about something. They didn't notice our approach.

"Hey, lifeguard!" I shouted, popping off the Flexileg once again. Meena offered her shoulder for balance.

Carlos turned, his grin morphing into a scowl when he realized it was me.

"Catch!" I said, tossing him my leg, turning, and diving into the chilly waves in one fluid motion. With Izzie and Meena on my heels—well, *heel*—we chased after Alain and Frank.

"Hey, Charlie's Angels! Wait up!" Homer shouted, splashing as he dove in after us.

After our swim, Alain, six foot three and strong from a winter of junior hockey, took it upon himself to piggyback me to the picnic table where lunch was ready.

"Didn't your mother ever teach you not to put your feet on the table?" he chided, setting me down on the bench with a small thud.

I laughed at the question, not bothering to tell Alain that it was Carlos who had dropped my Flexileg—still attached to my muddy Nike cross-trainer—on the picnic table next to a big bowl of potato salad and a pitcher of fruit punch. Nor did I tell him that my mother had taught me diddly-squat, except maybe how to live without one.

"Oh, dear."

I glanced over in the direction of Dan's voice and caught him staring as I smoothed on a clean prosthetic sock over my stump and shoved it back into the Flexileg casing.

"There's a problem?" I asked. Because now that the other WESTEX participants had seen my calf stump in all its ugly splendor—and no one had gagged or giggled—I was feeling a bit cocky about it.

Dan chewed his lip. "Wow. I'm thinking of the liability. What if your... uh... artificial leg gets broken, or you twist your other ankle, or—"

"Or," Meena interrupted, "what if an eighteen wheeler crashes into the van? Or one of our campsites gets buried in a landslide? Or Frank is eaten by a bear?"

Frank blanched—no easy feat on a sunny beach in June. "*NOT funny!*"

"Okay, okay." Dan put up his hands defensively. "I see your point, Meena. I guess I'm just surprised that Rainey's... leg... wasn't mentioned on her medical form."

Simple explanation: When I was accepted for WESTEX at the last minute, I didn't have time to get an appointment with a GP. Lynda had completed my form. Even *I* was surprised when she ticked the "no" box beside the question asking if I had any physical disabilities or special needs that would inhibit my full participation in the program. But it wasn't like she'd lied. I could use my prosthesis to walk, run, and climb on dry land with the same ease most folks use a fork or spoon to eat. And when the Flexileg wasn't feasible, I had crutches. And now it seemed I also had Alain's strong back.

"If Rainey gets sent home, we all go home!" Meena piped up.

"Yeah!" the others chorused, before I could tell Meena to save her activism for world poverty and endangered wildlife. I knew she was just trying to help, but I said it before: I can stand up for myself.

"It seems, Dan, that you haven't read the fine print." Brooke rifled through some papers in her backpack. She extracted my registration forms and scanned them quickly. "It does say, *right here—*" Brooke shoved the papers in Dan's face, "—on the *glowing* recommendation written by her school principal, that Rainey has a 'congenital amputation and wears a prosthesis on her left leg.' It also says she's had '*no trouble* participating fully in gym class and intramural sports.'"

"Uh... sorry, Rainey," Dan said, frowning as if he had only just realized that being WESTEX headmaster meant being responsible for more than giving geography lectures and leading campfire songs. "Stuck my foot in my mouth, I guess."

That, of course, cracked me up. Slowly the others began chortling, too. "Shit, I did it again," Dan mumbled, his ears glowing the exact color of the fruit punch.

"We're *all* glad to have you here, Rainey," Brooke said.

"Speak for yourself, Screech," Alain laughed, flashing her a smile so sweet she actually smiled back. "The girl weighs a ton."

I whacked him on the shoulder. "Hey, who asked you to be my mule?"

Brooke waved us off. "All of you, go dry off and come back pronto for lunch. We're on a schedule."

After a quick picnic, Dan and Brooke excused themselves to prepare a few more getting-to-know-you games. The rest of us sat around scarfing banana splits we bought from an ice cream truck parked by the playground.

"Well, guys, we sure aren't traveling with the Anorexia Triplets," Homer remarked, as Izzie, Meena, and I tore into our monster sundaes.

"Gotta keep our strength up," Izzie giggled.

"Yeah," Meena added, wiping a blob of hot fudge off her chin. "We're gonna leave you guys in our wake during the next swim race."

Alain reached across the picnic table and pinched her tiny waist. "Keep packing it away like that and you can just drive across the water next time on your spare tires."

"Piss off," Meena replied, flicking a pineapple chunk at his head. Alain caught it in his mouth. Great reflexes. Gotta love that in a guy, even if he is a bit of a head case.

Frank changed the subject. "So who, or what, do you all think you'll miss the most this summer?"

"Easy," Homer said. "Mom's spring rolls." His parents operated a Chinese buffet in Scarborough.

"*The Young and the Reeeeestless*," Izzie admitted.

"My dreads," Meena said, running her hands over her closely clipped skull. "We parted ways yesterday—I didn't want them collecting bugs and twigs and other summer souvenirs."

"I'll miss my girlfriend," Frank piped up. "She a business major at U of T. She's *nineteen*," he bragged.

"Yeah, *riiiiight*," Izzie smirked.

"What's so funny?" Frank demanded.

"Let me guess," Izzie said. "You met her on-line?" WESTEX didn't allow laptops, video recorders, Blackberrys, or iPods. Too much distraction was the theory.

"*So what if I did?*"

"You've met her in person, though, right?" Homer asked.

"Not yet... but..."

"Sounds like true love, man. Go for it," Alain laughed, pounding Frank on the back good-naturedly.

Frank was indignant. "You got something—or *someone*—better to miss?"

Whoa... Alain's normally wide-open face slammed shut like a bank vault. For a few tense seconds, it looked like he might pick Frank up by the front of his golf shirt and toss him in the lake. Instead, Alain picked up his plastic ice cream dish and licked it clean. Sticky caramel stuck to his nose. "Easy," he replied, one wary eye still on Frank. "My darkroom."

"You develop your own photographs?" Izzie asked him. "*Coooool.* I've always been curious about how a darkroom works."

Alain's face opened for business again. He winked at me across the table. "It's amazing the sorts of things that have developed in my darkroom."

Meena nudged me. It was my turn to say who/what I'd miss the most. "Uh... Simon?"

"I *kneeeeew* you had a boyfriend!" Izzie, the gossipmonger, screeched.

"Simon's *not* my boyfriend," I retorted. "He's my stepmother's Golden Retriever."

"Carlos?" Homer asked. Carlos had been so quiet down at the other end of the table that I'd forgotten for a few minutes that he was there. A miracle.

"Yeah?"

"Your turn."

"Jessie," he said softly. "That's who I'll miss the most." He stared out over the water.

"Who's Jessie?" I asked, trying to sound nonchalant, all the while thinking, *Rainey, you fool, he does have a girlfriend. They're probably even* engaged *or something.*

"Nobody!" Carlos rose so fast he knocked over his can of
7UP. "I'm going to go fix that broken back rest now."

"What was that all about?" Meena asked when Carlos was
gone and we'd sopped up his sticky mess with paper napkins.

Izzie tossed her hair and raised a knowing eyebrow at me.
"See how he *ruuuuuns*?"

Dan and Brooke re-joined the group and introduced a team-
building exercise. For the next forty-five minutes, we were too
busy strategizing—well, mostly *arguing*—with each other about
the best way to survive the night after a hypothetical northern
wilderness plane crash to miss anyone or anything.

CHAPTER NINE

WESTEX reached the region of Muskoka shortly after four that afternoon. We would be staying at Arrow Lake Campground for a week, orienting ourselves to the camping lifestyle, getting a start on the academic component of the program, and exploring Algonquin Provincial Park.

The nylon "mansion" that Meena, Izzie, and I would share that summer took us thirty minutes of sweating and cursing to erect that first time. It had three separate "rooms" divided by zip-on walls, and a small vestibule in front where we could stash our packs and muddy sneakers. It was musty, dusty, and carpeted with dead bugs. Across the campsite, Homer, Alain, and Frank hadn't fared much better with their tent, which was missing a pole and had to be propped up with a fallen tree branch. Brooke, Dan, and Carlos each had their own tents, miniaturized versions of our own, set up on the "prime real estate" at the very back of the site, away from the stink and the banging door of the outhouse across the road.

"Hell *Sweeeeet* Hell," Izzie groaned.

The guys lost the coin flip and were assigned to unpack the "cookstuff" boxes, raid the coolers (which would need to be restocked every three or four days as we passed through towns with grocery stores), and prepare our first dinner: pasta with canned meat sauce. Carlos, using a double-burner propane stove, boiled rotini and heated the Prego. Frank set the table with metal dishes and cutlery bent and dented from previous WESTEX trips. Homer made a salad and nearly sliced off the tips of two fingers. Alain set two old Coke cans filled with wildflowers on the picnic table as a centerpiece.

"What *is* that?" I laughed, pointing to the leafy green weed he'd included in his arrangement. "Poison Ivy?"

Alain elbowed Carlos. "She's going to be a handful," he laughed, nodding at me.

Carlos frowned and went back to stirring his cauldron of tomato sauce.

"What's in there, Carlos?" I asked, making a stab at conversation. "Eye of newt, hair of the speckled toad... ?"

No response.

"... moose testicles, rattlesnake venom, baby vomit... ?"

So much for trying to be friendly; I was invisible. Carlos passed his ladle to Alain and slunk off in the direction of the outhouse.

"What the hell's his problem?" Alain asked me. "What you said was funny."

"You think everything is funny." Well, except for that one exchange with Frank.

He wasn't laughing now, either. "I saw you talking to Carlos this morning during drop-off. I asked him how he knew you. He told me you worked together at Pineview. My little brothers played basketball there a few winters ago."

"What else did he say?" Could Alain drop a few hints about why Carlos was treating me like pond scum?

"Not much. Just that you taught arts and crafts to little kids."

"He treats me like I have some sort of contagious social disease," I admitted.

Alain shrugged. "Maybe Carlos has issues. Or, maybe he's just an asshole. I wouldn't take it personally, Rainey. I doubt whatever it is has anything to do with you."

"Who died and appointed you camp psychologist?" I asked. I think I liked Alain better when he was being a doofus.

"I'm no psychologist; I'm a photographer." Alain waved his fingers spookily in front of my face. "I *SEE* things. There's something about the way Carlos looks at you when you're not paying attention. It's—"

"Disgust?" I suggested.

"No. More like... regret?"

"You see a lot," I said skeptically.

"I'll tell you what else I see," Alain added. "You've got something eating at you, too..."

Don't we all, Alain? I wondered.

"... something that has nothing to do with Carlos. Want to spill it?" he asked.

I shook my head.

Alain elbowed me playfully. "Saving it for a 'Rainey' day, huh?"

From what I'd witnessed, Alain was ninety-nine percent goofball, one percent brooding mystery man, but my gut feeling was that he was someone I might be able to trust with my "something" one day.

Maybe.

CHAPTER TEN

After dinner, Meena, Izzie, Homer, Frank, Alain, and I set off through the trees on a scavenger hunt to locate the nearest outhouses, the shower hut, the canoe launch, the coin laundry, and the public beach. Dan added that we should invent a team name while we were gone. Previous WESTEX groups had named themselves the Adventurers, the Explorers, the Mountaineers.

"Don't you just *love* the great outdoors?" Homer said, taking an invigorating breath, then doubling over, hacking out the bugs he'd inhaled. "Why don't we call ourselves the Bug Suckers?"

"Or the Fly Swatters," Meena groaned, slapping at her head. The deerflies were voracious despite everyone's efforts to repel them with liberal doses of Deep Woods Off. "*Eau du Happy Camper,*" Alain called it.

"Anyone want a swig of my sports drink?" Frank asked, bringing up the rear. He'd brought a whole case of blue Gatorade with him—a prize from his job, he said, for selling the most bottles of environmentally friendly toilet-bowl cleaner that spring.

"He might be the king of cleaning supplies, but he doesn't seem too particular about spreading his own mouth germs around," Meena whispered to me.

"I'd rather have a *beeeeer!*" Izzie called back to Frank.

"Hey, that's it!" Alain said. "For our team name. 'The Canadian Six-Pack.' All in favor?"

Motion carried.

We arrived back at the campsite an hour later to find Brooke and Dan setting up for the first of what would be nightly after-dinner team meetings. "Daily opportunities for us to recap the day's events, air grievances, and make group decisions," Brooke explained. "And... eat dessert!" she added, whipping a paper towel off a tray of just-made Rice Krispie Treats. The Six-Pack— and the ants—stormed the picnic table like it was Vimy Ridge.

A while later, Dan licked his sticky fingers and handed out pamphlets he'd picked up at the campground office. The front of each brochure, in large bold print, read: WELCOME TO BLACK BEAR COUNTRY.

"But we're only three hundred kilometers from Toronto!" Frank exclaimed, peering nervously into the surrounding forest. He was, hands down, perhaps the least woodsy person *on the planet*. He'd nearly fainted during the hike when Alain had picked up a baby garter snake and dangled it in front of him. "Here, hold this so I can get a picture," Alain told him, one hand holding out the snake, the other fiddling with the lens cap of his expensive-looking digital SLR camera, one of two cameras—the other was an old-fashioned Minolta loaded with black and white film—that he toted around everywhere. Frank squealed like he'd been handed a live grenade. Why he'd applied to join WESTEX—and worked so hard selling enviro-stuff to pay for it—was anyone's guess.

"The average black bear weighs between three and six hundred pounds," Dan read. "Bears are omnivores. They'll eat anything: nuts, plants, berries, fish, carrion—"

"Carri-what?" Izzie asked.

"Dead animals," Meena explained.

Alain poked me. He had a Rice Krispie stuck to his chin. "Yummy road kill. Crunchy on the outside, chewy in the middle. Good source of protein and eight other essential nutr—"

Dan interrupted. "The black bears' ongoing search for a free lunch brings them into contact with campers who are careless with their food storage and garbage disposal. Bears become 'nuisance bears' by habitually visiting campsites where they have previously found food."

"They are *conditioned*," Meena said.

Dan beamed. "Correct! And this *conditioning* poses a threat to the safety and enjoyment of park visitors. It usually leads to the bears' being captured and relocated. Or shot."

Frank bolted up, banging his knee on the top of the picnic table, rattling everyone's plastic juice cups. "You know what?

I thought I could do this. I can't. I'm going home."

Dan laid one of his own hairy paws on Frank's shoulder. "Sit back down," he said, not unkindly. "There *are* ways to reduce your likelihood of a bear encounter."

Frank lowered himself slowly back onto the wooden bench.

"First," Dan explained, "all food and fragrant items must be stored in the van. Not so much as a stick of gum or tube of toothpaste in the tents. A bear's sense of smell is much better than a human's. Also," he added, "cooking areas must be set up downwind from the tents and kept spotless. Garbage is to be secured in the van until it can be driven to the designated dump spot at the end of each day."

"But what if the campers before us were slobs?" Izzie asked. "What if the bears are *already* conditioned to raid this site? What if they're stalking us right now, just waiting to *pouuuuunce?*"

"Offer Frank up as a sacrifice?" Alain suggested.

"*NOT* funny!" Frank shouted at him.

"Never run from a bear; it will give chase," Brooke responded. "Don't climb a tree; black bears can climb faster. Try to scare the bear away. Yell. Bang pots and pans. Slowly back away. They're great bluffers. They'll snort and even mock-charge. But it's rare for one to attack a human, unless the human has threatened its cubs, or stands between the bear and a known food supply."

"But what about while we're hiking, Dan?" Homer asked. "What if we encounter a bear on the trail?"

Use compassionate verbal strategies, I giggled to myself.

"Always travel in groups. Talk and sing as you hike the trails. If bears can hear you coming, they'll avoid you."

Brooke smirked. "Shouldn't be too much of a challenge for you rowdy lot."

When our meeting ended, the sun was low in the sky and the air had grown cool. "Next lesson: fire-building," Brooke announced. Everyone dashed to pull sweaters from their packs.

In order to preserve the forest floor and wildlife habitat, campers were prohibited from using deadfall for campfires. Bundled kindling and firewood needed to be purchased from the park store. Brooke fished some money from the cash box she kept in her pack and asked Carlos to make a quick trip to the store on the other side of the campground.

"What do we use for marshmallow sticks?" I asked.

"That reminds me," Brooke said, overhearing. "Here, Rainey." She pulled another five-dollar bill from her cash box. "I used up our stash of marshmallows for the Rice Krispie Treats. Go with Carlos and pick up another bag from the camp store to last through the week."

Me and my big mouth.

The tension inside the van was thicker than a twenty-dollar cheeseburger. Carlos spent the entire three-kilometer ride to the store flipping between the only two static-free radio stations available: CBC news and some bleeding-heart country crap. At the store, we went our separate ways—Carlos to the woodshed, me to the grocery area.

Carlos was finished his business first and sat drumming his fingers on the steering wheel when I returned with the marshmallows. I got in the van without comment, flinging the bag onto one of the back seats.

Carlos shot me a smug look.

"What?" I shot back. "Marshmallows don't bruise."

He stared at me for another few seconds, then, sighing, he got out of the van, and motioned for me to climb back out, too. "We need to talk," he said, leading off with long strides towards the end of the parking lot where a wood-burned sign read: "Scenic Lookout." An arrow pointed down a gravel trail through a forest of maples.

Two minutes into the trees, the trail widened into a ledge overlooking a narrow river canyon.

Wow... this is *beautiful,* I thought, peering down over the wooden guardrail, taking special note of the lines of the tree branches and the curve of the river and the... wait a minute! An unnerving shiver rocked my spine. What if Carlos wasn't *just* a jerk? Did he bring me here to toss me over the ledge? I'd plunge a hundred meters to my death. He'd claim it was an "accident." He'd say I'd leaned too far over the railing and lost my footing.

"You, uh, said we need to talk?" I asked, stepping away from the barrier and smacking my head where blackflies were making a five-course meal of my ears.

Carlos hesitated for a long minute. Then another. I watched his face warily. Storm clouds reflected in his eyes, despite the clear twilight overhead. "I want to... apologize, I guess," he said, finally.

I wanted to take Carlos seriously, but he sounded like an android, or a hack actor reading from a script. His words were spot on, but the sincerity was hurting.

"Well... I'm sorry, too, for asking you out," I said. "I didn't realize you had a girlfriend."

"I don't have a girlfriend. Not since last March," Carlos replied.

"I just asked you out as a friend, anyway. It's not like I had a *thing* for you," I lied.

"Come on, Rainey. You did so have a *thing* for me," Carlos retorted.

My face burst into flames. Whitehot fury erupted from the deep pit of embarrassment nestled deep inside my rib cage. So much for spontaneous human combustion's being a myth.

Trust Carlos to not even notice. "Anyway, *that's* why I couldn't accept your invitation," he continued. "I knew you wanted more than a day at a sports symposium."

Egotistical jackass! Except... there wasn't even a shred of arrogance in Carlos's voice. Just... regret? Was Alain right?

"Well, I know I'm not exactly a perfect female specimen,"

I said, gawking down at my prosthesis.

Carlos kicked at the dirt with his shoe. "Christ, Rainey, you know I didn't even know about your leg until this morning, and besides, that doesn't matter to me. This isn't—"

"Then what?" I interrupted. "Is it that you don't like tall girls? Or maybe you prefer redheads? Or does..." *Watch it, Rainey,* I told myself. *You're losing it.*

"Look, this is not about you. I just want you to know that I can't get involved with you—with *anyone*—right now."

"So what do you want me to do about it, Carlos?" I hissed. "Quit WESTEX? Pack up and go home so I won't ruin *your* summer?"

"Don't talk crazy, Rainey. You earned your WESTEX spot. I just mean that your being here complicates things. I need this summer to sort out some things for myself—*by* myself."

"Okey dokey," I huffed. No sense mentioning to Carlos that my life had turned itself inside out, too. That the warm fuzzies/white-hot lust I'd felt for him at Pineview belonged to a different Rainey. A more naïve one. A less focused one. A Rainey who didn't know her mother was in Squamish.

"So?" Carlos asked.

"So what?"

"So... are you... okay?"

"It's getting dark, Carlos," I said, avoiding the question. "We'd better get back to camp."

CHAPTER ELEVEN

Dan spent most of Day Two reviewing the academic component of the WESTEX program. Plunking our textbooks—already mud-spattered and water damaged from previous WESTEX voyages—down on the picnic table, he emphasized that the majority of our history, geography, and outdoor education requirements would be met through field studies, museum visits, and outdoor adventure experiences.

And we'd all be required to keep a journal to reflect daily on what we learned about Canada, the outdoor life, and ourselves.

"*Academic* journals, folks," Brooke explained. "We want you to comment on the successes and struggles of team dynamics, but they are *not* places to describe romantic coups or list the shortcomings of your trip leaders. Keep a separate journal for that if you wish. These *assigned* journals will be handed in upon arrival back in Toronto. You'll be given a mark for each area of study based on your observations and analysis of your learning experience, plus extra credit for skill acquisition, team participation, and leadership development."

"If anyone thought this trip was going to be a day at the beach, you were right." Dan grinned. "But you won't be lying on towels soaking up UV rays."

"*Daaaaamn,*" Izzie interjected, then went back to picking a wad of sticky pine sap out of her hair. That would teach her to stop whipping it around all the time.

"You'll be classifying rock and soil samples, identifying plants and aquatic life, and learning wilderness survival."

"Life's a beach," Alain said, tossing his Expos cap up in the air and catching it on his head.

On Day Three, we rented canoes at Arrow Lake's main dock. Dan paired those of us with canoe experience with those who had none. I sat confidently in the stern after years at Camp Wenibawabie, matched with Frank, whose only canoe experience was watching the old movie *Deliverance* on late-night TV. "Not exactly confidence inspiring," he admitted.

"Just hold the paddle like I showed you!" I yelled up to him in the bow. "Left hand on the grip! Bottom hand around the throat! Dunk the blade further into the water! Use your muscles! Stroke! Stroke! Stroke!"

"*WHAT IS THIS! THE ARMY?!*" Frank yelled back. For such a twerpy guy, he had an awfully big mouth.

But was Frank on to something? Did I have a career in the

Armed Forces? I could handle giving orders and doing pushups and kicking ass, but—from a totally frivolous perspective—I'd never looked good in camouflage. And there was the leg thing; the army *created* amputees, but did it accept the previously amputated into basic training? Couldn't you just hear my father? "Don't *shoot* the Taliban, Rainey. Use compassionate verbal strategies."

Once Frank got the hang of paddling, I steered us further out onto the lake. There, we were joined by Izzie and Homer in one canoe and Alain and Meena in another. Dan and Brooke cruised amongst us, dispensing stroke pointers and safety tips. Carlos waited on shore for one of us to start drowning so he could showcase his lifeguarding skills—though I was pretty sure if it were me drowning, he'd let me sink.

When Dan gave a signal that it was time to head back to shore, Alain, in protest, yelled "*PIRATES*!" The Six-Pack began drenching each other using canoe paddles like beaver tails. Water flew like fireworks through the air.

Until Frank lost his grip on his paddle and leaned so far out over the canoe to grab it we—SPLAT!—capsized. Thank God I'd left my Flexileg on shore.

Dan halted the game immediately. "Are you two okay?" he called as Frank and I surfaced.

I laughed and spouted a mouthful of lake water up in the air.

Frank's life vest had ridden up so high his skinny face was

poking out an arm hole. He yanked it down and shook water from his hair like a dog.

Brooke frowned. "That canoe needs to be righted and brought to shore."

"Holler if you need a hand." Dan sat back smugly, his paddle at the ready, waiting for one of us to flounder so he could offer up his expert advice.

He could keep it.

Alain waved me over. Minutes later, he and I briefed Frank and Meena on the finer points of canoe-over-canoe rescues.

"I already know that Rainey think's she's Captain Highliner, but where'd *you* learn this?" Frank asked Alain as I maneuvered our swamped, upside-down canoe so that it was perpendicular to Alain's.

"I grew up canoeing," he replied. "My grandfather's farm in New Brunswick backs onto a river."

On three, Frank and I pushed down on the near end of our submerged craft, causing the far end to lift out of the water, so Meena and Alain could hoist it up and over the sides of their craft. From there it was a simple matter of flipping it right-side-up and sliding it back into the water. Piece of cake.

Alain plucked Frank's wayward paddle from the water and passed it back. Then he turned to me. "Last summer, I bought an old fiberglass fourteen-footer at a garage sale for fifty bucks. I keep it at a friend's summer house over on Ward's Island. You should come out in my canoe with me when we get back to the city. The sunsets over the CN Tower are awesome."

Meena started humming the theme song from *The Love Boat*. I grabbed a fistful of weeds from the bog and hurled them at her.

The next morning, Carlos drove us all to Huntsville. Tourist season was in full swing and the small cottage town was bustling. While Brooke and Dan made several supply runs, the Six-Pack made fast work of the Muskoka Museum and explored the upscale sporting goods stores and craft boutiques along the main drag. Izzie went all out arranging for UPS to deliver a souvenir T-shirt and a life-size blow-up alligator to her boyfriend Sammy, way up at that sailing camp in Quebec.

"It's not enough that you call him every morning and make those disgusting slurpy-kissy noises into the phone while the rest of us are eating breakfast?" Meena asked.

We ordered chicken burgers at an outdoor café. Near the end of our meal, a woman with teased-up platinum hair, thirty if she was a day, sat down with a fruit shake at the next table. Her super-sized boobs spilled out the top of her black Lycra tank-top. The guys stared.

"Here, take a napkin and wipe the drool off your chin," I said, giving Alain a sharp kick under the table.

He picked up his Coke and drained it in five seconds flat. "Hot out here, isn't it," he remarked.

Meena nudged me. "Look at the puddle of dribble on Frank's shirt."

"Hey, Frank! What would your imaginary U of T girlfriend think about you *ooooogling* Miss Boobfest?" Izzie giggled.

"She's not *imaginary*," he shot back.

Miss Boobfest was oblivious to the male attention; she was too busy staring like a confused four-year-old at my legs.

Here's the thing: I knew when I decided to wear shorts that hot morning that I should expect the usual curious and/or concerned glances from strangers. Not a problem.

But rude stares are something else. You'd think I'd be used to them by now. Sticks and stones and all that shit.

Ha. When the Carlos-mobile pulled up to the curb a while later to fetch us, I stood up with the others and gathered my belongings. "Look at the fake leg!" Miss Boobfest stage-whispered to a passing waiter. Even turned away, I could feel her hot-pink fingernails pointing at me, her ignorant eyes boring into my Flexileg.

I wheeled around to face the bitch. "At least my *TITS* are real!" I yelled, then flounced away to the van without a backward glance. Greg would say that my compassionate verbal strategies were lacking, but what the hell, I was too tripped up with rage to care.

At the van, Meena and Izzie were clapping. Dan looked confused. Brooke was chewing on her lip, probably to keep from laughing. Homer and Frank were fighting over the window seat and hadn't noticed a thing. Carlos? Who cares? I ignored them all.

"You're one tough chick, Rainey," Alain said as he settled next to me in the van.

"Tough as nails," I lied.

Then, for two days, it rained non-stop. The Six-Pack spent hours under big plastic tarps strung high up over the picnic tables. Once Meena was reassured—about forty times—that the rumbling in the distance was trucks on the highway, *not* thunder, the Six-Pack hunkered down and made a fair start on our reading assignments.

And Carlos brooded. With no day trips or swimming sched-uled until the weather improved, the good-humor mask he'd been wearing in public began to fray around the edges. Sure, he helped with the chores, and participated in mealtime conversations, as long as they didn't get personal, but he made no effort to show up for our nightly team meetings, our smoky campfires, or even the poker-for-Skittles tournament that lasted well into the next morning. He most often disappeared into his tent right after dinner with his portable radio and a sports magazine.

"And a bottle of *booooze,*" Izzie hazarded to guess. "Didn't you smell him before dinner? I asked if he'd share and he told me to get lost, that he'd been sucking rum-and-butter Life Savers. *Riiiiight.*"

I tried not to pay attention to Carlos. I knew he wanted me to keep my distance. It wasn't so hard to do; the program schedule kept me hopping. Even so-called "free time" was spent breaking in my sketchbook and watercolor pencils, updating my journal, and just getting to know the others.

And *worrying*. Busy as I was, and as hard as I tried, I never really succeeded in shaking off the nagging anxiety about what to do about my mother. That little scrap of paper with her address and phone number on it was burning a hole in my pack.

And in my stomach.

CH_APTER TWELVE

WESTEX's last full day at Arrow Lake Campground was my seventeenth birthday.

I hadn't mentioned it, but someone must have snooped through the registration papers because at six that morning, Frank, Alain, and Homer charged into the she-tent like a herd of stampeding buffalo.

Before I'd even had a chance to wake up fully—forget about putting on a sweater or my Flexileg—Homer and Alain carried me, kicking and cursing, through the woods to the beach front.

"One! Two! Three! Happy Birthday!" They swung me far out into the lake, bedclothes and all.

I came up sputtering, my teeth chattering. "Come on in! Water's great!" I beckoned to them once I'd caught my breath. I planned to drown them all, one by one.

Homer shrugged. "Can't. There's no lifeguard on duty."

"There is now." A groggy Carlos appeared on the beach, raking his fingers through his bedhead. "You idiots made enough noise to raise the dead."

Well, good morning to you, too, Mr. Sunshine.

"Just keeping the bears away," Frank declared, emerging from the beach trail. He held up my prosthesis. "Thought you might be needing this."

"Kick Alain and Homer in the ass with it, would you?" I shouted.

"Izzie and I brought you a *towel,* girlfriend," Meena called, as they brought up the rear.

Izzie laughed, waving it around like a flag. "That T-shirt you sleep in is *daaaaangerous.* It needs a hazard label: 'Transparent When Wet.'"

"At least her TITS are real!" Frank yelled, his voice likely carrying clear across the lake.

I ducked under the water up to my chin.

"Let's go fishing, men!" Alain shouted. Within seconds I was hauled, kicking and cursing again, back to shore.

Izzie tossed me the towel. "Cover up, Miss June, before Alain gets his camera."

"Where's a Hooters job fair when you need one, Rainey?" Frank snickered.

"Shut up, you piglet." That from Carlos. Like I needed him to defend me?

I wrapped myself up tight as a sushi roll and turned to Frank. "Hooters would likely consider me underqualified."

"It's all fun and games until someone loses her shirt," Meena mumbled.

Izzie laughed. "Let's *hope* that's not *all* Rainey loses this summer."

Nice. I knew letting myself get pulled into Izzie's late night girl-talks would be bad news. "Why don't I just get 'I'm a virgin' tattooed across my forehead?" I sneered at her.

"See." Frank poked Alain in the ribs. "I told you you weren't the only one."

"Shut up, you piglet," Alain said.

At seven-thirty, after gulping down bowls of clumpy oatmeal loaded with raisins—or were those chewy little lumps bugs?—WESTEX piled into the Carlos-mobile. Our agenda: a day-long tour of the Highway 60 corridor through Algonquin Provincial Park.

We'd been inside the park gates about ten minutes when Frank screamed, "*STOP THE VAN!*"

Great! He's sitting behind me and he needs to puke, I thought.

"Look! Over there!" Heads swiveled as Frank pointed to a marshy area beside the road.

"It's a mother moose!" Alain exclaimed, grabbing for his camera. "And her two... uh... mooslings? Moosettes? Moosies?"

"Her two *calves*," Meena corrected.

Alain snorted. "You could kick some serious ass on *Jeopardy*, Meena."

"I'm counting on it. I'll need the money to get through vet school."

Carlos pulled the van over to the gravel shoulder. We all piled out to gawk at the moose. I flipped open my sketchbook and pulled my set of watercolor pencils from my pack.

Dan cleared his throat. "Did you know..."

Here we go again, I thought. Dan was a walking, talking encyclopedia of trivia. He asked, "Did you know..." at least fifty times a day, in reference to everything from earthworms to historical architecture to outdoor cooking. We hadn't been gone a full week and already our journals were bulging.

"... that moose are the largest of the five known species of deer in North America? Males can grow to fourteen hundred pounds and seven feet at the shoulder. The average life span is ten to fifteen years."

"Like dogs," Frank said.

"But not likely much good at Frisbee," I said, dipping a finger into my water bottle and using my wet index finger to smudge strokes of red and brown and yellow together to capture the color and texture of the moose's hide.

Dan continued. "The hairy flap of skin you see hanging below the neck is called a dewlap."

Homer laughed. "My grandmother has one of those."

"Where are the antlers?" Alain asked, fiddling with the buttons on his camera.

Dan nodded. "Good you asked. Only *males* have antlers. They grow each summer in preparation for the fall mating season. Their length and breadth play an important role in determining which bulls get—"

"Laid?" Frank suggested.

"*Seeeee*, girls. Size *does* matter," Izzie giggled.

Dan explained. "Bull moose charge each other using their antlers to gouge their opponents into retreat. Occasionally, a lesser bull is gouged to death. Worst case scenario: the antlers of two opponents become locked together, and they both die of starvation."

"Sounds like a stupid reality TV show," Homer remarked. "*Extreme Dating: Moose Edition.*"

"Here's what I don't get," Frank said. "Why, with the whole park to roam in, do moose come so close to the roadway? They eat twigs and leaves, right, so it can't be the road kill or garbage that's attracting them."

"It's the salt," Meena answered.

Dan lit up. "Correct again, Meena. After the long winter, moose are mineral deficient. The highway run-off contains salt residue from cold-weather maintenance."

Dan lectured for another few minutes until the moose grew tired of being ogled and wandered back into the pine forest. I blew on my sketch to dry the damp areas.

"I hope you found this information interesting," he concluded, before herding us all back into the Carlos-mobile.

"It was moose-merising," I said.

Carlos pulled into a trailhead parking area a few minutes later, killed the ignition, and tilted his backrest into sleep position. Dan, Brooke, and the Six-Pack piled out of the van for our first scheduled activity of the day: a seven-kilometer hike.

Dan took the lead, marching the rest of us along a rugged loop trail through rocky pine forests and marshlands, stopping periodically to point out loon nesting grounds and beaver dams, and to preach about the tragic effects of acid rain on local fish and loon populations. "Nature's classroom!" he called out at one point, spreading his arms wide, as if to bear hug the planet.

Halfway through the hike, while the rest of the Six-Pack clambered one at a time up a low lookout tower to view the rock strata of the river gorge below, Alain hung back on the ground. "Rainey?" he called up to me. "Take a picture from up there, would you?" He pointed westward, then reached up to pass his digital camera to me. "I've already set it up for you. Just aim and shoot. "

"I'll come down now, Alain. You should climb up and get the shot yourself." I was afraid of dropping his camera into the gorge by accident. It would probably take over a year of shifts at Pineview to replace it.

He urged me once again to take the camera. "You've got a good eye. I trust you."

Reluctantly, I took the shot he wanted.

"Thanks," he said sheepishly when I climbed down the lookout steps and passed the camera back to him.

"What's the deal?" I asked him. "You afraid of heights or something?" I was just joking, but there went that odd flash of sadness in Alain's eyes again, and his jaw set with anger, making me wish I'd kept quiet.

But just as soon as it appeared, it was gone. He snapped the lens cap back on his camera. "Or something," he replied.

At noon, WESTEX stumbled out of the trail into the parking lot. We woke up lazy-ass Carlos, made a quick picnic, then continued east on Highway 60 towards the Algonquin Logging Museum.

The outdoor exhibits, recreating the park's forest industry from the "caboose shanties" and log chutes of the mid-1800s to the high-powered chainsaws and backcountry road systems of today, were crowded with tourists. Ahead of us on the trail was one of those *Leave It to Beaver* families I'll never relate to: A perky Mom. A patient Dad. A boy about ten, bursting with enthusiasm over the ugly old saws and bark-strippers. And a newborn baby, asleep in a sling-type contraption across Mom's chest. Dad and the boy rushed toward a display of antique axes when Mom stopped to adjust the sling's straps. She called for Dad and the boy to wait up, but they were already out of earshot.

She turned to our group. "Would you hold Janie a second

while I fix the halter?" She held the sleeping infant out to Carlos, who was closest. The baby was no bigger than a ten-pound sack of potatoes, decked out in a pink Baby Roots T-shirt and Mickey Mouse diaper, her tiny toes bare and wiggly.

Carlos looked suddenly sorry that he had let himself be talked into joining us that afternoon, but he took Janie anyway, holding her out at arm's length, as if she were radioactive.

Mom took the baby back a moment later, oblivious to Carlos's discomfort. She rushed to catch up with her family.

"You'll need to practice holding a baby if you ever have one of your own," Meena remarked to Carlos. I'd been thinking the same thing. How could a guy who was so good with the kids at Pineview be so uncomfortable holding a baby?

His eyes shot flames at Meena. "*Mind your own goddamn business!*" he shouted, before making quick strides towards the exit. Meena shot her middle finger at his back.

Dan joined our huddle, grinning, clueless to the tension that had just passed. "Brooke and I've been talking to a museum guide. Did you know that 'wolf howls' are held in Algonquin Park each August? People gather along a back road and a guide leads them in a howling exercise. Sometimes, the wolves howl back."

"owwww-ow-ow-ow!" Alain called, Frank and Homer joining in. Someone's dog let loose, too. Up ahead, baby Janie began to wail. And somewhere in a nearby pine, a red squirrel gave everyone hell.

"So much for the peace and quiet of nature," Brooke remarked, returning from a trip to the washroom. She checked her watch. "It's time we all headed back to camp. I just need to make a quick phone call. Why don't you all check out the gift shop and we'll meet at the van in fifteen minutes."

At the gift shop entrance, Homer and Alain steered me away from the door.

"Maybe you could go and... see if Carlos is okay?" Homer suggested.

"No way!"

Alain nudged me towards the parking area. "Don't be a party pooper."

Okay, okay. It was obvious that the Six-Pack were conspiring to chip in for a birthday present. And would it hurt to let Carlos know that I was there for him if he changed his mind about sharing his troubles? Maybe I had a flair for social work and didn't know it?.

Wouldn't my father be thrilled?

I spotted Carlos perched against a picnic table fifty feet from his van, staring into a clump of pines.

I walked over and perched next to him. "Want to talk?" I asked.

He turned his head just long enough to freeze me with an icy glare. "Nope."

"Okay. Just... I'm here for you if you... change your mind," I choked out.

"I won't change my mind."

I stood up to go. I wanted to tell Carlos, "Piss off and get over yourself, already." But stupid me decided to honor my father's pacifist policies and give his old "compassionate verbal strategies" one last shot. "Well, I hope whatever it is gets better," I said, reaching out to give Carlos's shoulder a squeeze of support.

"*Get away! Just keep the fuck away from me!*" Carlos jumped off the table, knocking my arm away with such force that I lost my balance. Tripped over my boots. Fell to the ground, scraping my elbow on the gravel.

"Shit! Rainey, are you okay? I'm sorry." He put a hand out to help me up.

Ignoring him—and his hand—I struggled up on my own and stomped back in the direction of the gift shop.

The others were on their way out, carrying bags of souvenirs. Brooke hurried past me, looking grim.

Alain wrapped an arm around my shoulder. "Hey! You okay? Did Carlos give you a hard time? You look a little shook up."

I wasn't injured—no broken bones sticking out, or blood trailing from my scraped elbow—but I was furious. At myself. I couldn't believe I'd let Carlos get to me—again. "I'm fine. Just peachy," I said.

Alain ruffled my hair. "Don't let that dickhead spoil your birthday."

He was right. I'd come on this trip with an important agenda. I *needed* to fulfill it. And I *wanted* to have a good time fulfilling it. So instead of making any lofty birthday wishes for myself, I would grant Carlos his. I would "keep the fuck away" from him. I'd die of thirst before I'd even ask him to pass the juice at dinner. So there.

"Time to go!" Dan yelled from the van.

"You know, there are plenty of fish in the sea," Alain added, grabbing the enormous gift bag he'd propped between his feet, and quickly setting off vanward so I wouldn't see what was in it.

"Alain?" I called after him. He turned back.

I had only intended to say thanks. What came out was, "Nice gills."

CHAPTER THIRTEEN

Late that afternoon, as the van pulled up to the Arrow Lake check-in window for the last time, a park ranger poked his head out the gatehouse door.

"You the WESTEX group from Toronto?" he asked Carlos.

"Yup."

"You got a Rainey Williamson in there?"

"Yup."

"Well... tell her to come inside," the ranger beckoned. "Delivery."

Confused, I climbed over a few sets of legs, exited the van, and followed the guy into the gatehouse. He brought me around the service counter into the staff area and opened an old refrigerator.

"A red-haired woman showed up this afternoon. Tall. Gorgeous. Looked like Geena Davis. Not *now*—Geena's *old* now—I mean, from her *Thelma and Louise* days. She had a big blond dog with her, too. Anyhow, she insisted I put this in here for you." He pulled what I recognized as Lynda's Tupperware cake tray from the middle shelf and lifted up the cover. "She was afraid to leave it at the campsite in case the wildlife got to it before you did."

Oh. My. God. It was a huge chocolate cake smothered with fluffy icing and strawberries.

"So..." the guy asked, "that was your... older sister?"

"Stepmother," I replied, still stunned.

"Lucky dad, kid. Anyway, Geena—"

"Her name's Lynda."

"*Lynda* said she was sorry to have missed you. And to tell you Happy Birthday. Nice lady, *Lynda,* driving all the way up here from Toronto."

Here's the truth: I was mortified. What had Lynda been thinking? WESTEX wasn't preschool. Seventeen-year-olds didn't get class parties.

"No one ever made *me* a cake like that," the guy added.

Here's another truth: Before Lynda, no one made me a birthday cake at *all.* Greg always took me out to dinner on my birthday, and then, while they were alive, we'd go for cake at Grandma and Grandpa Jenkins's afterwards. They always bought a birthday cake from the grocery store. Each was the same: vanilla cake, white frosting with pink candy roses, and *Happy Birthday, Rainey* spelled out in green. I loved my grandparents, and I loved those cakes, but they never seemed to remember that I liked chocolate best.

Leave it to Lynda to think of everything.

A lineup of cars was honking to get through the gate. "Well, kid, you better go eat your cake before the icing melts. Have a good day."

It sure couldn't get any worse.

I called my father on my cell phone the minute we reached the campsite.

"Rainey! Happy Birthday!" he shouted in my ear.

Greg had taken me to the Mandarin for a birthday lunch the previous Saturday. Afterward, he'd shelled out a small fortune at MEC for a top-quality backpack, a waterproof windbreaker, and new hiking boots for the trip. Lynda wanted to go to the restaurant with us; she'd been crushed when she was called away to deliver a baby at the last minute.

I'd silently cheered. I missed spending time alone with my father.

"I got Lynda's cake," I told Greg. "I didn't actually see her and Simon, though. We were at Algonquin Park all day."

"I told Lynda she was nuts to drive all that way when you'd probably be off on some outing."

I knew that Lynda didn't mind the long ride. One time she told me that she loved driving, especially in the country after a bad day at the hospital. It helped to clear her head. And as much as I bitched and moaned about Greg's weekend absences when he and Lynda were dating, most times it was Lynda who'd made the four-hour drive east to Mollglen.

"Lynda was up all night fixing that cake." Greg added. "She even got a colleague to cover her emergencies today so she could make the trip."

"Is she home?" I asked. Might as well say thanks. I wasn't a total ingrate. Or I didn't want her to think I was, in any case.

"At the hospital," he said. "Call her there. She'd love to hear from you."

That's what I was afraid of. "Okay. And Greg? I made a... decision."

I had? When? I barely had time to decide what to wear in the morning—not that it mattered out here in the bush.

"You aren't getting your belly button pierced, are you?"

Right, Greg, and I'm bent over a log right now having a grizzly bear tattooed on my butt. He had to stop reading those online parenting magazines. "I decided that I'm not going to call Sara," I said. "I don't want to see her."

Silence on Greg's end.

"Are you still there?" I asked, when I couldn't take the quiet any longer.

"I *did* tell you that it was your decision," Greg said.

"Right."

"But... well, may I ask *why* you decided against it? You don't need to decide yet. Maybe it's a little early in the summer to be making—"

"It's just..." *Just what? Just that I'm a chickenshit? Just that I'm losing sleep over all the what ifs? That I needed to check something off my* TO DO *list today and it might as well be that? Oh, come on, Rainey, make up something, something good.* "I'm just... happy... the way things are right now," I croaked. "You, me, Lynda, Simon, maybe a baby before long. You guys are all the family that I need."

Another silence, even longer this time. Then a throaty cough. "You're not getting too much sun, are you, Rainey?"

Lynda's answering service told me she'd been called in to assist with a delivery, so I got away with leaving a message on her voicemail. I told her the cake was spectacular (no denying that), and I let her know how sorry I was to have missed her visit (a big fat lie).

Shockingly, it crossed my mind to say something else, too.

But I didn't.

CHAPTER FOURTEEN

That evening, our nightly team meeting was set aside in honor of my birthday.

The Six-Pack "surprised" me with a sweatshirt from Algonquin Park; they'd used a fine-tip magic marker to sign their best wishes on the back. Carlos was sent to the camp store for more firewood and came back with a case of 7UP. A conciliatory gesture? Like I cared?

Alain pulled a huge stuffed moose from a bag. "*Bonne Anniversaire!*" he shouted.

Frank reached across the table for the plastic fly swatter and held it out to Alain.

"Time to give her the birthday bumps?"

Alain grabbed the swatter and whacked Frank with it. "Get real. I give birthday kisses." And before I had a chance to protest, he tossed the swatter over his shoulder and kissed my right ear.

"*Un,*" he said.

Then he kissed my left elbow.

"*Deux!*" everyone joined in.

Then three quick kisses on my right forearm. One on each knee. Another on each cheek. Five across my forehead. One on my nose. One on my chin... that made sixteen.

"Hmm..." Alain mused. The light of the setting sun cast ripples in his dark blue eyes. I had a sudden urge to sketch dolphins jumping in and out of the ocean.

That he planted number seventeen on my mouth didn't surprise me. But the fact I found myself kissing him back sure did. Repeat after me: I had sworn off guys for the summer. What surprised me even more was that what seemed like ten years later, amid loud claps and jeers, we were still lip-locked and showed no signs of coming up for air.

At last, Alain broke free and took a bow. On wobbly knees, I started cutting the cake and passing it around, pretending like nothing had happened. When I passed Carlos his piece of cake, he waved it off and began chewing at his thumb like his life depended on it.

I got my own piece of cake and sat in the spot Alain saved for me across the table from him, ignoring Izzie's sly glance and Meena's surreptitious thumbs-up.

"This is the best cake I've ever eaten," Alain said, his mouth stuffed full. Little globs of icing were stuck to the corners of his lips. It took every scrap of self-control I had not to lunge across the table and lick them off.

"Let me guess; your stepmother's a caterer?" Izzie asked. "Does she do proms? Because next *spriiiiing*, I'll be wanting–"

"She's an obstetrician."

Suddenly, Carlos choked on his splinter or hang nail or whatever it was he was chewing at. Homer pounded on his back until Carlos caught his breath and was able to take a swig of 7UP to clear his throat. He excused himself to rest up for "the long drive tomorrow."

What the hell was that about?

Unless... did Carlos get some girl... Jessie?... *pregnant?* Was he running from his baby? *I'll kill him,* I thought.

Alain's smearing a fingerful of icing onto my nose brought me back to reality. "This turned out to be an excellent day," he said to me.

I reached under the table and gave his knee a squeeze. "My day turned out not too shabby, either."

But, despite my resolve not to see her, I wondered if somewhere in Squamish, Sara had remembered my birthday.

CHAPTER FIFTEEN

The Six-Pack spent the rest of that last night at Arrow Lake Campground sitting by the fire. Fueled by hot chocolate and leftover cake, we talked and laughed for hours, finally straggling to our tents shortly after midnight.

I couldn't sleep—again. Thoughts and images and feelings tumbling around in my brain like socks in a dryer: Carlos's hostility. My scraped elbow. Alain refusing to climb up on the lookout. Lynda's cake. My vow to stay away from guys that summer. (Gee, Rainey, how's *that* going?) My lack of career focus. My awesome moose sketch. My decision not to contact Sara.

Sara, Sara, Sara. Why did it always come back to Sara? After years of hiding all my curiosity and concern about her in the back closet of my mind, she was suddenly the last thing I thought about at night and the first thing I thought about in the morning. Did I hope that by stating my intention *not* to contact Sara, it would put an end to my messed-up feelings about her? That the stress hitching a free trip on my shoulders would just slide off like a banana peel?

Well... yeah.

But now it seemed even worse. Had I made the right decision? Had I made it for the right reasons? Had I let Greg down? Had I let *myself* down?

At the crack of dawn, I left the tent as quietly as possible and walked down the trail to the beach. Rays of early sun cut through the evergreens at the far side of the lake and danced across the water towards me like a silent party. I wondered if I should go back for my sketchbook and watercolor pencils.

"Couldn't sleep either?" a voice asked, making me jump.

Brooke. Sitting on the beach to my right. I'd been so struck by the light off the water, I hadn't even noticed her there.

I nodded my head in response, pulled off my Flexileg, and plunked down next to her in the damp sand. For a few silent minutes—well, silent except for the songs and chirps and squawks of a million hungry birds—it was pretty noisy, actually—we stared out across the lake. "Brooke?" I asked. "Why do you do this each year? Eight weeks in the woods every summer is a lot of time away from real life."

"Look at that sunrise, Rainey. Who's to say what's real or not?"

I doodled fishes in the sand. "I guess. What I meant was—"

"I know what you meant," Brooke cut in. "What seemingly sane adult would work all school year as a high school guidance counselor, then opt to spend her summers leading a program like WESTEX?"

"Well... yeah. Don't you ever just want to take a break?"

Brooke gave me an appraising glance and picked a stone out of the sand. She hurled it far out into the lake. After the *kerplop,* she watched the ripples until they disappeared. Then she spoke. "Nine winters ago I went through a terrible time. There was a... death. Then a messy divorce, and a month later I was in an even messier car accident. Broke a leg, both arms, my collarbone."

I didn't know what to say, so I slapped at a mosquito buzzing my right ear and waited for her to continue.

"When spring came around that year, I knew it was time for a change. And I don't mean a new purse; I mean something major. I heard about a new summer academic program that was being piloted, an eight-week camping trip to the West Coast for high school seniors. The school board was looking for a guidance counselor/chaperone."

"You were perfect for the job."

"I didn't know the first thing about camping that first year. Remember: I grew up in suburban St. John's. I moved to Toronto at nineteen. Communing with nature was limited to growing marigolds on my apartment balcony."

I shrugged. "WESTEX took you anyway."

Brooke threw her head back, laughing. "And I've *loved* it. Every sunburned, bug-infested, bad food moment. I *still* love it. I'll come on these trips as long as they'll have me. I learn something new every summer."

"What are you learning *this* summer?" I asked, flinching as a fat white gull swooped over our heads and landed in the sand nearby.

Brooke took her time responding. "I'm learning that what worked for me doesn't necessarily work for everyone."

"Like who?"

She shook her head. "Look, Rainey... I shouldn't be telling you all this."

"Carlos? Is he?... Did he?..." *Did that shithead get his ex-girlfriend pregnant and then take off?* I wanted to ask, but I knew Brooke wouldn't tell me. And the baby theory made no sense as an explanation for why Carlos was avoiding me specifically, since as far as I knew, you couldn't get pregnant just by *imagining* having sex with someone.

Brooke eyed me for a good ten seconds. "His sister's a good kid. I thought I could trust her recommendation. And Carlos is a good driver and conscientious lifeguard, but..."

"You think he's running from something?" I kept up, sifting cool sand through my fingers. "That's what Izzie thinks."

Another long silence. Brooke sighed. "You can't outrun yourself."

"I don't understand."

"It's not for you *to* understand, Rainey. Just consider... maybe Carlos isn't as strong as you are."

"I'm not strong."

Brooke shook her head at me. "Kid, I *heard* you chew out that bitch at the restaurant the other day. And I *watched* you on that seven-kilometer trail yesterday. We covered some rough ground at a pretty fast clip. You only limped when you thought no one could see you."

"I *don't* limp." I was *not* Wimpy Gimpy Girl. And the Flexileg was designed for sports and rough terrain. The problem the previous day was my new hiking boots. The soles were higher than my usual cross trainers and threw off my center of gravity, affected my balance, and gave me blisters on my real foot. Greg had warned me about breaking in the new boots before leaving Toronto, but I'd blown him off.

"I imagine you learned pretty early in life how to suck it up," Brooke went on. "Some people don't adapt so well to life's curveballs. And Rainey... I *saw* Carlos knock you over yesterday. That's why *I* couldn't sleep last night."

Ah, crap. So much for putting that sorry episode behind me. "Brooke, it was an *accident*," I responded. "I don't think Carlos *meant* for me to lose my balance. It's my new boots. They—"

"No matter," Brooke interrupted. She said nothing more, but I could see how conflicted she was about wanting to support Carlos but not wanting his behavior and attitude to affect the safety and well-being of the group.

"Brooke, whatever you do, don't fire Carlos." All I needed

was *that* on my conscience. "It's still early summer. And I'm okay," I insisted, brushing dirt off my hands. "I've sucked it up, as you put it."

Frowning, Brooke glanced at her watch and jumped to her feet, scaring the gull back up into the air squawking.

I rose, too, slipped on my Flexileg, and brushed sand off my butt. "I just wish I knew why Carlos has been so... what's the word?"

"*Antagonistic* toward you?"

"Right," I nodded. Brooke and I headed single file up the trail toward the campsite. "I'm not his *enemy*."

Brooke stopped in her tracks and turned to face me. "Here's something else to consider, Rainey: Maybe, by trying to keep his distance, Carlos is doing you a favor."

CHAPTER SIXTEEN

Breakfast, cleanup, pack-up, and WESTEX was heading northwest on the Trans-Canada. By noon we'd passed Sudbury. By late afternoon, we'd made the stretch of Lake Huron's north shore and through Sault Ste. Marie, stopping only long enough to answer various calls of nature and pass around sandwiches slapped together from breakfast leftovers. Exhausted from the heat and the sheer effort it took to stay civilized for so long, an amazing cheer went up two hours later when Carlos finally slowed the van and turned left off the highway into the campground at Agawa Bay.

Our assigned tent site was right on the beach, just thirty meters from Lake Superior's east shore. A brisk wind kept the biting insects away and blew sand in our eyes.

"As you know, we'll be here for three days," Dan announced at our team meeting that night.

"*Fiiiiinally.* Time to relax on the beach," Izzie said, taking in the long stretch of sand.

"Reality check," Brooke replied. "You've all been signed up for a two-day wilderness survival course. Starts first thing tomorrow. Seven AM."

Dan puffed his chest out like a proud pigeon. "My old buddy George runs a survival school just up the road from here. He can't wait to meet all of you."

"What the hell is this? Boot camp?" Frank groaned.

"It's whatever you make of it," Brooke replied.

Dan grinned. "When life gives you lemons, make—"

"Make out!" Alain hollered.

Day One of our wilderness survival course was strictly academic. Crowded around wooden tables inside a weather-beaten shed full of ancient AV equipment, dusty animal skeletons, and astronomy charts, the Six-Pack learned about what to do if we got lost or injured in the wilderness and how to treat and prevent bee stings, poison ivy, and hypothermia. We classified edible vs. poisonous plants, reviewed what to do in the event of a bear encounter, and honed our map and compass skills. We even learned what to do to prevent being hit by lightning—information that started Meena hyperventilating. Through it all, Dan's "old buddy George" was patient with our questions and gave us many opportunities to apply our knowledge to hypothetical scenarios.

Day Two was wet, blustery, and cold; in other words a great day to huddle in our tents with frothy mugs of hot chocolate and trashy paperbacks. Nice fantasy. The Six-Pack was forced to "suck it up," as Brooke would say, and spend all day outdoors. As a large team, we practiced building fires in the rain, blazing trails, and responding to mock first-aid situations. Then, in teams of three participants to one leader, we were transported by Jeep into the woods and dropped at two separate points, exactly three kilometers from a ranger station. Equipped with only a canteen of water, a map and compass, and a first-aid kit, each team was instructed to find its way safely back to base. Meena, Frank, Dan, and I, mud-spattered, teeth chattering, wet hair plastered to our skulls, arrived back just five minutes before Alain, Izzie, Homer, and Brooke.

Our survival instructor was pleased with everyone's performance.

"Not bad for a bunch of city punks, eh?" Homer beamed as he accepted his certificate, his nose dripping with rain.

None of us thought we'd actually *need* any of those wilderness survival skills that summer.

The wet weather carried over to our last full day at Agawa Bay. We spent the morning hunkered down under the tarps again, reading and bitching about the rain and just trying to stay warm. Though WESTEX didn't travel through eastern Canada, we were still responsible for knowing the history and geography of the Maritime Provinces. Alain was too quick to boast that the east coast was where Canadian civilization began with the arrival of the French explorers in the sixteenth century. "My ancestors," he bragged, tossing his ball cap up in the air and catching it on his head, the way he did at least fifty times a day, whenever he felt a burst of euphoria.

"Chimpanzees are French?" I laughed.

"The French *did not* initiate Canadian civilization," Meena said sourly. "The First Nations aren't called the *First* Nations for nothing." She squinted up at the gray sky over Lake Superior and brightened. "Hey, everyone! I think it might be clearing." Meena had been on self-appointed sky watch for two days now.

"Forget vet school, Meena. Become a meteorologist," Frank giggled.

"I didn't come on this trip to become some bimbo weather girl."

Maybe I should become a weather girl, I thought. Make the name work for me.

"Haven't you heard that old, saying, Meena," Dan interjected. "*Make your own weather?* Even if there's a hurricane or blizzard outside, you can carry the sunshine in your heart if you choose to."

The look Meena gave Dan could have caused a blizzard in Panama. It was enough to make you run for a jacket.

Meena's weather predictions were right; after lunch, the clouds disappeared, leaving the sky a brilliant blue. Dan made some calls to a nearby wilderness outfitters and rented sea kayaks and a guide to take us out on the lake. The guide spent a good half hour reviewing basic strokes and emergency water skills, and telling us about the tragic wreck of the *Edmund Fitzgerald,* which it turns out isn't just a Gordon Lightfoot song, after all.

From the lake, the rugged shore, rocky ledges, stands of gnarled jack pines, the sun bouncing around in the waves was... wow! A visual explosion of light and texture and color. I would have been happy to spend the rest of the summer out on the lake with nothing more than my sketchbook and watercolor pencils

Alain felt it, too. He spent almost an hour out there alone with his cameras, uncharacteristically quiet, setting up his shots and executing them like a sniper. Dan thought he'd taken a huge risk bringing his precious cameras out in his kayak. But Alain just shrugged, saying his cameras were a part of him. A third eye that let him see the world more closely.

Or maybe all those lenses and filters and crop functions helped him keep his distance.

CHAPTER SEᵥENTEEN

Our last night at Agawa Bay, a drunk guy from Wawa dropped by our campfire about an hour after Brooke and Dan had ended our nightly team meeting and turned in for the night. Boasting that he and his buddies drove down to the campground each weekend to get wasted, Drunk-guy explained they'd run out of beer. He was disappointed that we couldn't offer up anything more potent than tea or hot chocolate.

"What are ya?" he slurred. "A bunch of geeks?"

"Well... yeah." Homer shrugged.

"*Speeeeeak* for yourself, Homer." Izzie tossed her hair over her shoulder haughtily.

"You wanna go take a walk?" Drunk-guy asked Izzie.

"Take a hike," she retorted. "*Alooooone.* I'm taken."

"Then what about you over there?" Drunk-guy staggered over and draped a beefy arm over Meena's shoulder. "Anyone tell you that you look like Alicia Keys—only bald? Come on; wanna go check out the moonlight?"

Meena flung a stream of obscenities—and her mug of steaming hot chocolate—at the guy's crotch and flounced off across the road to lock herself in the outhouse.

"What the hell's her problem?" Drunk-guy stammered, wiping at the massive brown stain seeping down the front of his jeans. "You burned my dick, chick!" he shouted at the outhouse, then giggled at his stupid rhyme. He turned back to the campfire and addressed the rest of us. "Is she a dyke?"

For the record, she wasn't. In fact, in a rare moment of weakness during one of Izzie's late-night gossip-o-ramas, Meena had even admitted to *wanting* to hook up with a guy that summer. But only someone smart. And decent. And ambitious. (Okay, she wanted *Homer,* a fact to which he seemed totally oblivious. If Homer was having a love affair with anyone that summer, it was with Mother Nature. I don't think he'd complained about anything—or even stopped grinning—since WESTEX left Toronto.)

Not to be deterred, Drunk-guy slid down beside where Alain and I were perched side-by-side on a log. There were some who might say we were holding hands—but I didn't think thumb-wrestling counted.

"Nice legs, baby," Drunk-guy said to me, running a grubby hand over my knee. His hot breath smelled like beer and onions.

"Here," I said, bending down quickly, popping off my Flexileg, and pulling it out from where it was hidden underneath my pant leg. I offered it up to him. "Take one home with you."

Drunk-guy bolted off the log so fast he lost his balance and almost fell into the fire. Screaming, he scrambled up and ran off down the road and into the night like he'd seen a ghost.

I laughed so hard I fell backwards off the log, taking Alain down with me.

"*Bed! Now! All of you!*" Dan roared from his tent in the far corner of our campsite.

"Never wake a sleeping bear," Frank remarked solemnly.

A half hour later, Izzie, Meena, and I had finished in the shower house and were making a beeline for our tent, when I heard my name being spoken further down the beach.

"You go ahead," I told them. "I'll catch up in a sec."

The camp road and the beach were divided by a thin wall of brush, supplying me with adequate cover to watch through the branches.

I'm not really spying, I told myself. *Not if I'm tonight's hot topic.*

A full moon shone like a spotlight on Carlos and Alain, who were returning to the campsite from the lake with buckets of water to douse the stubborn campfire embers. Their voices carried inland on the breeze. They were talking about me all right. Me and Drunk-guy.

"Nice, the way you stood up for Rainey, your *girlfriend,*" Carlos taunted, a sneer in his voice.

"Rainey?" Alain laughed. "She can stand up for herself."

Ten points to the hockey-playing photographer.

"You've known her long enough to know that?" Carlos shot back.

Alain dropped his heavy bucket on the beach, hopping out of the way as water sloshed out onto his feet. "You've been hassling me about Rainey for the past half hour. Why?" he asked, clearly exasperated. "You treat her like she's got rabies."

Carlos halted and kicked at the sand. "Look... I'm just working through some problems right now."

"We've *all* got problems."

"Right. What's your big problem, Alain? A b in chemistry? A zit on your chin?"

Alain picked up his bucket and started up the beach to the fire pit. "Just forget it."

"No. Come on, Jocko," Carlos called after him. "Tell me your problems. Got an uncomfortable itch? Run out of spending money already? Miss your mommy?"

"Listen, Carlos, just shut the hell—"

"Glitch with one of your precious cameras? Worried that choosing WESTEX over summer hockey camp will get you cut from the team?"

Alain dropped his bucket in the sand again and kicked it over, spraying water all over himself and Carlos. "*YOU WANT TO KNOW ABOUT MY PROBLEM, ASSHOLE?*" he hissed.

My legs were telling me to turn and run, but my knees

wouldn't bend. Curiosity—and concern—about this darker, angry side of Alain glued my shoes to the gravel. I stood transfixed, barely breathing.

"My Dad was in construction, overseeing one of the downtown condo projects," he started. "Eight months ago, just last September, he had a heart attack at work, and stumbled against a guard rail. The rail broke and he fell. *Seventeen* stories."

Oh my God. That's why Alain wouldn't climb up to the lookout.

"My mom had a breakdown. She wouldn't eat. She didn't shower. Wouldn't even leave the house for a month. My twin brothers are thirteen. They started ditching school, shoplifting, smoking."

Carlos cut in. "Hey, man, if you're looking for sympathy, I—"

"*I don't want your fucking sympathy!*" Alain raised his voice and took a step closer to Carlos. If they had been moose, they'd be ready to lock horns. "You asked to hear my problem! You want to hear it or not?"

Carlos held up his hands defensively. "Your move."

Alain stepped back. His voice was clipped and raw. "Mom pulled it together this spring and decided to move with the twins back to New Brunswick, to my grandparents' farm. They left Toronto two weeks ago, when school let out. I applied to come on this trip because I didn't want to spend the summer alone in Toronto."

"Why didn't you just go with them?" Carlos asked.

"Sure, Carlos, like I never thought of that? Mom wouldn't let me go with them. Flat-out refused. She used the insurance money to pay off the house in Toronto and set up a trust fund to pay for my expenses through to the end of university. She insists that my dad would have wanted me to stay put. That changing schools and hockey teams now would hurt my future. That if I followed her and the twins back to the farm, even for the summer, I'd end up a farmer, not a photographer, and *definitely* not a hockey player."

Carlos cut in. "So why—"

"Why aren't I *happy?* Seriously, how many other kids my age have a house of their own, paid off, and enough cash in the bank to support themselves for the next six years? Too bad that fucking money can't bring back my dad or put my family back together again." Alain's voice cracked. "I feel so... out on a limb."

He picked a rock off the beach and let it fly out into the darkness of the lake. "I may just be the class clown on this trip, Carlos. The dumb jock who probably got picked because I promised to take some pretty pictures for next year's brochure. But I thank my lucky fucking stars that I'm here. I want to make the most of this opportunity, not waste my time sulking about things I can't change. I want to make my dad proud."

"So, what's your point?"

Alain growled in frustration and jabbed his index finger into the front of Carlos's shirt. "My *point* is I'm pretty sure *everyone* here has problems. But you, my friend, are the only one tripping about them. I don't know what—or who—it is that has you so riled up—"

Carlos crossed his arms over his chest. "I don't want to discuss it."

"So don't. But fucking learn to deal with it, would you?"

"The way you have? By hitting on Rainey?"

"Are you *jealous?* Because you've had plenty of opportunities to spend time with her, Carlos. But you keep blowing her off and making her feel bad. She deserves to be happy."

"And you make her happy, I suppose?"

Alain's voice dropped to barely a whisper. "I don't know. But she makes *me* happy."

Holy smokes. Suddenly, the moon seemed even brighter, the stars twinklier, the air fresher, my heartbeat faster.

Damn. Izzie was right. I'd lasted a week.

Carlos picked up his bucket and stormed up the beach to the fire pit without another word. His water hit the embers, sending up a cloud of ash. Flinging the bucket aside, he stalked off to his tent. Alain followed closely behind him, scooping up sand in his empty water bucket and dumping it on top of the fire, too. He stood by the pit for a long time, stirring mud into the coals with a stick of driftwood.

Go on, Rainey, I told myself. *Blow your cover. Tell him that being out on a limb won't be so bad because you'd be happy to*

*toss out your no-guys-for-the-summer policy and climb out
there with him.*

And I was just about to when Alain put his bucket down
softly in the sand, mumbled "'Night, Dad," to the stars, and
disappeared into the guys' tent.

CHAPTER EIGHT_EEN

In the morning, Alain stuffed his face with breakfast and cheerfully recited his "Joke of the Day."

"Okay," he started, swallowing a mouthful of toast. "The answer is: SIS-BOOM-BAH! The question is..." He drumrolled his fingers on the picnic table. "What sound does a sheep make when it explodes?"

"Eeeeew," Izzie groaned as Frank pelted an orange slice at Alain's head.

Though his mouth was smiling, Alain's eyes were tired. His hair was more rumpled than usual. Blond scruff stubbled his chin. I hadn't seen him toss his ball cap up in the air all morning.

I pulled him aside the first chance I got. "There's no time now," I said, gesturing to where Dan and Carlos were piling our belongings into the van's cargo trailer, "but, later... can we talk?"

"Cripes, it's me, isn't it? I know I haven't had a shower, but I brushed my teeth." Alain sniffed his pits skeptically.

"You're fine. But let's... do lunch."

"Picnic table for two? Peanut butter on whole wheat? Apple juice and happy banter? It's a date."

WESTEX stopped for lunch at a roadside picnic area near White River, the tiny town where—according to Dan—an orphaned black bear she-cub was bought from a hunter for twenty dollars by a World War I soldier named Harry Colbourn. Lieutenant Colbourn named her Winnie, after his hometown of Winnipeg. She traveled with him to England and was placed in the London Zoo when Lieutenant Colbourn was shipped to active duty in France. Christopher Robin, the son of the writer A.A. Milne, was a frequent visitor to the zoo. Winnie became the inspiration for—you guessed it—Winnie-the-Pooh.

"I've seen all those cartoons. Winnie-the-Pooh is a guy, isn't he? And he isn't a black bear. He's... yellow. Look, Dan." Frank pointed across the picnic area to a Disney-inspired statue. "I told you, he's *yellow!*"

"Winnie is *stiiiiill* a *BEAR*, Frank," Izzie laughed.

"And his/her relations are probably still wandering this neck of the woods," Meena added.

"Holding a grudge," I giggled.

Frank ate his lunch in the van.

Alain and I took our lunch to an empty picnic table upwind from the porta-potties. Alain picked a daisy from the tall grass and offered it up to me like a dozen roses.

"So," he asked, his mouth already full of sandwich as we slid onto the splintered benches opposite each other. "What's the mystery?"

"No mystery," I responded. "It's... well... I heard you and Carlos arguing last night when I was coming back from the shower."

"Damn. I knew I couldn't play the joker card all summer." Alain set his forehead down on the picnic table, knocking his ball cap off. It landed upside down. "Pierre Boudreau" was written in faded magic marker on the underside of the brim.

When he raised his head back up, a tiny wood chip was stuck to Alain's right eyebrow. It would have made a funny sketch if the rest of his face hadn't been twisted in such pain.

"That ball cap; it was your dad's?"

He nodded.

"I'm sorry about what happened—to him," I said.

"Yeah... well. Carlos was goading me. I thought sharing a slice of my own fucked-up life with him might make him realize he's not the only one with problems." Alain glanced over my shoulder to where Carlos was alone at another picnic table, eating with his back to the rest of us. "But he's a tougher nut to crack than I thought. Maybe I should have just slugged him," he grinned, stuffing a final piece of sandwich in his mouth.

I didn't want to talk about Carlos. "You must be so sad

sometimes." The smell of the daisy on the table was over-whelming, sending me back in time to Grandma and Grandpa Jenkins's funeral three years before.

Alain stuck the straw in his juice box and drained it. "My father was great. Funny. Athletic. Smart about people. He wouldn't want me spending the rest of my life bummed out."

"That's a pretty mature attitude."

"It's the hundred-dollar-an-hour attitude. My hockey coach sent me to a shrink. He didn't want my so-called 'grief' to flush my point record down the toilet."

I took a deep breath. "There's something I want you to know," I said.

"I hope it's good news," Alain said, wiping juice dribbles off his chin with his sleeve.

"It's this: Even if Carlos kissed a frog and turned into the prince of a guy I thought I knew back at Pineview, I've moved on. A few months ago, he was a seemingly friendly face when I sorely needed one, but now that I know him better... well, Izzie would call *him*—has called him—Mr. *Loooooser.*"

Alain frowned. "What does that make me?"

What *did* that make him? "Wow... let me think... Mr. Funny? Mr. Smart?" The wood chip detached from Alain's eyebrow and fluttered to the picnic table. "Mr. Adorable?" I added.

Alain groaned. "Shit, Rainey. Teddy bears are adorable. Puppies are adorable."

"Okay, you're *not* adorable. What do you want to hear? That you're a Mr. Heart-stopping Hunk of Mega-muscled Man-flesh?"

Alain flexed his biceps. "Yeah. I like that. What else?" he begged shamelessly.

"Mr. First-Rate Kisser?" popped out.

Alain's smile faded. *Oh no,* I thought. *I've said too much. Those seventeen birthday kisses happened days ago. He was just kidding around.* Refusing to meet his eye, I glanced left and right, scoped out a place to hide. Maybe if I just slid under the picnic table?

"Know what you are to me?" he asked.

I shrugged and sat on my hands so he wouldn't see them shaking. The air was so clean and fresh; why was I having trouble breathing?

He didn't speak until I'd mustered the nerve to look him in the eye. Then he said, "You, Rainey, are the best thing to happen to me in a long time."

CHAPTER NINETEEN

After leaving White River, Dan turned in his seat and lectured us on the physical and socio-economic landscapes of Northern Ontario. No book illustrations were necessary as we drove through blasted rock, rugged stands of pines, and raw areas of forest recently destroyed by wildfire. One tiny mining town after another sported, if little else, a police station, a few tired bungalows, a Bates-like motel for stranded travelers, and a run-down gas bar/diner combo catering to Trans-Canada truckers. The only bright spots in many of these hamlets were the shiny-green LCBO signs above the liquor stores.

Oddly, Frank fired an imaginary machine gun out the window at each one.

"My mother would love it up here," he remarked when Carlos stopped in Terrace Bay to refuel and let us use the washroom. It was the first time since the trip began that Frank had made any reference to his family.

"She's a nature-lover?" Homer asked, scanning the rocky

hills of pine and aspen. The six of us were taking turns at the pop machine.

"She's an alcoholic," Frank replied, counting his loose change and punching a few quarters into the slot. "When I was a little kid, she only drank evenings and weekends." He punched in another quarter. "But three cheers for tele-commuting. She told her boss she wanted to do her data-entry job from home because she needed to be there when little Frankie came home from school." Plunk went another coin. "Bullshit. She just wanted to drink all day. So that's what she does; drinks and types. Rum and Coke—that's her poison of choice. She drinks from a coffee mug that says *Number One Mom,* thinking I won't know," Frank cackled.

"Does she know she has a problem?" Homer asked. The rest of us were still speechless, not so much at Frank's revelation as at the way he just spewed it out at us, like it was bile that he couldn't keep down for one more second.

Frank hooted and punched the Hires button with his fist. "Her whole *life* is a problem. She hates her job. She hates my banker father, who was transferred to Germany last year and is remarried to an aerobics instructor. She hates the city, but doesn't want to move. She hates the subway, but won't buy a car. *And* she hates that I came on this trip, worked my *ass* off all year to afford it, and risk my life in bear country, just to get away from her for a while." Kerplunk! His root beer appeared at the bottom of the machine. "It was come on this trip or kill myself. Or her.

You know those girls who drowned their alcoholic mother in the bathtub a few years back? I envy them."

"They're in jail, Frank!"

"So?" He grabbed his pop and snapped the tab. "Cheers," he said. We all drank deeply.

Settling back into the van minutes later, my mind wandered west, to my own mother. Was she an alcoholic, too? A drug addict? Something even worse?

And why did I care? Hadn't I decided not to contact her? Why, then, was my mind still brimming with questions I'd never know the answers to? Not unless...

Forget it, Rainey, I scolded myself. *You already decided. Cut her loose.*

From my seat in the back, I reached forward and poked the back of Frank's T-shirt. He swiveled around. "How's your mom doing now that you're away?" I asked him. "Have you checked in with her?"

"Twice. Totally shit-faced both times. I'd hoped that without me to cook her dinner, and clean her puke, and put her to bed when she passes out on the floor, she'd get help. Or at least cut back. Oh well, can't win 'em all." He shrugged and turned back forward.

Frank might have been a non-jock, a liar about his love life, and total chickenshit when it came to wild animals, but he was no wimp when it came to his mother.

Not like me.

A half hour east of Thunder Bay, Dan instructed Carlos to take a turn north to Amethyst Mine Panorama, one of North America's largest amethyst deposits, the guide book said.

Dan cleared his throat. "Did you know... that the gemstone we call amethyst quartz was named after an ancient princess?"

"What was an ancient princess doing up *heeeeere?*" Izzie asked. "Not a castle or palace in sight."

"Good you asked," Dan replied. "Princess Amethyst traveled to the shores of Lake Superior to worship at the shrine of the goddess Diana. But little did she know, the arrogant wine god Bacchus had unleashed man-eating tigers to destroy the first humans they could catch."

"*NOT funny!* There are no *tigers* in these woods," Frank said.

"Tiger Woods, get it?" Alain piped up, elbowing him in the ribs.

Dan continued. "This story is a *myth,* Frank. Anyhow, hearing the roar of the tigers, Princess Amethyst climbed into a nearby quartz cave to pray for help. The goddess Diana heard her prayers and sealed the princess safely into the cave. In the end, Bacchus was forced to make amends by calling off the tigers, freeing the princess, and pouring red wine on the cave. That's why..." He raised an eyebrow in question.

"Amethyst is purple," Meena concluded.

Dan wasn't finished. "Legend also states that the wearers of amethyst will always be protected from the consequences of over-indulgence."

Frank spent a small fortune at the gift shop for an amethyst bracelet and matching earrings for his mother. He vowed to mail them to her from Thunder Bay ASAP. "It can't hurt," he said.

Another few minutes west on the Trans-Canada was the Terry Fox Monument, set on a hill overlooking Lake Superior.

Everyone knew that the west-facing statue marked the spot where, in September 1980, Terry Fox, the twenty-two-year-old B.C. athlete and right leg amputee, was forced to end his Marathon of Hope to raise funds and awareness for cancer research. His journey, which began in Newfoundland in April the same year, was intended to span the country. When cancer spread to Terry's lungs, he had covered over fifty-three hundred kilometers.

Brooke spoke. "I was *there,* in Newfoundland, when Terry dipped his artificial leg into the Atlantic and started his run. I was your age, a high school senior. Every year WESTEX stops here, and every year I marvel at the distance that handsome young man covered, and at the impact he had in such a short time."

"Terry Fox died of cancer in June of 1981, a month shy of this twenty-third birthday," Meena said, reading from a pamphlet she'd nabbed from the guest station.

"But how many lives have been saved as a result of his dream?" Brooke replied.

Everyone was uncharacteristically quiet; this wasn't the time or place for roughhousing and banter. What struck me most, looking past the monument, and out over the highway to the rugged shoreline and choppy waters of northern Lake Superior, was the beauty and desolation of the spot where poor health had forced Terry to abandon his journey. Even without the monument, it seemed the sort of spot where one could come to think deep thoughts.

Alain sidled up beside me and gestured to the statue. "He set the bar kind of high, *non?*"

I'd been thinking the same thing. Even with my good health and today's superior prosthetic technology, I doubted I could *walk* forty kilometers in *one* day, let alone *run* over forty kilometers *every day* for five months straight.

"I didn't mean just for you," Alain added when he noticed me studying my left shoe. "I meant for everybody."

We'd all have a lot to put in our journals that night.

CHAP**T**ER TWENTY

Sammy called as WESTEX was setting up camp at Thunder Hills Campground just east of Thunder Bay.

He broke up with Izzie. *Hell* broke loose at WESTEX.

The guys pretended not to notice Izzie's meltdown. Not easy; she was milking the drama cow down to her last drop.

Meena and I *tried* to show our support. We took Izzie aside. Passed her tissue after tissue. Let her hang her anger out to dry.

"That *ROTTEN SCUMBAAAAAG LOOOOOSER!*" she cried. "Sammy met someone else, he said, like it was *nothing*. We've been together for six months! He's only been working at that stupid sailing camp in Quebec for *threeeee* stupid *weeeeeks!* I hope they go sailing off into the sunset and get eaten by *SHARKS!*"

"I'm not sure that there *are* sharks in the St. Lawrence River, Izzie," Meena said.

"Not helpful," I said, elbowing Meena.

"I'll be the only *spiiiiinster* on this trip!" Izzie moaned. "Rainey has Alain. Meena has Homer."

"I do *not* have Homer," Meena said.

"Well, you *waaaaaant* him. And how could he not want you? You're *waaaaay* smart. And what did that drunk guy say last night? You look like Alicia Keys—only bald. It's—"

"Izzie!" Meena was irritated now. "It's *not* going to happen."

"Why wouldn't Homer want—"

"*Because he's gay,*" Homer said. Meena, Izzie, and I whipped our heads around to face him. "Sorry for sneaking up, girls," he grinned. "but I overheard my name being tossed around like a Frisbee."

"You're GAY!" Izzie shrieked, distracted at last from her own heartache. "*Reeeeeally?* You knew this, already?" she asked Meena

"He had to tell me." Meena frowned. "I did everything short of a lap dance to get him to realize I could be more than a good field study partner."

Izzie seemed pumped by the news. "There are *ooooodles* of gay guys in the performing arts program at my school, Homer. Are you seeing anyone? 'Cause if not, I could probably hook you up."

Cringing at her bluntness, Homer shook his head. "I'm still pretty fresh from the closet."

"Slim pickings here," she added, arms waving towards Dan and Carlos, who were reviewing maps at the picnic table, and Alain and Frank, who were busy at the camp stove, adding what looked like *way* too many dried jalapenos to a huge pot of chili.

"Getting into pre-med is more important to me than anything right now."

"So lay off him, Izzie," Meena said sharply.

"Why didn't you tell us before now?" she prodded.

"Didn't need to." Homer shrugged. "Besides, I figured it would be better for me if you got to know me first as Homer the science geek, not Homer the... homo."

I hear ya, Homer, I thought. Here's a rule of life I learned in kindergarten, along with my ABCs: Quirks with the potential to be... uh... *socially limiting* are best downplayed when trying to make a good first impression.

"How are your parents with it?" Izzie continued her interrogation. "Do they know?"

"Why don't you mind your own damn business?" Meena said to Izzie, standing up on the balls of her feet so she could get right in Izzie's face. "Forget acting and singing, Izzie. Why don't you and your tabloid mentality go look for a job at the *National Enquirer?*"

Homer put a hand up. "I don't mind questions, Meena. It's better than having people make wrong assumptions."

"Like who?" Izzie asked.

"Like my ultra-conservative parents." Homer kicked at the dirt with his Tevas until his toes were covered in gray dust. "When I told him I was gay, my father didn't speak to me for three months. My mother *still* cries sometimes when she looks at me. I would have put off telling them, at least until I finished high school, but they kept trying to set me up with daughters of friends from church. It was... ghastly. I finally just blurted out 'I'm gay' one night at dinner. They didn't even know what I meant at first. I had to explain it to them."

"Yikes." I cringed. That *was* rough.

"When my father dropped me off for this trip, he gave me spending money, wished me luck, and told me if I wasn't 'fixed' by the end of the summer, not to bother coming home." Homer's shoulders slumped.

That was the most he'd said at one time since beginning the trip. He seemed exhausted by his rant. Like he could use a nap.

"That's *terrible!*" Izzie threw her arms around him.

Homer disentangled himself. "No biggie, Iz. I've got a cousin that I can move in with. He's not gay, but he's open-minded. And he's got a great DVD collection. Maybe my parents will come around some day." His voice was glib but there was no disguising the hurt in his defeated shrug.

"Do *they* know?" Izzie asked, nodding toward Alain and Frank.

"Yeah. From the get-go. I didn't want it to come as a surprise later in the summer in case they had 'issues' sharing the tent with me. They're okay with it, I guess; it's not like I've been prancing around in a purple Speedo, belting out Broadway show tunes. Alain made jokes, of course. Wanted to know if he was my type."

"Is he?" I asked.

"Don't worry, Rainey; he's all yours."

"What about Frank?"

Homer laughed. "I could kick Frank's ass from here to Manitoba if I wanted to, and he knows it. Not that I'd want to," he added quickly, before excusing himself to help the guys finish dinner.

Immediately, Izzie switched back to tragic, dumped-girlfriend mode. "I don't think I can survive being single," she groaned to Meena and me. "I've always had boyfriends, since I was eleven. I'm a dumper, not a *dumpeeeee.*"

"Welcome to the real world," Meena smirked.

"I never knew that rejection could feel so... *iiiiicky,*" Izzie mused.

"Iz, I wrote the book on rejection," I offered, glancing over at Carlos; we'd effectively managed to ignore each other all day. God, all those hours I'd spent obsessing over him last spring. Hours that I'd never get back. Hours I could have spent painting a masterpiece. Or learning an instrument. Or even just... flossing.

"Any helpful hints?" Izzie asked. "I suppose tossing myself headfirst off a high rocky ledge tomorrow isn't an option?" she asked.

Cripes, Izzie, don't let Alain hear you talking like that, I thought.

Meena scowled. "Just get over yourself, Izzie. Face it; rejection is a part of life."

"One of the *craaaaappiest* parts."

"It's like what my grandmother used to say," I piped up.

"What doesn't kill you makes you stronger."

"Gee, thanks, *Oprah*," Izzie huffed.

Alain loped over to tell us dinner was ready. "Look at this flyer!" he added excitedly, passing it to me. "It was tacked to a tree near the outhouse."

A horror film festival was being held at the ramshackle drive-in theater we'd passed on the road to our campground.

"Yes!" Izzie pumped her fist in the air. "Now *that* would *cheeeeer* me up."

"I asked Carlos if he'd drive us, but he said he's too tired," Alain explained. "But so what? We'll just sneak out after Brooke and Dan go to bed. The guys are for it. Are you in?"

"I don't know..." Meena hesitated. "I'd been hoping to review my Manitoba history before we–"

"Well, *I'm* in," Izzie cut in.

"Me, too." I grinned.

"Oh, all right," Meena relented.

"And..." I added, "I have an idea."

CHAPTER TWENTY-ONE

Shortly after ten PM, Dan was snoring. And we didn't worry about waking Brooke. "I sleep with earplugs," she'd warned us the first night. "If you need me, yell *loudly*. Or bang on my tent. I'm a light sleeper and don't want to be roused every time one of you farts or slaps a mosquito."

Alain called a huddle. "Everyone have a flashlight? Toilet paper?" he asked. He and I had raided WESTEX's emergency TP supply. "Homer, do we have your portable radio?"

"Check."

The Six-Pack snuck off on foot, traipsing along the gravel camp road in the growing dark, dodging cars and trailers returning from town, talking loudly during quiet stretches to warn off any large, hungry creatures that may be out looking for a late-night snack.

It took forty minutes to reach the drive-in. The place was packed with cars and pickups. The stink of beer, popcorn, and hash wafted up over the area like a mushroom cloud. According to the flyer, the second movie, *Revenge of the Scum-Sucking Zombies 2,* was set to start.

"We can't admit you without a vehicle," the old guy at the booth said, his words whistling out the gap in his mouth where his front teeth should have been.

We hadn't come all that way just to be turned away. "Time for Plan B," Alain said, rubbing his palms together in anticipation.

"I don't know about this," Meena said. "It seems kind of—"

"Stay behind if you're *chiiiiicken,*" Izzie clucked.

"I'm NOT—"

"So shut up about it," Frank grumbled, looking just as wary as Meena. "Let's just get this over with."

The drive-in was encircled with a low barbed-wire fence. Keeping the poles in sight, we cut through the deep brush to a spot where we were least likely to be noticed and scrambled over onto the drive-in property.

"Now I know why WESTEX makes sure our tetanus shots are up to date," Homer remarked good-naturedly, inspecting his various scrapes and snags before flipping on his battery-operated radio. He fiddled with the dial until he picked up the screams and moans of the zombie-actors on the weather-stained screen. A perfect backdrop for our caper.

"This is going to be *sooooo* much fun!" Izzie squealed, hopping up and down. "You think there are any cute guys in those cars?"

she asked me. So much for her heartbreak over Sammy.

"Rainey, where the hell did you learn to pull off stunts like this?" Frank asked.

Alain grabbed him in a playful headlock. "You wimpy, city-raised kids never had to create your own fun."

Quickly, the six of us rolled toilet paper around each other's arms, legs, heads, and torsos until we all resembled poorly wrapped mummies.

"Now, spread out," I gestured. "Ready? One, Two, Three... *GO!*"

We sprinted towards the cars, legs wide, arms outstretched like the creatures on-screen. We ambled through the rows of vehicles, trailing toilet paper as people screamed in surprise and honked with annoyance. Some girls threw candy out their car window at Homer and Izzie, who were yelling "Trick or Treat!" Alain grabbed someone's discarded beach ball and started what could only be described as Mummy Volleyball with Meena and me. And Frank—oh my God—totally let loose. He jumped into the open bed of some guy's pickup and break-danced to some internal disco beat.

It's all fun and games until some crotchety old security guard sets his Doberman on you.

"*COURS!*" Alain bellowed.

Six mummies raced back towards the fence, four of us face-planting when we tripped in gopher holes. (Frank and I more than once.)

Despite this, we'd have all made it out of the drive-in
Scott-free if Izzie hadn't been hell-bent on being first over the
barbed-wire. In her haste, she snagged her sweater and was
still struggling to free herself when the snarling Doberman
caught up to our bottleneck and backed us all up against the
metal. The movie forgotten, the drive-in crowd turned their
attention to the Six-Pack. Why watch zombies destroy San
Francisco when you could watch a real-life drama unfold?

The security guard—turned out he was the same old toothless
guy from the ticket booth—zoomed up to us on an ATV, cut the
engine, and scratched the now passive dog under its chin. "Good
boy, Bullet. We caught us some hooligan trespassers." He
beamed a powerful flashlight across our guilty faces.

"This way," the man ordered us, firing up the ATV once
again, and pulling a fast U-turn.

"Smart-*aaaaass* dog," Izzie grumbled as Bullet eagerly herded
the six of us toward the shack that served as both drive-in office
and concession stand.

And now, holding cell.

CHAPTER TWENTY-TWO

A half-hour later, the Carlos-mobile spun into the drive-in, spitting gravel. "Get in!" he ordered the six of us, who were still dripping toilet paper. Singling me out with a special glare, he added. "What are you, five years old?"

"Not so fast," the security guard / ticket-taker / Just call me Hank, called out as Carlos slammed the now loaded van into reverse and began backing out of the parking lot. Hank stuck his head in the van, flashing us all a gap-toothed grin. "We have an agreement, right?" he asked Carlos.

He nodded smugly. "Brooke told me about your arrangement. She said to assure you that they'll all be here tomorrow." He glanced in his rearview mirror and scowled at us. "Bright and early."

Good. That meant Brooke wasn't going to kill us. Not tonight, anyway.

"Excuse me? *Haaaaank?*" Izzie called up to the front of the van. "What exactly will we be doing tomorrow?" She hadn't figured out yet which of crying, acting indignant, or flashing her boobs might get her out of whatever Hank and Brooke had planned for our punishment.

"Don't worry, Missy," Hank cackled. "I'll supply ya'll with rubber gloves."

Carlos delivered the Six-Pack back to the campsite a little past one AM. Remarkably, Dan was still sawing logs in his tent, oblivious to everything. So far so good.

Brooke had restarted the fire; the flames framed her face in an angry portrait. Her mouth was twisted in a knot.

She sent Carlos back to bed, gestured for the rest of us to join her by the campfire, and snarled through her teeth at us. "You stupid, stupid children! Such bad, bad judgment! I was so ashamed—and embarrassed—when a park warden showed up here an hour ago, shining a light in my tent, wanting to know who was responsible for the six kids at the drive-in. Do you know how lucky you are—how lucky we *all* are—that the police weren't called? And I can't believe you hiked to the drive-in after dark!" She crossed her arms over her chest. "I have a mind to send you all home."

The Six-Pack sat frozen on their logs.

Brooke's expression softened, but only slightly. "I *won't*. Not this time. But... I do expect better from you in the future." Her eyes shot sparks at Alain and me. "I'm pretty sure I know who masterminded this bird-brained scheme." She paused before readdressing the group. "But you are *all* guilty by reason of participation."

Mumbled "sorrys" all around.

"I don't want *apologies!*" Brooke hissed. "I want your word—your *solemn* word, Izzie, so wipe that smirk off your face—that nothing like this will happen again."

"It won't," Meena said.

"It won't," the rest of us echoed.

"Tomorrow is Canada Day," Brooke stated. "WESTEX was going to be visiting Thunder Bay and staying out late for the fireworks celebration, but instead, you'll all be up to your sorry asses in garbage while Dan, Carlos, and I enjoy a leisurely day off."

Turned out that instead of calling the police and having us charged with trespassing and mischief, Hank was sentencing the Six-Pack to clean up his drive-in. Not just our own toilet paper trails, but the *whole* drive-in—a week's worth of popcorn buckets, soda cans, beer bottles, used condoms... anything people had dropped out their car windows. Plus—yuck!—Bullet's poo.

Gross, but at least we weren't going to jail.

"Now douse the fire and get to bed." Brooke rose and retired to her tent without another word.

Izzie whispered to me a moment later. "Tonight was *fuuuuun.*"

"Speak for yourself," Meena growled, but I remembered how her eyes had danced with laughter during our game of Mummy Volleyball. She could be a lot of fun when she wasn't just waiting for a question to answer, or an injustice to fix, or a storm to rain down. "My mother would be so disappointed if she found out."

What would my mother think about tonight's hijinx? I wondered. Ah, why did I even care; she'd never find out about it, anyway. I'd made my choice.

Homer grinned like it was Christmas morning. "I had a great time, too!"

"Rainey and Alain are a bad influence on us," Frank pouted, then burst out giggling.

In the morning, we held our breath while Brooke took Dan aside and told him the supposedly "gifted" Six-Pack were just a bunch of good-for-nothing juvies, after all.

If she was looking to have her fury supported, she was sorely disappointed. Instead, Dan busted a gut laughing.

"True, it was dangerous," he admitted, wiping tears of laughter from his eyes. "And yes, don't *ever* pull a stunt like that again—you want to get me fired? *But,*" he chortled, tears running down his cheeks, "I haven't heard of kids doing anything so old-fashioned crazy since my buddy Fred and I used to spend Saturday nights cow-tipping near Peterborough."

"You should have been reported to the SPCA," Meena retorted.

Dan blushed. "Ah, we all do foolish things when we're young. Eleanor Roosevelt once said, 'You can do foolish things, but do them with enthusiasm.'"

Brooke's voice was ice. *"Are you sure, Dan, that's the attitude we want to promote here at WESTEX?"*

I felt bad for Dan the Doofus; he was just trying to build rapport. "Happy Canada Day," he waved as the Six-Pack set off to the drive-in, again on foot. The road was safe during daylight hours, Dan and Brooke agreed, probably just so Carlos could sleep in. "Just remember your bear safety," Dan added. "Stick together. Stay on the road. Be noisy."

"Want to make homemade firecrackers tonight? I know chemistry," Homer joked as we headed up the road.

Alain nudged Meena. "Or maybe we could all go *bear-tipping?*"

"*NOT* funny!" Frank replied.

CHAPT_ER TWENTY-THREE

The next day, WESTEX hiked a steep, rough trail across the Sleeping Giant peninsula. I ignored Dan's frequent "concerned glances" over his shoulder. Didn't he know that amputees are climbing Mount Everest these days?

Lunch was set out in a clearing. As we sat on boulders and logs, wolfing down fruit and bagels, Dan lectured us on several variations of the legend of the "Sleeping Giant," the rocky outcropping resembling—you guessed it—a sleeping giant, that jutted out into Lake Superior just east of Thunder Bay.

"What part of him are we sitting on now?" Frank asked, when Dan wrapped up and announced an hour of free time before we made our way back to the van.

Brooke consulted her map. "His chest."

Frank frowned. "Then we better not wander too far. I don't want to fall into his belly-button."

"Here. Brought you a drink."

I was sitting on the ground on a cushion of pine needles, my back against a thick trunk, putting final touches on a sketch of a squirrel I'd baited with a piece of peanut butter sandwich, when Alain tossed a juice box at me. It landed on my open sketchbook.

"Thanks," I said, putting it aside while I made a few final touches to my drawing.

Alain peered over my shoulder. "Hey! Great work!"

"I'll draw *you* sometime, too. My plan is to sketch *all* the wildlife I encounter this summer."

"Can I sketch you, too?" Alain asked.

"Sure," I replied, closing the sketchbook, and wedging my pencil behind my ear. I pierced my juice box with the straw and proceeded to drain it in one long sip.

"Can I sketch you like in the movie *Titanic* when Jack Dawson sketches Rose?"

Naked! Apple juice squirted out my nose. "NO!"

Alain plunked down next to me at an angle so that both our backs were held up by the same gummy pine trunk. "You gonna be some hotshot artist when you grow up?" he asked.

Well, wasn't *that* the million-dollar question? It embarrassed me that I was the only one of the Six-Pack who didn't have a high-powered career path all mapped out. Alain was going to be a hockey player and/or a photographer. Meena was going to be a veterinarian. Homer wanted to be a brain surgeon. Frank planned to become a billionaire selling environmentally-friendly cleaning products. Izzie was going to make it or break it in Hollywood. But me? I was sketching. That was my future—sketchy. Like a fuzzy dream made of light and shadow and color. It was all Lynda's fault. She never should have bought me that sketchbook and all those watercolor pencils. It was just something else distracting me from my WESTEX goal to settle on a practical/lucrative career.

I shrugged.

"Well, what's your fantasy job? I won't tell anyone. Pig farming? Exotic dancing? Ghostbusting?"

I chewed my fingernail. The worst Alain could do was laugh. "It's like you said. I want to be a hotshot artist. An illustrator," I said. "Children's picture books. Movie posters. Wall murals..."

Alain squeezed my shoulder. "Well, you'd be great at it."

I felt a bit squirmy inside. I wasn't used to anyone but Lynda— and she didn't really count—taking my artwork seriously.

"Will you be applying to OCAD next fall?"

"God, how cool would *that* be," I sighed, visualizing myself lugging a big, black portfolio bag around the Ontario College of Art and Design in downtown Toronto, jaunty with self-satisfaction and bursting with creativity. "But I'll probably end up at York or U of T. My father doesn't want to see me 'paint myself into a corner.'"

"That sucks."

"Yeah. He'd rather I learn technology and savvy business skills like he did. Be a computer chip off the old block."

Alain nodded. "That's not all bad, you know. You need technology and savvy business skills to be a success at anything these days, even an illustrator. Hell, even a hockey player."

"Cripes, Alain, you sound like my guidance counselor." I was so sick of people telling me what I needed. "Like I tell my dad, if all else fails, I'll open a doggy day care."

He laughed. "If *I* can't make a living as a hockey-playing photographer, I'll audition to be a subway musician."

"You play an instrument?"

"Promise you won't laugh? My grandfather on my mom's side is Scottish. Very Scottish. He eats haggis and wears skirts— I mean kilts—on Robbie Burns Day. He taught me to play his old bagpipes two summers ago when I went back to New Brunswick to help him out on the farm. I was just fooling around, but he said that I was pretty good. That I had a lot of hot air."

"I'd toss a few loonies in your baseball hat to hear you play," I giggled. "But only if you wore a skirt—I mean a kilt—too."

Alain tossed his Expos cap into the air and caught it on his head. I wondered how many thousands of times he'd practiced that move to get it right every time.

CHAPTER TWENTY-FOUR

We spent the next few days at Whiteshell Provincial Park in Manitoba—the "Friendly" province, if the license plates could be trusted. We worked on our canoe skills at Falcon Lake, caught up on our reading during a day of rain, and debated the rebellions and execution of Louis Riel, the infamous Métis leader, around the fire late one night.

One night at our after-dinner team meeting, Brooke lectured us about some of the famous and important women who influenced Manitoba. "Thanks to the efforts of Nellie McClung, Manitoba women, in 1916, were the first in Canada to be given the right to vote and hold public office. And you've all read Margaret Laurence and Gabrielle Roy in Can Lit."

"Don't forget Bobby Clarke," Alain piped up.

"Not a woman," Meena said.

"So? He's a hockey legend. He was from Flin Flon. Played for the Flyers from '69 to '84. Scored 358 goals. Had 852 assists."

"And Burton Cummings," Dan said. "Also not a woman."

Brooke smirked. "Not a hockey player, either."

"Who?" Homer asked.

"No, Homer. 'The *Guess Who.*'" Dan grinned at the Six-Pack. "Before your time."

Our Manitoba studies were in preparation for a three-day stay in Winnipeg. Instead of camping, we'd be billeted with senior summer students from a suburban high school. We'd be staying in *real* houses in *real* beds with kids who *hadn't* spent the previous three weeks living outdoors. Even showered and in clean clothes, the Six-Pack were scratched, insect-bitten, and wind-burnt—not at all the fresh-from-the-mall big-city kids the Winnipeg group might be expecting.

My billet's name was Sharon Greene, a.k.a., Miss Manitoba, a living, breathing, multiple-award-winning overachiever. She was super-model skinny, hell-bent-on-being-valedictorian smart, Christian-youth-group-leader bubbly, and wanted a career teaching children with disabilities. "It's just so *nifty* that I got paired with you!" she exclaimed, gawking at my Flexileg. *Nifty?* Was I billeted with a 1950's sitcom daughter? "Were you born with special needs?" Sharon asked.

The only special need I had at that point was to slap her upside the head, but I kept my cool.

Mrs. Greene was a homemaker. "My mother could show that jail-bird Martha Stewart a thing or two about baking apple pie,"

Sharon boasted that first evening at dinner. I thought Lynda's apple pie was better, but I didn't say so. I was trying to remember my "compassionate verbal strategies."

For three days, WESTEX visited museums, explored parks and historical sights around Winnipeg, loitered at "Portage and Main," and attended the Winnipeg Folk Festival—sometimes one-to-one with our billets, but most often in a large group. The high school provided bus transportation for these outings, so Carlos, being redundant, had been granted three days off to stay with a cousin who lived an hour away, near Brandon.

"Anyone want to place bets on whether or not Carlos comes back for us?" Frank asked. Okay, so I wasn't the only one wondering.

But there he was, at the crack of dawn on departure day, parked in the high school parking lot.

We'd all seen the map and checked the weather forecast. It was going to be a long, hot, windy drive from Winnipeg to Saskatoon.

Despite this, Carlos seemed unusually alert. Chipper, as my Grandpa Jenkins would say. His Mr. Nice Guy mask patched up and secured firmly in place. He was even pleasant to *me*, asking how I'd enjoyed Winnipeg and my billet. I told him everything had been just "nifty."

As we piled our packs into the cargo trailer, Alain poked me, cocked his head towards Carlos, and mimed taking a hit off a joint.

"No way." First Izzie suspects he's been drinking and now... Didn't Carlos have enough problems?

Don't get me wrong, I'm no teen crusader against mind-altering substances. I'd even smoked weed with Derek in his basement back in Mollglen when we were not quite fifteen and had just started dating. He'd stolen two joints from his older brother who played drums in a garage band—the Nose Pickers or the Butt Lickers, I could never remember. I looked at it as a science experiment. I wanted to know what it was that made drugs so great that people would steal, kill, and go to jail for them.

My experiment was a flop; all I got for my efforts was a short-lived coughing fit and a nasty taste in my mouth. But for Derek, that afternoon sparked a weekend drug habit that I convinced myself wasn't a problem. We had a deal: he wouldn't pressure me to join him and I wouldn't pressure him to give it up. "No pressure"—that was Derek and me. Even when he dumped me, his reasons were clear; it would be too much "pressure" to keep our relationship going long distance. Grrrr.

Alain laughed. "Look at his eyes—they're as glazed as a jelly doughnut. And he's, like, giggling to himself."

"Wouldn't we smell it on his clothes or in the van?" I asked.

"Like you can smell *anything* in that van besides the laundry bags and foot stench?"

"He can't drive stoned, can he, Alain? We didn't sign up for the Magical Mystery Tour."

He shrugged. "We can't accuse him. We have no proof."

Well, I'd be sure to fasten my seatbelt extra tight. "You ever smoke?" I asked Alain.

"I've tried it."

"Like it?"

"Nothing on earth beats a hockey high. Except maybe..." He winked at me as we slammed the trailer hatch closed and headed for the van.

"Yeah, yeah." Sex. It was on my mind, too, strangely juxtaposed with a million facts about Canadian history and geography. But Alain and I weren't there yet. Not even close. How could we be? We were never alone. Stalled at first base. And me with all those condoms in my pack.

CHAPTER TWENTY-FIVE

The Carlos-mobile sped past fields of bright yellow canola and blue flax, turning off the main Trans-Canada onto the Yellowhead at Portage la Prairie by mid-morning.

Emerging dusty, windblown, and cramped from the ride, necks sore from gawking around at the grain elevators and wind farms, *my own eyes* sore from watching Carlos's driving like a hawk, we stopped for lunch about an hour past the Manitoba-Saskatchewan border.

"*Loooook!* Sunflowers," Izzie remarked. There were fields and fields of them, tall and sturdy, swaying like modern dancers in the wind.

"My grandparents used to call me 'Sunflower' when I was a kid," I remarked to Alain as we carried pitas and fruit to a small spot of shade under an aspen tree.

He laughed. "Kind of a whacked nickname for a girl named Rainey."

"I was always taller than the other girls and had this shock

of yellow hair that stuck out all over," I explained. "They told
me they called my mother 'Sunflower,' too, for the same..."

What the hell was I saying?

Alain wiped peanut butter from his fingers onto his shorts.
(I could hardly criticize him for this, since my own shorts were
always covered in smudges of watercolor pencil.)

"Your parents are divorced, right?"

I lay back in the grass and closed my eyes. "I don't think my
parents were ever married."

"Do you see your mother often?"

"I... uh..."

"Oh, God, I'm so stupid," Alain said. "Is she—"

"Dead? No. But..." I wasn't ready for this discussion. *But you
started it,* you moron! I reminded myself. And how could I *not* tell
Alain about my mother after he'd been so honest about his own life.

So... still on my back, with eyes still firmly closed so they
wouldn't blurt out more than I intended about my feelings, I
told him what I could. That Sara was only eighteen when she
had me. That she ran away six months later. That she apparently saw me in the Flexileg print ad last fall and tracked my father
to Toronto. That I'd only found out the night before WESTEX left
home that she lived in Squamish, B.C.

"You must be so excited!" Alain shouted. I turned my head
and cracked one eye open at him. The bright sun framed his
head like a halo. He looking so happy for me, like meeting my

mother for the first time was something I should be ecstatic about.

I sat up and shook my head at him fiercely. "I'm not calling her."

"Aren't you curious?"

"Curiosity killed the cat."

Alain leaned back on his elbows. "Wow... I hope you change your mind."

"*Why?*" I demanded, ripping a fistful of dry grass from the ground. Greg said it was my decision, and I'd made it. I wasn't looking to have that decision critiqued, even if my reasoning did seem to the average person to have as many holes as the scarf I'd knit my father for Christmas back in sixth grade.

"Aren't you interested in knowing what she's like?"

"She's *awful,* Alain! What sort of mother leaves a nineteen-year-old guy to raise a baby alone? What sort of a daughter leaves town without saying goodbye to her own parents?"

"Isn't there anything you'd like to *tell* her, or *show* her, even if it's just to let her know how well you've turned out without her?"

Before I could stop myself, I did something I hadn't done since Greg told me we were moving to Toronto. I bawled. "What if I call her, or go see her, start to care about her, to need her, and she rejects me again! Damn her." *And damn you too,* Alain, I thought. *Derek wouldn't have pressured me like this.* He would have just said "whatever" and gone off somewhere to smoke a joint.

"I didn't mean to upset you," Alain said. But I could see that he still didn't understand. How could he? He'd grown up in a normal family. He'd give almost anything to be with his mom and brothers in New Brunswick, or to be able to see his dad again. "If you want, I'll go with you," he added, laying his hand on mine.

I yanked my hand away. "*I'm not going!* It's enough that Greg loves me."

"It's not just your dad who loves you," Alain sighed.

"I know," I sniffed, shoulders sagging, eyes to the ground. "Lynda loves me, too." Whether I wanted her to or not.

Alain reached over and lifted my chin so I had no choice but to look him in the eyes. "*I* love you," he said.

CHAPTER TWENTY-SIX

We'd only be staying in Saskatchewan overnight, forgoing the tents once again for motel rooms in Saskatoon.

Alain and I went on what, under normal conditions, would be called a "date." After gorging ourselves at a nearby Pizza Hut, we set out on foot along a recreational trail paralleling the South Saskatchewan River. It was a warm evening, clear and dry. People were out in droves.

The sky was still bright when we walked passed a booth renting in-line skates.

"Want to?" I asked.

Alain chewed his lip like a starving person who had just been offered a turkey dinner. "You can skate?" he asked me.

"I'm not bad," I said. Not very good, either, but exercise was exercise after a day cooped up in the Carlos-mobile.

Alain grabbed my hand and we rushed to the booth.

For a while, we skated along slowly. I needed to get a feel for the skates. Find my center of gravity. Work at maintaining my balance. Alain was as loyal as Simon, happily tagging along at my side, even though I could sense that he was itching to bust free at full speed for the sheer joy of it.

"Alain, just go. I'll catch up," I insisted after a while.

He kissed my cheek and took off like a rocket, dodging pedestrians, leaving cyclists and slower skaters—like myself—in his dust. *He must be a thing of beauty to watch on the ice,* I thought. Ah, he was a thing of beauty anyway, what with all that messy, white-blond hair sticking out the back of his dad's old Expo cap, his animated eyes, the slightly off-center nose he said was busted in a hockey brawl.

I gained some momentum and caught up to him thirty minutes later. He was flaked out on the grass by the river, panting from exertion, looking as thoroughly content as Simon stretched out on the back porch after a long game of Frisbee.

Showing off, I waved and skidded to a stop—or tried to—the way good skaters do. Instead, I tripped off the pavement and—*ooomph!*—landed flat on top of Alain.

"Just thought I'd drop by," I said.

"I think you broke my ribs," Alain groaned.

"Are you in pain?"

"Actually, you on top of me feels... pretty good."

So that's what's poking into my stomach. I rolled off him and sat up quickly. Smoothing my hair, I took in the scenery. "I never realized that Saskatoon was such a big city."

Alain sat up beside me. "It kind of rises out of the prairie like a big shiny oasis. Like... Oz." He started humming. "We're off to see the Wizard..."

It was dusk now. I looked up into the clear sky and strained my eyes to find the first evening star. "This is turning out to be such a great summer," I murmured. *If only this Sara thing wasn't hanging over my head, I thought. Or if it were possible to use my watercolor pencils to sketch out a lucrative/practical career plan.*

"Yeah. It'll really suck when it all ends." Alain reached over to flick a piece of grass out of my hair.

An alarm went off in my head. "What do you mean?"

No response.

Neon lights flashed behind my eyelids: *Danger Ahead!*

"Alain?"

"*Oui?*" He rolled onto his back contentedly and closed his eyes.

"Am I just... part of your trip?"

He rose back up on his elbow and eyed me with confusion.

"Am I just part of your all-inclusive package?" I demanded. The setting sun suddenly seemed too hot, too bright. "Transportation, accommodation, food, instruction, park fees, summer fling?"

He let out a tortured sigh. "Rainey, could we not talk about this now? Let's not spoil the night."

"Okay," I said, my words cold as January despite the heat. "Let's not." I rose and brushed dirt off my pants. Without another word, I clomped over the grass to the paved path, and skated off back in the direction of the rental booth.

Alain called after me. "Rainey, wait! I changed my mind. Let's talk."

Screw him.

It took him less than ten seconds to catch up. Alain kept pace and didn't say a word to me until after we'd returned our skates.

I stomped off toward our motel, still angry but feeling horrible, too, as if I'd let us both down somehow, as if I'd broken some sacred code of boy-girl relations. Why did I keep doing that? First Derek. Then Carlos. Now Alain. *That, Rainey, you idiot, is why you vowed to keep away from guys this summer. Now look at the mess you've made.*

"Rainey?"

I kept going.

Alain cursed in French.

Brooke said I was strong, that I could suck it up. She was wrong. I was a mess and a coward. And about fifty other rotten things. There should be a rehab facility for relationship-challenged females like me. A week ago, I'd told myself that I'd be there for Alain. That I'd help him hang on when he felt out on a limb.

What I didn't realize then was how far out on my own limb I was that summer.

Alain stepped out in front of me, blocking my path.

"Piss off," I said.

He grabbed my shoulders. "I can't promise you forever right

now, Rainey. But I will promise you that if you run away from me now, whatever we've got going is over. Now."

I lost it. "Is this about my leg?" I demanded. "You're going to dump me at the end of the summer because you aren't sure how your friends will react to you dating a—"

"*ARE YOU FUCKING CRAZY*?!" he shot back.

I looked into Alain's eyes. They were cold and hurt. Sighing, I pointed to a nearby park bench. We sat down.

After what felt like a decade of silence, Alain turned to me. "*What the hell was that all about back there?* I told you less than five hours ago that I loved you. Doesn't that mean anything to you? Incidentally, you didn't say it back to me, so if anyone should be insecure here, it should be *me*. How do I know you aren't just spending time with me until Carlos snaps out of it and comes to make his move on you? Or maybe I'm just some *distraction* so that you don't have to deal with the issue of contacting your mother."

Whoa. He was just so... wrong!

I took a deep breath. It stuck in my throat. My next words came out garbled. "I love you, too, Alain."

He looked unconvinced. "Why was that so hard for you to say?"

"Because it scares me to death."

"Why's that?" Apparently, I wasn't going to be let off easily.

"*Because I wasn't supposed to let myself fall in love with anyone this summer, Alain!*" I shouted.

He started to say something, but I cut him off at his first syllable. "And what's *worse,* I don't think I've ever *been* in love with anyone before. Okay, sure, I had a thing for Carlos last spring, but he never gave me a chance. And, yeah, I had a boyfriend back in Mollglen, but it wasn't.,. serious."

"So what's the problem?"

"The *problem,* Alain," I shouted, "is that I'm trying to piece together my messed-up jigsaw puzzle of a life this summer! I thought I knew where you fit. Now I'm scared that you don't fit at all. You aren't — and *you can't be* — just a fling for me. I only have time this summer for stuff that matters."

I could just imagine Alain thinking, *Right, Rainey, you hypocrite. Like the drive-in escapade. That certainly was right up there with finding a cure for global warming.* But instead, he just frowned. "If I matter so much to you, why did you shut me out so quickly back there?" Alain asked.

"You said, 'Let's not talk about this.'"

"*This* being our future, right? Don't you know that things will be different when we go home?"

"Yeah. Daily showers again."

"Don't be a smart-ass. I mean... we won't get to see each other every day. We don't even go to the same school. And I have hockey. The house needs painting. I want to try selling some photographs so that I don't have to rely on my trust fund to buy fucking toothpaste. You live four subway stops away.

Wouldn't it be better if we agreed to call it quits at the end of WESTEX and cut our losses? If we try to stay together, you'll just end up hating me and I don't think I could handle that."

"Why would I end up hating you?"

Alain looked at me like he thought I had brain damage. "I have hockey games every weekend. Practice and training almost every day, sometimes twice. Photo workshops. Visits to New Brunswick. Every girlfriend I've had—and there haven't been many, in case you want to get mad about *that*, too—ends up dumping me because I won't hang out at the mall after school or set up regular weekend dates. Or spend hours like this one, arguing about where our relationship stands."

"Alain?"

"I know. I'm a selfish asshole. I've heard it all before. I won't apologize for it."

"Alain," I repeated. "I grew up in a hockey town. I know about the practices and games and clinics, plus school, homework, jobs, and family. I don't play hockey, Alain, but I do have..." I counted on my fingers, "... volleyball clinics, a job at Pineview, my artwork, flyball league with Simon, monthly orthopedic appointments, and a stepmother who insists on spending time with me. In other words—"

"You're busy, too."

"I don't *want* a boyfriend who hangs around all the time like a cheap accessory."

"What *do* you want, then?"

The joy of being seventeen was having the vocabulary to make incredibly mature-sounding speeches—even after spending the preceding half hour shouting and whining like a pissed-off preschooler—without having the experience to know what I was getting myself into. I swallowed hard and pressed on the way some heroine of a teen TV drama might. "I want to watch you play hockey... sometimes. I want to help you paint your house; I'm good at that sort of thing. I want you to text me a 'joke of the day.' I want to get together when it's *possible*, even if it's just to walk Simon. Or do homework. Or watch DVDs. Or—"

"Make out?" Alain was coming around. Whew.

I needed to finish my rant. "You have these big plans, Alain, and I want to support them, just like I hope you'll support mine—once I figure out what they are. And if it doesn't work, we'll breakup. Maybe we won't even make it through the rest of the summer. But—"

I had to halt my monologue then because Alain kissed me. Really well, and for a really long time. I wasn't sure what it was I'd said right, but I'd have to say it more often.

"Anyway," I sighed, pulling away to wipe a blob of spit from my lip. "I don't need—or want—you to promise me forever. I just don't want to buy into this relationship if you're only looking for a summer rental." Hmmm. *Maybe I have a future in real estate?*

Alain laughed. "Rainey?"

"And I get that some girls expect too much of your time, Alain. But maybe I can be the one who's different. Maybe—"

"Rainey?"

"Yeah?"

"Just shut up about it! You had me at the part where you want to help me paint the house."

When it got dark, we returned to the main street in search of a Cineplex and a funny movie; there'd been more drama in the past hour than either one of us was prepared for. While we waited for the lights to go down, Alain stopped shoveling popcorn into his mouth long enough to put his arm around me and say, "I'm sorry I threatened to call it off tonight if you didn't stop and talk to me. It was bullying."

"No, Alain. I'm *glad* you called me on it. I don't want to be someone who runs when the going gets rough."

I didn't want to be like my mother.

CHAPTER TWENTY-SEVEN

With the exception of Dan, who could probably sleep through a nuclear holocaust, the males were in foul moods the next morning.

While Dan settled our bill at the office and Carlos gassed up the van, the rest of us dug into muffins and fruit in the guys' room. "A wailing baby next door kept us awake all night long," Homer griped.

"Who knew that something so small could scream so loud for so long?" Frank added.

Alain yawned. "Carlos stomped out at three AM to sleep in the van. I guess uncomfortable sleep is better than *no sleep at all*, which is what *I* got."

Brooke grinned. "Welcome to fatherhood, boys."

Her smile vanished when she turned and spotted Carlos, back from his trip to re-fuel, leaning against the door frame. He gave her a murderous look, turned on his heel, and stomped back outside.

Brooke started after him. "I'm sorry, Carlos. I wasn't thinking!" she called.

"Bite me," Carlos shot back, slamming the door behind him. Baby cries erupted again from next door.

Brooke sank onto one of the beds and bit her lip. "I deserved that," she sighed.

The Six-Pack knew better than to ask what the confrontation had been about. But Carlos's secrets were emerging whether he wanted them to or not. And I wasn't sure anymore that I wanted to know them. Not if they had to do with his running out on a baby. A baby named Jessie?

But hadn't he said he'd *miss* Jessie the most?

Dan burst into the room. "Let's go, happy campers! Grab your packs and hustle. Carlos is ready to leave without us!"

"I'll just bet," I mumbled.

Past rolling plains and dusty villages, from Saskatoon northeast to the Alberta border, we were Dan's captive audience-on-wheels. "Did you know... that the province of Alberta was named after Queen Victoria's daughter, Princess Louise Caroline Alberta? Or that the town of Vulcan, Alberta, boasts the largest replica of the *Starship Enterprise* in the world?"

Which reminded me: it had been a long while since I'd called Greg.

I phoned during an early lunch at Lloydminster. It was past noon in Toronto; I knew Greg would be out on the back porch with Simon. Theirs was a regular lunch date. Lynda never let

Simon eat table scraps, but Greg snuck him leftovers and peanut butter crackers when she was at work.

He answered, chewing. "Rainey! How are you, kid?"

"Did you get my postcards? How's Simon? Did you know that there's a town in Alberta that has the biggest replica of the Starship Enterprise in the world?"

"Vulcan, right?" He swallowed. "Listen, Rainey, I'm glad you called. There's something I have to tell you."

Oh, cripes, what now? I thought.

"It's kind of sudden, but I've been asked to do a major consulting project. I'm going to Japan for three weeks. I leave this weekend."

Japan? "Is Lynda going with you?"

"I wish she could. *Lynda* wishes she could. But she's committed to speaking at an obstetrical conference at U of T. It's just as well; if you have an emergency, it's best if one of us can be reached in Toronto."

"You've never been out of the country for so long before, Greg," I said.

"I'll be home before you are. You won't even miss me."

"I miss you *now*, Greg," I said, which was at least a bit true.

"You *sound* awfully happy."

"Yeah, well." I debated telling him about Alain. Nixed the idea. Greg had enough balls in the air right now without knowing that his daughter was in cahoots with a junior hockey player with rock hard abs and his own house. "How's the Web site doing?" I asked instead. Greg's *Star Trek* Web site was rated one of the best in the world. Not that many normal people would care.

"Over three thousand hits yesterday," he bragged. "But I'm not going to have time to monitor the site when I'm away. Lynda promised to keep an eye on things for me."

"Aren't you glad you married Wonder Woman?" I asked.

Greg ignored my sarcasm. "How's the course load?"

"It's a lot of work. But it's fun. I've made some great friends."

"Any problems with the Flexileg? Are your knees okay?"

"Don't be a worrywart, Greg. You know I can keep up."

In the background I heard happy woofing.

"Lynda just came through the door," Greg said. "Want to say hi?"

Not especially. "Yeah, I guess. Have a great time in Japan."

"Rainey, is that you?" Lynda said into the receiver a few seconds later.

"Did you get my message about the birthday cake? Everyone loved it. Thanks again." I'd done oral history exams that took less effort than uttering those three sentences.

"You're *very* welcome!" Lynda replied. "My pleasure. I guess Greg told you about his business trip?"

"I'll try to keep myself out of trouble while he's gone."

"You know that I'm here for you, Rainey," Lynda said.

"Uh-huh."

"Call me anytime. I suspect you've got some rough water ahead in the next few weeks."

"Well... I *am* going rafting on the Athabaska in a few days."

"That's not what I meant."

I knew it. And I knew that Lynda knew that I knew it.

"Greg told me that you decided *not* to contact your mother?"

"So?"

"Think you'll change your mind?"

"No."

"Well, it might be rough for you, anyway, just to know she's there, so close by."

"I'll be *fine.*" *Then why is just thinking about it now making your heart beat so hard in your chest that you might break a rib?* I thought.

Lynda sighed. A rare phenomenon. "Maybe you're too old to need advice from your wicked old stepmother, Rainey. But I love you. And if you let me, I can be one hell of a good friend."

"Lynda?" What I thought I should say—*knew* I should say— was on the tip of my tongue. But all that came out was: "Right."

CHAPTER TWENTY-EIGHT

WESTEX drove straight through the town of Hinton, Alberta, turned north, crossed the fast-flowing Athabaska River, and reached Foothills Park in time for dinner.

Through a ridge of spruce backing our campsite, we could see mile after mile of green hilly forest, ending with the sun ducking over the gray Rockies, only another half-hour's drive west, Brooke promised.

To our left, a campsite was occupied by an elderly couple grilling steak outside a large RV. On the right was a younger trio, a man and two curly-haired women, one thin, one very, very fat. Neither group seemed thrilled to be camping beside a group of teenagers. They watched us suspiciously as we set up the tents and cooking area, as if waiting for the beer and boom boxes to emerge.

After a late dinner of beef and vegetable stew, Brooke called our nightly team meeting to order around the campfire. The temperature had dropped so low we could see our breath. Dan had warned us that nights grew cold here in the foothills, but the sudden shift from the dry summer heat of Saskatoon to the frigid single digits of Alberta left us huddling close by the fire, clutching mugs of hot chocolate like they were all that came between us and death by hypothermia. *I should have packed mittens,* I thought, pulling the sleeves of my polar fleece jacket down over my fingers. *And long johns.*

"Regarding day trips, Dan and I are splitting you into two groups for the next three days," she said. "You can cover twice as much ground—literally. Evening activities will be unchanged: team meetings followed by leisure activities of your choice, *provided* that those activities are *legal* and respect campground policies and the environment. If you leave the campsite, Dan and I *must* know where you are going, and what you are doing."

"Alain, Izzie, and Frank will be Group A," Dan read off his clipboard. "Frank, Meena, and Rainey are Group B."

Brooke handed out handwritten schedules. "As usual, Carlos will be driving you to the starting points of your daily activities, picking you up afterward, and performing lifeguard duties as necessary. Dan and I will act as resources to both groups on an as-needed basis, but we won't be active participants. By now, your groups should have the outdoor skills and problem-solving abilities to complete your missions cooperatively and independently.

"Any questions?"

"Anybody know any ghost stories?" Alain asked.

Dan and Brooke excused themselves to go to bed.

The Six-Pack had already heard a few eerie tales that summer. At Algonquin Park, Dan told us about Tom Thomson, the famous landscape artist who drowned in the park's Canoe Lake in 1917. As he was an experienced outdoorsman, there remains speculation that his death, in only a few feet of water, was *not* accidental. Then, while passing through Saskatchewan, Dan explained that the fertile Qu'Appelle Valley north of Regina got its name when a young native warrior was out paddling across Katepwa Lake. He heard the voice of his dying lover calling to him. When he reached shore and was told of her death, he drowned himself in the lake. People say that their voices can still be heard calling to each other in the wind.

"I know a ghost story," I said. "And it's absolutely true."

"As true as Frank's girlfriend," Meena giggled.

"*NOT funny!*"

Homer shone his flashlight in my face. "You're up, Hitchcock."

I set my mug on the ground and cracked my knuckles. "In the 1940s, when Camp Wenibawabie was only a few years old, the year-round caretaker was an old guy named Orville. He had a dog, a Black Lab named Coal. Orville thought that the dog was all he needed for company during the off-season. You've seen *The Shining?*"

Nods all around.

I leaned forward. "Okay, so just like the Jack Nicholson character in the movie, Orville went crazy. Totally bonkers. Cabin fever, I think it's called. When he took walks in the forest, he'd hear the squirrels talking to each other—and to him. 'Hey, Orville, how about a drag off your pipe?' they'd ask. Or 'Hey, Orville, don't you think it's time to set out the mousetraps?' He'd see a group of birds on the roof of the tool shed and imagine they were plotting to call the camp owners and tell them he was a slacker."

"What about the dog?" Frank asked.

"Coal loved the old nutcase. That is... until the day Orville mistook that big, beautiful dog for Satan... *and chopped his head off with an ax!*"

"*Disgusting!*" Meena shouted, pelting me in the forehead with a marshmallow.

"Shhhhh! Settle down!" An annoyed voice traveled over from the site occupied by the elderly couple.

"Orville buried the dog's body deep in the woods," I whispered. "But the cold and the deep snow discouraged him from making the long trip again. Instead, he threw Coal's head down the well near the dining hall."

"Great. Now I'm going to have nightmares," Frank groaned.

"Go on." Alain rubbed his palms together. "This is getting good."

"Orville died soon afterward. Hypothermia, probably. He was found on the riverbank in the spring when the camp's owner dropped by for a pre-season inspection." I paused, then whispered, *"The raccoons and ravens had picked his bones clean."*

"Rainey, you are one *siiiiick* puppy." Izzie shivered.

"Summer was coming," I continued. "The camp owner had Orville's remains taken to town for burial and hired a new caretaker."

"That's *it*? Pretty lame ending, Rainey," Homer said.

"It's *not* the ending." I said. "The camping season began a few weeks later. Things had... changed. Campers who got up at night to use the outhouse would run back to their cabins scream-ing, *'There's a black, headless dog running across the fields! Wagging its tail!'*"

Frank put his hands over his ears.

"Others reported hearing faint barking coming from inside the old well."

"Poor Coal, trying to reunite his body parts," Meena said solemnly.

I shrugged. "I went to Camp Wenibawabie for eight summers; I never saw or heard any ghost dogs. But... my last summer there? The old well was finally filled in and cemented over. One morning, my friend Julie and I passed by the site on our way to the craft building." I picked up my mug and took a long sip of hot chocolate.

Homer sat forward expectantly, so far forward that I thought he might singe his eyebrows in the fire flames. "And..."

"*THERE WERE FRESH DOG PRINTS IN THE CEMENT!*" I yelled.

"Shut up, you damn kids!" a gruff old man barked from the campsite next door.

Somewhere in the distance, a lone wolf howled.

CHAPTER TWENTY-NINE

The next morning, Homer, Alain, and Izzie were dropped off at the fairgrounds in Hinton to attend a regional rodeo. Alain was excited about seeing the bull-riding and calf-roping contests. "Homer and I are excited about seeing the *cooooowboys,*" Izzie giggled.

Alain rolled his eyes. "I've been paired up with Will and Grace."

Frank, Meena, and I were driven west into Jasper National Park. We gaped at the Rockies, visited the Jasper Yellowhead Museum, and picked up rental mountain bikes to make a windy uphill journey to Pyramid Lake. Brooke assured me that it would provide excellent scenery for sketching. No lie. Who knew so many shades of green and blue and brown could possibly exist in nature? Or that I could actually capture them all by simply creating layers of watercolor pencil on paper and smudging them with a finger wet with lake water.

How would I ever consider a skill that gave me goose bumps just a hobby?

The next morning, Alain's group was dropped off at Maligne Lake for hiking and a boat cruise to Spirit Island. My group was registered for a guided rafting tour down a section of the Athabaska River.

"Uh, isn't this *dangerous?*" Frank asked, his face chalky as he tightened his crash helmet and stepped into the rubber boat.

"Ever seen *The River Wild?*" the guide asked.

Frank shook his head. "Why? Does everyone die?"

The guide winked at Meena and me. "Not everyone."

Despite Frank's never-ending squeals of terror, it was a spectacular day: wet, cold, exhilarating. I could have stayed out on that river for the rest of my life. For three long hours, I was convinced that career-wise all I needed in my life was to become a river guide. All thoughts and concerns—of home, school, Carlos, Sara, *everything*—were lost to the wind and waves.

Our third day at Foothills Park dawned bright and beautiful. Alain snuck into my tent at sunrise and slobbered all over me until Meena beat him off with pillows.

"Damned *wiiiiildlife,*" Izzie groaned, pulling her sleeping bag up over her head.

"Let's go," Alain said to me.

"Where to?" I wanted to know, pulling on my Flexileg and throwing a sweater over the tank top and shorts I'd been sleeping in.

"Loons. I need loon photos. Calendar publishers like loons."

We hiked down a narrow gravel trail through the forest to the water. Three loons were gliding in figure eights, diving for breakfast about twenty feet from shore. They might have been fashion models the way Alain was talking to them. "Yeah, baby, that's right, come a little closer... now swim together, that's the way... you with the big beak, just turn your head a little to the right..."

"I'm going swimming," he announced suddenly. Setting his camera carefully on the ground, he ripped off his T-shirt, kicked off his Tevas, and stripped off his shorts.

I was just wishing I'd brought my sketchbook—what an excellent life drawing Alain would make!—when he dove into the lake.

"*Merde!* It's freezing!" he shouted when he surfaced. What did he expect, skinny-dipping at seven AM in a glacier-fed lake? But he stayed out there treading water, buck naked, his lips frozen in a grin.

"Come on in!" he beckoned.

"No way!"

"Chicken!" Alain shouted. "Bwock! Bwock! Bwock!"

The loons began squawking, too. Egging me on.

Okay, okay. I'm no Wimpy Gimpy Girl. Tossing my sweater aside, I pulled off my tank top, kicked off my shorts and Flexileg, and dove in after him.

CHAPTER THIRTY

Later that same morning, over bagels and scrambled eggs, Dan explained our day's activities.

Alain, Izzie, and Homer would be mountain biking the back trails of Foothills Park to a wild bird sanctuary. My group would be canoeing a wide, winding creek five kilometers from above the park office to Moose Lake near our campsite. Our mission: to locate and catalogue water insects and foliage in our journals.

Frank, Meena, and I jammed lunch, bottled water, a spare paddle, our cell phones, and a first aid kit into our packs and pushed off from the dock at the park office at ten AM. The air was warm, the winds calm, and the creek route seemed straightforward. Hiking trails paralleled the banks that would allow us access to picnic areas and outhouses as needed.

I took the stern of our sixteen-foot aluminum craft and tossed Frank the bow paddle. Meena agreed to sit in the middle and record field notes in our journals. According to the information we were given at the camp office, recent heavy rains had made even the shallowest portions of the creek navigable by small craft—good news for us: no portaging. (Just picture it: me on crutches, and Meena and Frank, with their muscles concentrated between their ears and a combined weight of less than two hundred pounds—trying to portage a canoe anywhere?)

All morning, the three of us did our school work, belted out crazy camp songs, and waved at hikers and other small crafts passing by.

"So, Frank, how's your imaginary girlfriend?" Meena asked, splashing him with her paddle when she caught him ogling three girls in tie-dyed thongs sunbathing on shore.

"She's NOT imaginary. *Wasn't* imaginary. We... broke up," Frank said, swiveling around in the bow seat to face her.

I laid my paddle down and pretended to be aghast. "What? When? You must be so *devastated*."

Ignoring me, Frank gazed into Meena's eyes with an expression startlingly reminiscent of Simon when he knew Lynda had a pot roast in the oven. "Can we go somewhere and talk privately?" he asked.

"Uh... no. We're in a canoe."

"Then I'll tell you later," Frank told Meena.

"Tell me now."

"Well... it's like this," he said. "It just wouldn't be fair to keep Karen... waiting for me..."

"Finally," I laughed. "Mystery Chick has a name."

Frank continued ignoring me. "... when it's... it's..." He paused.

"When it's *what?*" Meena asked.

"God, the suspense," I laughed.

"Oh... okay." Frank leaned toward Meena. "When... it's you... I... want," he whispered.

Meena: "Me?"

Me: "Meena?"

Frank's face and ears turned as red as his hair.

Meena looked sick. I don't think she thought badly of Frank; she just didn't think about him at all. "Let me get used to the idea for a while," she croaked, sticking her nose back into our field notes.

It was my turn to hum the theme song from *The Love Boat.*

By one PM, we were three-quarters of the way through our journey. After a quick lunch break on shore, Meena had taken the bow seat. Now she shrieked, pointing her paddle at the sky like a rifle. *"OH NO! LOOK!"*

Angry purple clouds were gathering over the foothills.

We paddled faster. Maybe we could beat the storm back to camp. But before long, sudden gusts of hot wind began tossing us sideways towards the thick, reedy marshlands lining the creek on both sides.

Meena was antsy. She bounced up and down in the bow seat, paddling in a panic, splashing water everywhere, making it difficult for me to keep an even keel. "Do you think we'll see lightning?" she kept asking Frank over her shoulder.

"Do I look like the weatherman!" he yelled up to her. He must have been a bit put out by Meena's lukewarm response to his earlier declaration of love.

A low rumble in the distance.

Meena dropped her paddle into the canoe and drew her knees up to her chest. She covered her ears with her hands.

Frank shoved our field notes into his pack and reached forward over Meena's shoulder to take her paddle. He began stroking as fast as he could—which unfortunately wasn't very fast. "Hey, Captain!" he called back to me. "Maybe we should take cover?"

"Let's keep going awhile," I said. "The storm is still miles away."

Bad call. Ten minutes later, the low rumbles turned to BANGS. The dark clouds morphed into eerie swirls of gray-green.

The sky opened fire. In a matter of seconds, raindrops turned to ice pellets, then to jawbreaker-sized hail that nailed us on the head and began filling the canoe. Meena rocked and cried and beat at the sides of her head with her fists. We had to get to land—FAST!

"Over there!" I pointed my paddle toward a small clearing in the marsh. A trail marker indicated that it was another takeout spot for paddlers wanting to take a lunch break or gain access to the main road. The creek bank was steep and muddy, but there were some thick berry bushes we could tie the canoe to.

Frank and I tossed our packs and my crutches up the muddy

creek bank, then scrambled up on our knees, pushing Meena ahead of us. Her wails were all but drowned out by the sizzle of lightning, the CRASH! BOOM! of thunder, and the onslaught of hail.

"*We need shelter!*" Frank screamed.

Braced on my crutches, I pulled our laminated map from my pack. "There should be an outhouse about a hundred feet—"

"*There it is!*" Meena screeched and broke into a run as another bolt of lightning cut the sky in half.

"You go ahead with her, Frank!" I yelled over the storm. "I'll catch up." My crutch tips were sinking three inches into the mud with each step.

"I can't just leave you here alone to get fried by lightning. I know tossing you over my shoulder like Alain would is out, but..."

Wow... I'd underestimated the Frankster. Who knew that a pain-in-the-ass scaredy-cat when it came to ordinary things could shine in an emergency? He'd just grown a foot in my books. "Ever been in a wheelbarrow race?" I asked him.

"Sure."

"Then let's go!" I dropped the crutches and got down on my hands and knees in the mud. Frank hoisted me up by the calves and we ran—me on my hands—through the muck to the outhouse.

Once barricaded inside our cramped quarters, I dug a flashlight out of my pack. My hands were filthy and scratched and my wrists screamed in agony. The stink was overwhelming. But at least we were out of the storm.

Keeping his shorts up, Frank sat down on the sticky toilet seat, lifting the crouched and shaking Meena up by the armpits and taking her on to his lap. She clung to him like Velcro, whimpering and digging her nose into his shirtfront with each streak of lightning and crash of thunder.

I retrieved my cell phone from my soggy pack and hunkered down on the grimy cement floor. I didn't want to think about how many germs were crawling all over me.

I tried Dan's emergency number. No answer. I hunted around in our packs for Frank and Meena's phones. Tried the number again. Nothing.

Another ZAP of lightning. Another BOOM of thunder. Meena buried her face under Frank's armpit.

"Now what, Captain?" he asked me.

It was half an hour before the rain and lightning moved on. As the last of the thunder subsided, so did Meena's fear. "You want me to explain what that was all about?" she asked in a small voice.

"Not especially," Frank said. Clearly, he'd already had enough excitement for one day.

She started crying again and told us anyway, in great gulps. "When I was eight... still living in Jamaica... my older brother... Jahmar... was struck by lightning. He was... killed... instantly. It was *all... my... fault!*"

"Who are you? God?" Frank asked.

"That was sensitive," I sneered, whacking his leg.

"Look, Rainey, I didn't *make* my mother an alcoholic, no matter what she says. *She* did. And Meena didn't kill her brother with a bolt of lightning. Mother Nature did."

And I didn't make my mother run away when I was six months old. Or did I?

"But it is my fault!" Meena insisted. "Jahmar was twelve. He and I had been playing in the field behind our house. When it started to rain, Mom called us in. Then I remembered that I'd left Amina in the field."

"Amina?" I asked.

"A little cloth doll that my grandmother made for me. I started to cry that Amina was going to drown in the storm. So Jahmar ran back outside to get her for me. I was watching from the window. There was a streak of lightning. He... fell down. I screamed for help, but he was already..." Meena's voice broke. "... gone... by the time Dad reached him. Amina was still in Jahmar's hand." Meena sucked in a long breath, then wailed, *"She was all... burned!"*

Frank shot me a helpless look over Meena's shoulder. I gestured for him to put his arms around her. Clearly, Frank would benefit from a few of Greg's "compassion" tutorials, too.

"I'm sorry," she whispered into his shoulder after a while. "I thought I'd be okay out here this summer—scared, but not *freaking,* you know? But I'm not okay. I'm crazy. Being outside in a storm brings it all back like it was yesterday. *If I hadn't started crying about that stupid doll, Jahmar would still be alive!"*

What would Greg say at a time like this? "You can't change the—"

Meena held up her hand. "Save it, Rainey. I know I can't change the past. But I can still honor it, right? That's what my mom says. Jahmar and I both loved animals. We always talked about opening a veterinary clinic together someday. There weren't a lot of kids out in the country where we lived. Jahmar and I played mostly with the dogs and goats and each other. He never treated me like a pesky little sister. He was my hero." She paused and wiped her nose on her sleeve. "He'd be really proud of—" She stopped.

"What's wrong?" I asked.

"Shhhh."

Heavy branches snapped outside the outhouse followed by sniffling-snuffling around the bolted door frame.

"What *is* that?" Meena asked, her eyes wide despite being red and swollen from crying.

The curious *sniff, sniff, sniff* reminded me of Simon when he smelled a stray Milkbone behind the couch. Only this sniffing was louder. *Snorting* was more like it. But not that annoying but harmless *snort-snort-snort* of Lynda's.

"Probably just a raccoon," I lied. What was it the wilderness survival guide taught us? To stay calm.

Frank groaned and clamped his eyes shut.

There were tiny cracks in the outhouse walls where the clapboard had weathered. I peeked out and came eye to eye with... *whoa!*

It was a black bear, probably a male, judging by its size, about four, maybe five hundred pounds.

The hairy black creature backed up cautiously and gave another loud snort. Globs of spittle flew in an arc above its head as it pawed at the mud. One of its ears was frayed at the top where it might have been in a fight.

Meena rose from Frank's lap, pushed me aside, and checked between the planks for herself. An odd croak escaped her throat. "Uh, yeah, it's just a... raccoon, Frank. A pretty big one, though."

"You're lying to me," Frank said, shoving Meena aside and sticking his eye up to the boards. "It's a BEAR!" he screamed.

"Let's scare him away," I whispered. "Isn't that what the wilderness survival guide said?"

"Then why are you WHISPERING!" Frank yelled, pounding on the outhouse walls with his fists. "GO AWAY, UGLY BEAR! GO BACK TO YOUR DEN! DON'T COME IN HERE, YOU HAIRY BEAST! DON'T MESS WITH ME, YOU FAT—"

Meena elbowed me. She cocked her head towards Frank. "Captain Testosterone to the rescue." Sarcasm was a good sign. She was feeling more like her old self.

Frank's rampage worked! The bear disappeared from our sightline. The sound of snapping branches and rustling foliage receded into the distance, just like the storm had. For a full five minutes afterward, the three of us huddled together in silence, totally stunned, afraid it would return. It didn't.

"The bear could probably smell the leftover sandwiches in our packs," I said, when I thought it was safe to exhale again.

"It could smell *anything* except all the shit in here?" Meena asked, wrinkling her nose.

"I'm not leaving. Ever. That bear is still out there somewhere," Frank said, when I suggested it was time to pack ourselves back into the canoe and head out.

"You plan to live the rest of your life in an outhouse?" Meena asked.

"Whose fault is it that we're in here in the first place!" he shot back.

"Listen lovebirds, I'm not staying here forever," I said, trying Dan's cell phone number again. Still no answer.

I opened the outhouse door a crack and glanced around cautiously. The muddy ground was covered in enormous bear tracks leading back to the forest. "Let's go," I suggested. "It's maybe only another half-hour or so to the take-out spot."

Though the rain and wind were no longer a threat, the air had chilled to bone numbing. My arms, already aching from the mad dash to the outhouse, were put to the test for what turned out to be another full hour of no-nonsense paddling.

We docked at four PM. Everyone was there to greet us.

Alain's group had been caught in the storm, too, but they'd found shelter with a friendly family with a large RV parked near the trailhead.

No one had worried about Frank, Meena, and me, even though we'd estimated an arrival time of two hours earlier.

"We knew the storm would have docked you for a while," Dan explained. "And I trust one of you would have called my emergency number if there'd been a problem."

"I *tried* to call, Dan," I explained. "No signal. Either we were out of range or your battery is dead and you don't know it."

Dan inspected his phone, then, groaning, ran to plug it into the charger in the Carlos-mobile.

Brooke frowned. "You tried to call? When? *WHY?*"

Meena and I let Frank, still high on bravado, tell the others about the bear, and how *he, personally,* had saved the day.

"Yeah, Rainey and I were just two goddamned damsels in distress." Meena sneered.

She really was feeling better.

Alain fetched my prosthesis and polar fleece jacket from the van. "You look exhausted," he said, wrapping the jacket around my shoulders and leaning in to kiss my neck. He pulled away quickly, like I'd morphed into a toad.

"Rainey? No offense, but you smell like... *shit.*"

CHAPTER THIRTY-ONE

While Meena, Frank, and I raced to the shower hut, Dan stormed the Foothills Park office to report our bear encounter. The game warden assured him that due to numerous reports that afternoon of a black bear roaming the area south of the outhouse, it had been tracked and tranquilized, and was being relocated north of the park as they spoke.

Our minds were set at ease. Even Frank's. In fact, we were all so confident that, the next afternoon, Dan agreed to hike with the Six-Pack to the now infamous outhouse so that we could make plaster casts of the bear tracks to take home as souvenirs. Carlos and Brooke agreed to drop us at the trailhead, drive to Hinton to re-stock the coolers, then return for us afterwards.

Upwind from the outhouse, we killed time waiting for our plaster bear tracks to set. Homer and Frank played Frisbee. Meena worked on her journal. Izzie worked on her tan. Dan sat on a rock, staring off into space, probably thanking his lucky stars that our bear encounter hadn't resulted in tragedy and a ton of paperwork. Alain took a few photographs, then set his cameras aside and silently motioned for me to ditch my bear sketch and follow him down to the creek bank. The ground had dried since the previous day's rain; I wasn't worried about sinking my Flexileg in mud.

Alain pulled me behind a berry bush and wasted no time sliding his hand under my tank top.

I welcomed Alain's touch, *craved* it. But what if a canoe paddled by? Or Dan decided to wander our way?

"Relax," Alain laughed. "No one is spying on us."

Branches snapped a little ways down the creek bank. "Someone's coming."

Alain nuzzled my neck. "I don't hear anything."

Then over his shoulder I saw it.

Coarse black hair. Wet snout. One ragged ear.

I dug my fingers into Alain's shoulders. "Look out!" I squeaked.

Alain whipped his head around. "Oh... *MERDE!*" he squealed and turned his body to face the monster head-on.

The bear didn't care that Alain and I both had wilderness survival certificates in our wallets. He only knew that we were blocking the way to his lunch in the berry patch, and was no doubt already *pissed* about being shot in the butt with a tranquilizer gun the previous afternoon and being sent packing to another county.

The bear must have given up a night's sleep to make it back to his old stomping grounds so quickly.

The bear snorted and bared his huge yellow-brown teeth at us. Its breath, even ten feet away from me, smelled like the rancid insides of a garbage bin. He shook his head, spraying a gallon of spittle through the air. A foamy glob of it landed on my arm.

Then he lunged at Alain!

We'd been warned about bluff charges, but this was the real deal.

I screamed "*BEAR!*" to alert the others, then watched in horror as the bear pummeled and slashed at Alain's head and chest with its enormous claws. Crimson blood seeped through Alain's shirt and down his cheeks. Alain punched and kicked with every ounce of his strength, which was considerable. But the beast outweighed him by at *least* two or three hundred pounds and had him pinned to the ground at the thighs. My screams and Alain's defensive punches only seemed to incense the bear further.

I had to do something. And "compassionate verbal strategies" weren't it. If I'd had a gun, I would have shot the bear dead. If I'd had a big stick or a heavy rock, I would have smashed the animal with it, but all I could see around me was sand and marsh and spindly shrubs.

So I did what I had to, what I *could*. I ripped off my prosthesis. While the bear's attention was focused on Alain, I *bashed* it over the head with all my might, losing my balance in the process.

In surprise, the bear lifted his great black head toward me. I rose up on my knees and smashed him again, right on the snout where Dan's "old buddy George" taught us it would hurt the most. The bear gave one ferocious howl and bounded off down the creek bank in the direction he'd come from. I sank back numbly into the sand beside Alain as the others came running.

Alain struggled to sit up. He looked dazed, his eyes glassy. His right cheek was deeply slashed, a wide flap of skin just... hanging, and his T-shirt was blood-soaked and ripped clear off his chest in the front.

"I love you," he slurred to me, right there in front of everyone. Then he grabbed his Expos cap off the ground where it had landed, put it on, and staggered slowly to his feet, wincing and gripping his ribcage, like the star of some low-budget slasher movie, except this was real. And way worse.

"You saved my life, Rainey," Alain said, then turned away to spit a huge wad of blood onto the ground. Then, grinning like he'd been eating sunshine, he addressed the others who had rushed to the creek bank. "Anyone get a photo of that little scuffle?"

I felt woozy. The edges of the berry bushes and the creek bank and my friends melted together like an impressionist painting.

Meena and Frank went running back for the first-aid kit in Dan's pack. Izzie and Homer rushed to help Alain up the hill. Dan punched numbers into his cell phone. "Shit, dead again." He shoved it into his shirt pocket.

"I'll call 911," Homer said, pulling out his own phone, which worked fine.

"Let's go, Rainey!" Dan called to me. "We have to get back to the trailhead! Alain needs an ambulance!"

I pulled myself up using the bush and waited a few seconds for the world to stop spinning. Then I slipped the Flexileg back on, took a step, and promptly fell back down again.

The Flexileg barely held my weight.

That sure brought the world back into focus.

I whipped it back off and inspected the casing. Oh, fuck. I'd cracked it on the bear's head. Greg was going to kill me when he found out. What was I going to use for the rest of the summer?

No time to think about any of that right now.

I shoved the broken prosthesis back on and limp-hopped to catch up with the others. *Wimpy Gimpy Girl! Wimpy Gimpy Girl!* I heard Derek's voice chanting in my head. While Meena and Dan ripped open gauze pads for Alain, I fished around in Dan's pack until I found his trusty roll of duct tape and kicked the Flexileg off again. Holding the crack together as best I could, I rolled the tape around and around, then tried the leg again. The Flexileg felt sturdier now—it held my weight—but the not-quite-even seam on the underside of the crack pinched the skin of my calf with each step.

"Suck it up, Rainey," I mumbled to myself, giving a phony thumbs-up to Dan when he shot a concerned glance my way.

Alain was all that mattered right now.

The seven of us, huddled close together, hurried along the short path to the trailhead, keeping an eye out for the bear. Dan borrowed Izzie's cell phone and was yelling at Brooke to gun it back to Foothills Park with Carlos ASAP. Joke was on him; she and Carlos were already waiting for us in the parking lot less than a kilometer away.

"Can your leg be fixed?" Meena asked, taking in my shoddy duct-tape job.

"Sure," I replied, with a lot more confidence than I felt. "I'll get a new casing put on when we get back to Toronto. It's insured." I crossed my fingers that Greg's policy covered "bear clobbery."

Alain staggered over to me, one hand pressing a wad of gauze pads to his chest, the other pressing a wad of gauze pads to his cheek. The fact he could still walk at all amazed me. "Rainey, how much is that... wonder-leg of yours... worth?" he asked me, his voice as slurry as a drunk's.

"Right now? Not a cent."

"No. I mean... I don't want to be... nosy, but—"

"Sixteen... give or take."

He eyes grew round. "You wrecked... a sixteen hundred dollar... prosth... th... leg... bashing a... b-bear over the h-head? To save... *me?*"

"Sixteen *thousand*," I replied.

He let out a low whistle. "Rainey, I..."

"Get over it. I'd have done it even if the leg had cost sixteen million dollars. Or a trillion."

"Even a... gaz... illion?"

"Alain? You're priceless."

Meena, Izzie, Homer, and I sat speechless in the emergency waiting area as Alain, who'd been accompanied by Brooke in the ambulance, was examined, X-rayed, sewn up, and medicated by the doctors at Hinton Hospital. Dan spent most of the time on a pay phone yelling at the Foothills Park warden. *"No! Forget re-locating again! That bear's a bloodthirsty killer! The trail needs to be closed immediately!"*

Frank was in the washroom puking. No one thought he'd be out anytime soon.

After two hours that felt like a week, Brooke bustled out of the swinging metal doors to tell us that Alain would be sore from the waist up for a week or so. He'd be taking preventative antibiotics for the rest of the summer. He had eighteen—eighteen!—stitches across his face and bandages galore. But he was one of the lucky ones, as far as bear attacks go. His blood loss looked way worse than it actually was. Bottom line, he'd be okay.

With a collective sigh, we bounded—I hobbled—up to feed quarters into the vending machines. Nothing like a near miss to make you crave sugar.

Izzie sidled up to me as I made my way back to my seat with
a Coke and a Mars bar.

"*Sooooo*... what were you and Alain doing down at the creek
bank together?"

"We were just... talking, Izzie. No big deal."

"Come *ooooon,* you can tell me..."

What the hell was her problem? Was she jealous of the attention that Alain and I were getting. Maybe she'd feel differently if
it were her with eighteen stitches in her face or a broken Flexileg.

"Alain must be *sooooo* upset about you coming to his rescue,"
Izzie said. "Guys don't like to be shown up by girls," she added
knowingly.

I already knew some guys were like that. Derek hated it when
I beat him at anything, from the stupid obstacle race when we
were seven to our math marks in tenth grade.

But Alain was different. As soon as he was officially dis-
charged from the hospital, he hugged me so tightly that I could
feel his heart pounding through the clean T-shirt a nurse had
rustled up for him in the lost-and-found box. He whispered in
my ear, "If I wasn't in so much pain right now, Rainey, I'd be all
over you."

Yikes.

CH_APTER THIRTY-TWO

Early the next morning, a warden stopped by our campsite to let Dan know that the bear with the ragged ear had been located. And shot dead.

I felt relief, but also a small stab of guilt. I understood that the bear had to be killed to prevent another attack. But I also understood that it was we humans blazing our trails and building our outhouses in their habitats that caused these bear scuffles in the first place. Maybe I should look into careers in animal conservation? *Would I have to become a vegetarian?* I wondered.

Now that Alain knew he was basically okay, he wanted to share his "great bear adventure" with his family. He flirted with the receptionist at the campground office until she let him use her computer to arrange a flower delivery to his mother in New Brunswick, with a note attached to call her son's cell phone ASAP.

I, on the other hand—or the other foot, as the case may be—wasn't planning to tell Greg—and definitely not Lynda—about my role in the "great bear adventure" until I got home. Or *ever,* if I found time and creativity to make up some minor accident or act of God to explain the damages to the Flexileg.

Dan and Brooke shook their heads at each other, dismayed at Alain's sudden enthusiasm to contact his mother. They'd wanted to call her from the hospital the previous afternoon, but he'd flipped out. His consents for emergency treatment were signed, Alain yelled, so there was no need to upset his mother if his injuries turned out to be nothing more than a few cuts and bruises. Something about Alain's uncharacteristic bad temper made Brooke and Dan leave it alone.

"So what if you'll be okay. Won't your mom still *freak* when she finds out?" Meena asked Alain. Her own mom called every night to see if Meena was feeling okay, eating right, staying safe. What had seemed like gross overprotectiveness earlier in the trip made sense now that I knew what had happened to Meena's brother. Meena would rather eat bugs for dinner than tell her mom about anything more than the pretty mountain scenery.

Alain shrugged. "I play hockey; it's not like I've never had stitches and bruised ribs before."

"The bear wasn't trying to steal a puck from you, you moron!" Frank interjected. "It was trying to KILL you!"

"And it's a great way to introduce Rainey to my family."

"She'll think you're dating a crazy girl," I said.

"Nah. She'll think I'm dating a gorgeous chick who's not afraid to kick ass. Like Xena. Or Lara Croft. Or Buffy."

I wondered if maybe Alain had an undiagnosed concussion.

Dan gave the Six-Pack a choice: take a day of rest, or stick to the schedule and explore the Icefield Parkway from Jasper to Banff.

"Let's go, man!" Alain exclaimed, high on life—or painkillers. He took his ball cap off, made like he was going to toss it up in the air, thought better of it, and put the cap back on.

"I vote yes," Izzie added.

Meena raised her hand. "Me, too."

"Let's do it," I said. If Alain could deal with bruises and stitches and sore ribs, I could suck up a little calf-pinching and stump-chafing.

"I'm in," Homer agreed.

Frank yawned. He'd sat up all night, according to Alain, wielding a big stick like a baseball bat, waiting for the bear and a dozen of the bear's extended family to drop by seeking revenge. "Who says that bears don't have a Mafia-type organization?" he asked.

"Um... actually," Frank said now. "I wouldn't mind taking a day off—"

"Frank?" Brooke broke in.

"Yeah?"

"Get your ass in the van."

"It's like we're traveling through a rack of postcards—or the glossy pages of a Western Canada coffee-table book," Homer remarked as we pulled into the parking lot at our first stop, Athabasca Falls, south of Jasper.

Just beyond the parking lot, the falls, fed by the meltwater of the Athabaska glacier, roared like a million lions. Potholes splashed foamy tentacles of ice water up at the tourists gathered on the walkways. Rays of copper sun danced in the wild water like ten billion new pennies being tossed in a fountain.

A series of steep stone steps led visitors down into a gorge. Alain took a pass, and while the others thought it was because of his injuries, he gave me a tortured look to let me know it wasn't. Slipping his digital camera around my neck, he said, "Give it your best shot," and quickly showed me how to make setting adjustments.

The steps were slippery going, not really worth the risk of death—or breaking Alain's camera—if I lost my footing and slipped over the barriers into the torrents. But I threw caution to the wind and trusted that the guardrails and my duct-tape job were up to snuff.

The things we do for love, as Greg would say.

Dan called a half-hour break after our hike, to relax and use the washrooms. "Definitely not five star," Homer asserted in reference to the Athabaska Falls facilities. He claimed that some day he was going to write a tourists' manual: *Shithouses of Western*

Canada. Points would be awarded for cleanliness, level of stink, toilet paper availability, flush technology, absence of flies, etc.

When Alain returned early to the van—I suspected to pop a few more painkillers—I stayed behind to sketch the rapids. I really got into it, using the small brushes, not just my finger, to capture details. I wanted someone looking at my drawing to *hear* the roar of the water, *feel* the mist. I was chewing my bottom lip in concentration, trying to decide which shade of blue to try next, when someone ahemed.

Carlos.

"Time to go?" I asked, thinking he'd been sent to fetch me.

He shook his head, his eyes drawn to my Flexileg propped up on the bench beside me; I'd taken it off to give my calf a breather. "What you did yesterday was so stupid," he said.

"What was I supposed to do, Carlos? Let Alain get mauled to death?"

"You could have been killed."

"I would have done the same for anyone."

"Even me?"

"Yes," I replied, turning my attention back to my sketch. I was in no mood for a debate.

Carlos changed the subject. "Did you and Farmboy have a nice swim yesterday morning?"

I hated that Carlos had started calling Alain Farmboy, like growing up on a dairy farm made Alain just another form of livestock. My urge to paint gone, I slammed my sketchbook shut. "You *spied* on us?"

"I'm a lifeguard," Carlos smirked. "It's my job."

Ice coursed through my veins like the Athabaska through the gorge. *"How did you even know we were out there!"*

"I haven't been sleeping well, lately."

"You sick creep."

"Look, all I *did* was leave my tent to take a leak. When I heard laughter and splashing down at the lakeshore, I thought I'd better check it out." Carlos grinned. "You have a nice body, Rainey. It's nothing to be embarrassed about."

"Just go, Carlos," I said, disgusted. "Report us if you want."

"I won't," he said. "You and Alain kept your mouths shut about..." He mimicked smoking a joint. "I know you both suspected something."

"Have you been on drugs the whole trip?"

"Relax. I only smoked one joint. My cousin in Brandon sold it to me. And I smoked it the night *before* we left Manitoba. It wouldn't affect my driving twelve hours later, would it?"

"How should I know? I guess we all got lucky."

Carlos changed the subject. "Do you really think that everything with Farmboy is going to end happily ever after?"

"Stop calling him Farmboy. His name is Alain."

"*Alien* is more like it. He looks like Frankenstein with all those stitches." Carlos turned and sauntered away.

"Hey!" I called after him. "You're a real asshole!"

Carlos turned back to face me, his eyes screaming with pain, like I'd shot him.

CHAPTER THIRTY-THREE

"What can you tell me about glaciers?" Dan asked an hour later. We'd just arrived at the bottom of the Athabaska Glacier, one tendril of the massive Columbia Icefield. It was so windy and cold that tourists were bundled in ski jackets, even though it was late July. Ominous signs warned visitors that the receding glacial ice above us was unstable, that to walk on top of the glacier was dangerous. But no fewer than a hundred people could be seen scattered across the bottom portion of the vast icefield like nuts on a marshmallow sundae.

With Dan around, we could never forget WESTEX was an educational trip. He'd even made us read our textbook chapters on glaciers and earthquakes round-robin at the campfire the previous evening.

"Glaciers cover ten percent of the earth's *suuuurface*," Izzie drawled.

"Glaciers contain three-quarters of the earth's fresh water," I added.

"If all the glaciers melted, sea level would rise more than seventy meters worldwide," Homer said. "Goodbye New York City, Toronto, and most of the other major cities on the planet."

Frank yanked his geography textbook from his pack and started flipping pages furiously until he found what he wanted. "In 1991, the body of a man dead for over five thousand years was found preserved in a glacier in the Alps," he read aloud.

"And the significance of that is...?" Dan asked.

Meena's hand shot up like we were all still in school. "The *significance* of the man found in the Alps," she answered, "is that glacial ice has retreated further today than it has in the past five thousand years. The effects of global warming on weather and ecosystems will be catastrophic."

Greg always says that the worst thing about know-it-alls is that they usually do.

The summer was almost half over and I still hadn't mapped a practical/lucrative career path that would meet with Greg's approval. So when WESTEX stopped for a late lunch at a rest area just north of Lake Louise, I wandered away from the others, sat on the ground with my back against a tree, took a clean breath of mountain air, and *demanded* that my brain speak to me. *Tell me, Brain, what the hell am I'm supposed to do with my life!*

But my brain wasn't up to taking orders. Instead, it became mesmerized by the shadows of clouds on the mountains. And the hundred shades of green in just one tree. The intensity of a raven's stare. I didn't realize until I looked down that I'd been sketching the bird on my dry arm skin with my fingernail.

Oh well, maybe tomorrow, I'd figure out my future.

Who was I kidding?

I took my prosthesis off again, afraid of the hamburger I might find underneath it after the steep walk up to the glacier. But it wasn't too bad—just a lot of chafing and a few blisters. I'd let the crutches take the brunt of my weight on the way down.

Alain joined me. "That looks sore," he said, plunking down beside me with a grunt. He took my stump into his lap.

"I've got Polysporin in my pack," I said.

Before I thought to stop him, he unzipped my knapsack and began rifling through its contents for the first aid cream. Suddenly, he stopped rummaging and looked up at me, amused. "Care to explain, young lady?" he said, pulling out the box of condoms.

"Lynda packed them." I snatched the box from Alain and stuffed it back into my bag before the others noticed. I'd never live it down if Izzie found out.

"Pretty cool stepmother." Alain grinned.

"She must have had a premonition about the sex-crazed maniac I'd be hooking up with this summer."

"And here I was wondering when I'd get a chance to sneak to the nearest drugstore."

Mauled by a bear less than twenty-four hours ago, doped up

on painkillers and fresh mountain air, and sex was *still* foremost
on Alain's mind.

I was finishing with the Polysporin when Alain's pocket rang.

"Mom. Right on time," he said, flipping open his cell phone.

Alain spoke to his mother in animated French for at least ten
minutes, making our bear experience sound like great fun and
insisting his injuries weren't too bad. But I didn't have to hear her
end of the conversation to know she was freaking. That she thought
Alain should get his butt on the first plane back to Toronto. Mrs.
Boudreau had lost her husband tragically less than a year ago; I
couldn't imagine how devastated she would be if the bear had
killed Alain. I couldn't even imagine how devastated *I'd* be.

After another few minutes of reassurances about his health
and mumbled "I'll be careful's" and "I love you's", Alain passed the
phone to me. "Mom wants to thank you for saving her precious
fils from the big bad bear. Talk slow; her English isn't great."

Greg hadn't sent me through the oh-so-*practical* French
immersion program at Mollglen Elementary for nothing, after
all. I was rusty, but managed to hold up my end of the short
conversation. Alain's mom said everything I'd always wanted to
hear from a mother but had never heard from Sara: that I was
quick-thinking. Strong. Gutsy.

When I hung up, Alain was wide-eyed. "*You speak French?*"
I shrugged. "Yeah. *Oui.* So?"

"You got any more surprises up your sleeve?"

Maybe we both did.

CHAPTER THIRTY-FOUR

Banff was busier than Toronto's Kensington Market on a Saturday morning. Carlos drove around in circles for at least twenty minutes, swiping at the sweat trickling down the back of his neck and mumbling about "fucking tourist traps," until he finally found a spot to park.

The Six-Pack hurried to a visitors' booth to get a map. The lady at the counter noticed me limping along, letting my battered crutches take most of my weight (which meant my armpits were killing me now, too), and offered me a free wheelchair rental. Horrified, I told her no thanks.

"Oh, come on, Rainey," Homer said. "I'll push you around."

Another rule of life—or *my* life in any case: NEVER accept help from anyone. It's better for people to think you're stubborn than to think you're Wimpy Gimpy Girl.

Except that you let Alain piggyback you on the beach, I reminded myself. Yeah... but it was worth public humiliation to feel up his shoulder muscles.

Except that you let Frank wheelbarrow you. Yeah... but we were in the middle of a terrifying lightning storm. And Frank was hardly someone to be calling anyone *else* Wimpy.

Except you're slowing everyone down and no one has the nerve to tell you.

"Oh, *okay,*" I told Homer. "But no wheelies. Unless I tell you to."

I plunked into the chair and the six of us set off up Banff Avenue to check out the restaurants and souvenir shops, glad that Brooke and Dan had ditched us earlier, to join a last-minute bus tour to the Banff Springs Hotel.

"Did you know..." Dan lectured earlier, "... that the Banff Springs Hotel was the first luxury hotel in the Rockies? It was built in the late 1880s by the Canadian Pacific Railway. Wealthy tourists flocked to the mountains by the thousands for the natural splendor and hot springs. Today, the hotel has over 770 rooms, 17 restaurants, 50 shops, a golf course, a bowling alley, *and* an on-site butcher and bakery."

"Makes our own living arrangements seem a bit... *lacking,* don't you think, Dan?" Homer grinned.

Now, two blocks on, Meena veered off towards a café that advertised homemade waffles and ice cream. She pulled Frank along with her and gestured for the rest of us to keep going. *Good for her,* I thought.

"*Hmmmmm,*" was Izzie's response.

No one looked more surprised by the turn of events than Frank.

We all had a blast, spending a fortune on souvenirs and eating junk food until our sides split. But by the time the Six-Pack met up with Dan and Brooke at the van at eight PM, exhaustion dulled everyone's eyes. The only sights we wanted to see on that long ride back from Banff to Foothills Park were the backs of our eyelids.

Except that Carlos was nowhere to be found. A ball of fun as usual, he'd refused to join Dan and Brooke on their hotel tour, saying he'd rather stay with the van and try to catch a nap.

Dan frowned now. "We'll give him ten minutes, then split up to look for him. He couldn't have gone far... oh, wait. There he is!" He pointed down a side road.

"Hurry, Carlos! We're running late!" Brooke shouted.

He sauntered up in his own good time. "Sorry, man," Carlos said to Dan, his eyes red and his voice groggy. "I took a walk to clear my head and woke up on a park bench."

"Give me your keys, Carlos," Brooke said. "I'll drive back."

"No, I'm... fine. I just... needed a nap."

She was adamant. "I'll drive."

"No. I can—"

"I *insist!* Three years ago, our driver sprained his right ankle at a campground near Moose Jaw; I drove his van all the way back to Toronto. Right now, all I want is to get everyone back to camp quickly and safely."

Still, Carlos balked.

"*GIVE HER THE GODDAMN KEYS!*" Dan snapped. Everyone flinched. Dan's reactions were inappropriate at the best of times, but they'd become even more erratic since yesterday's bear episode. There's no way he'd last eight summers with the WESTEX program the way Brooke had. Judging by the size of the vein sticking out of his forehead, stress might do him in before we reached B.C.

Carlos tossed his keys to Brooke and climbed into the van, shaking his head in frustration. He slid into the window seat at the very back and closed his eyes.

Making us all disappear.

Brooke said not a word the entire three-plus hours back to camp. She didn't need to. Her rigid posture and clenched jaw said it all.

"*Sooooo?*" Izzie asked Meena when the three of us had finally settled in our tent for the night. "How'd it go with Frank tonight? Are you in *luuuuuv?*"

"Stay out of it," she whispered back. "Nothing happened. *Nothing.*"

Meena was lying and I knew it, but I'd promised her I'd keep it quiet.

"Maybe he'll need some comforting from *meeeeee,* now? You think?"

It wasn't going to happen. Frank's assessment of Izzie earlier in the summer went like this: "If I wanted an over-emotional, mean-spirited, impulsive girlfriend, I'd date my mother."

"Not listening," Meena said, pulling her sleeping bag over her ears.

Meena had cooked up some psychological theory that Izzie's acting bug and guy obsession stemmed from lack of attention at home. Izzie's parents were in their late fifties and were always traveling to see Izzie's seven older sisters who lived out of town; according to Izzie, one or more of them was always having a baby, graduating from university, or getting engaged. Since she had the house to herself almost every weekend, Izzie had a lot of parties. "Where we do *waaaaay* more than play spin the bottle," she boasted.

Conversation exploded like fireworks at an impromptu "leadership" meeting between Dan, Brooke, and Carlos that kicked off outside Carlos's tent just after the Six-Pack had crawled into our tents for the night. The ten-foot distance and flimsy wall of nylon provided no sound barrier.

Apparently, Carlos had tried to crawl into his tent, too.

"Not so fast!" Dan was still livid.

"Look, man, I just need to get some—"

"Carlos," Dan hissed, "when I heard the school board had hired a *student* to provide transportation services, I took it on good faith that you were genuinely interested and capable of doing the job."

From Carlos: "I was... *am*... it's just..."

"I was under the same impression when your sister asked me to recommend you to the school board," Brooke cut in. "Carina was quite candid about your... situation, but I regret that she may have overestimated your enthusiasm and *underestimated* the depth of your troubles."

"I keep telling you, I was just *tired* today." Carlos did sound truly exhausted, not even able to muster much of a defense.

"I wasn't born yesterday!" Dan yelled.

"Shhhhh, Dan!" Brooke shushed him.

He lowered his voice, but just a notch. "You're on drugs, Carlos."

Izzie poked me. "And didn't I tell you, *weeeeeeks ago,* that I smelled rum on his breath?"

"No! I... took a couple of Benadryl from the first-aid kit to help me nap," Carlos said wearily. "I haven't been sleeping as well as I should. I thought it would wear off by the time you were ready to leave Banff."

"I know a pot haze when I see one!" Dan shouted. Brooke shushed him again.

"I'm *not* a liar! Check the fucking med box! Call the police, if you want!"

"There's no need for that right now," Brooke sighed. "Because the very fact you were too tired and disoriented to drive tonight—and that is, after all, your *job*—is grounds enough to suspend your employment. Combine that with the fact I've witnessed you act in a physically aggressive manner toward a WESTEX participant—"

"What happened with Rainey at Algonquin Park was an *accident*," Carlos interrupted.

Izzie nudged me in the dark. "What *haaaaappened?*"

I kept my ears trained on the drama unfolding outside.

"*Fiiiiiine.* Be that way." Izzie felt around until she found her CD player and pulled on her earphones. I guess no one else's drama was as interesting to her as her own.

"*There are no such things as accidents!*" Dan shouted.

"Dan, please. Get some sleep." Brooke spoke again, more gently. "You and I will talk in the morning and consult with the school board about Carlos's dismissal. I want to speak to him alone now."

"You're *firing* me?"

"That's up to the school board, but it will certainly be my recommendation," Dan offered.

Carlos was petulant. "You want me to leave right now?"

So was Dan. "You're free to do as you please."

"No, no, no, no," Brooke interjected. "Carlos, I want to speak to you first. And then you need some rest. Wait until tomorrow. Wait until the final word from the school board."

"Fine with me," Dan sulked. "But, obviously, pending the final decision of the school board, you, Carlos, are hereby *prohibited* from driving WESTEX participants in your van." Dan gave a final snort of indignation and shuffling noises receded across the campsite to his tent.

I was afraid to breathe. What would happen now?

Brooke's and Carlos's voices became less distinct. I heard the clatter of kindling being tossed into the fire pit and the whoosh of a match being lit. Light cast from the orange flames danced against our tent walls, broken only by the slower moving shadows of Brooke and Carlos as they sat down on the upended logs we used for seats.

"You want... tea?" Brooke asked Carlos. Her voice was barely a whisper.

A mumbled reply.

"Carlos, I hope when you... that you'll consider... counseling program."

"Drug counseling? I told you... *Benadryl*... allergy tablets."

"... *grief* counseling," Brooke explained. "... anger management classes. What happened... this spring... horrible, but... need to move on, Carlos. You're young and smart... There will be other girlfriends... babies. Think of... future. You say you want to be... teacher... coach. But you won't... with a rap sheet."

Carlos's voice broke into a loud sob. *"I wanted to be a father, too."*

He *WHAT*?

The thunk of a log being tossed onto the fire. I strained to hear the voices over the spit and hiss of flames. I struggled to fill in the blanks. "You'll... better one in a few years... finished school... job," Brooke said. "When you meet... woman... trust," she countered.

"I'm so fucking sick... everyone telling me... *move on!*" Carlos sounded like he was being strangled by his own words. "No one understands!"

"*I do... Carlos!*" Brooke's voice rose. "Eleven years ago, I got pregnant. My husband and I were ecstatic. I miscarried in my fifth month. And I... shut down. Refused to discuss it with anyone. A year later, I was divorced. My husband was tired of living with a ghost. He didn't mean the baby, Carlos. He meant me."

"Kayla didn't have a miscarriage, Brooke!" Carlos shot back. "She went behind my back and had an abortion. She killed my baby! *She killed Jessie!*"

I felt like I'd been punched in the chest with my own fist. I was so, so, so stupid, thinking the worst of Carlos. Assuming he'd knocked up his girlfriend and run away with WESTEX when he'd found out. For the first time since asking him to the sports conference, Carlos's behavior made a bit of sense to me. Despite his rude and reckless ways that summer, I wanted to scream out to him. Tell him that if a*nyone* knew that eighteen-year-old guys could be good fathers—even good *single* fathers—it was me.

Brooke began an agitated rant. "I understand that your *circumstances* are different, Carlos. But I know what it feels like to want a baby, to be so close... and then having that baby taken from you—by whatever means. Your sister knows about me. Maybe she was hoping I could get you to open up. Or that the change in scenery and the fresh air would clear your mind. But I've *failed* at my efforts. And you've failed yourself. And that failure is jeopardizing the WESTEX program."

Silence for a count of ten or more. If Brooke was waiting for some kind of apology from Carlos, none came.

"Try to sleep, Carlos," Brooke said a few moments later. I heard her knees crack as she rose from the log and doused the fire. Footsteps approached the tent area and a few moments after that, two separate zippers opened, then closed.

And a dark silence embodied the campsite like a womb.

CHAPTER THIRTY-FIVE

Another thing my father says: It never rains; it pours.

Homer, Alain, and Frank roused me at eight AM in a panic. It was Sunday morning, our last full day at Foothills Park, and I'd expected—*hoped*—to spend the day relaxing and catching up on my journal. Or maybe even deciding on a lucrative/practical career or two.

But I was doomed.

"Rainey, we need you!" Frank shouted. "*Now!*"

Yeah, yeah. I pulled on some sweat pants, a sweater, and my Flexileg, then poked my bleary head out the tent flap. The fat woman from the next campsite was with them. Her cheeks were red and her breath was coming in short gasps. She looked furious; who could blame her after all the late-night yelling at our campsite the previous night.

But that wasn't it. Not even close.

I joined the huddle outside the tent and Alain quickly brought me up to speed. The woman—her name was Vanessa—

had gone into labor.

She's pregnant, not fat, you idiot, I chastised myself. Leave it to the stepdaughter of an obstetrician not to know the difference.

Her sister and brother-in-law had gone to Jasper for the day, Alain continued. They'd forgotten the cell phone.

Vanessa broke into sobs, her bloated face twisted in pain and fear. "They left around seven... I told them I wanted to stay behind... to sleep in... I felt fine... but when I got up to use the... the outhouse... my water broke... I'm three weeks early! My husband is an army medic. He'd know what to do."

I swiveled my head around. "So... where is he?"

"He's in Afghanistan!!" she wailed.

"I called 911," Alain cut in. "They said there's a four-car pileup just east of Hinton. It'll be a while before they can send us an ambulance."

"I ran up to the camp office," Homer gasped. "No one's there until noon on Sundays, the sign said."

"So what can *I* do?" I asked.

Frank cut to the chase. "Didn't you say your stepmother was an obstetrician?"

They wanted me to call Lynda?

"She'll know what to do, right?"

Stupid question. "Lynda knows everything." I reached back into the tent for my cell phone.

"It's coming fast!" Vanessa shouted.

I dialed Lynda. No answer. It was mid-morning in Toronto. She was probably out with Simon. Or at the hospital. I left frantic messages everywhere for her to call me—ASAP.

Meena and Izzie crawled out of our tent. "Where the hell are Dan and Brooke when you need them?" Meena asked.

"There's a note on the picnic table," Homer replied. "They're taking a walk 'to sort things out.' I guess they mean about..." He cocked his head towards Carlos's tent.

"I tried Dan's phone," Frank said. "No answer—again. His phone is such a piece of shit; it's gotta be at least six years old. Ever notice how no one can ever reach Dan?"

"He and Brooke will probably be gone for *hoooours,*" Izzie said, picking up their note. "It says for us to make breakfast for ourselves and get started on our journals."

Vanessa grabbed her abdomen and screamed in pain. *"I need to get to the hospital! NOW!"*

I looked hopefully to the campsite on our other side, but the older couple with the camper were gone, their campsite bare. I pointed further down the road. "What about those people with the yellow truck?" I asked Vanessa.

"I'll take you."

Seven heads whipped around in unison. Carlos stood beside his van. His hair stuck up like a rooster. His clothes were wrinkled after a night of tossing and turning. But he seemed alert, eager even.

"I'll go with you," I told him. I'd seen my share of Lynda's grossly graphic childbirth videos—not that that made me some kind of expert on delivering babies—but at least I knew how slimy and bloody things could get. At the very least, I could drive if Carlos threw up or passed out. "With luck, Lynda will call back soon," I added. "It's a good half-hour to town, longer if the traffic is backed up. You may need... help."

Vanessa and I clambered into the van. Carlos pulled a Jays cap over his bed head and hopped into the driver's seat with more enthusiasm than I'd seen in weeks.

Without a backwards glance, he sped towards Hinton as fast as was safe, given the hilly terrain, all the while keeping an eye on Vanessa and me in the rearview mirror.

"Oh, no! STOP!" Vanessa screamed. *"The baby's coming! NOW!"*

At best, we were still a good twenty minutes from town. Carlos pulled to the shoulder and snapped on his hazard lights. I called 911 again. Fucking busy signal. Could things get any worse?

Of course.

"I can't wait! It's coming NOW! AAAAHHHHHHHH!"

Carlos ran to the back of the van and removed clean towels and the emergency first-aid kit as if on autopilot. While Vanessa tried to find a functional position on the front bench seat, he spread the towels beneath her and snapped on a pair of latex gloves like he was star of some TV medical drama.

I sat behind Vanessa, using my body to support her shoulders and give her the leverage she might need any second now. I encouraged her to breathe the way she'd been taught at her childbirth classes and tried to maintain my own breathing and calm the thumping of my heart in my ears. I didn't know if I was thrilled or horrified by what was about to happen.

"It's coming quick, all right," Dr. Carlos said, cool as a glass of lemonade despite the oven-like temperature inside the Carlos-mobile. He grinned at Vanessa. "One or two big pushes should do it."

And he was right. One huge, screaming push later, out popped a big, bloody baby boy. "Thank God for advanced St. John's Ambulance training and the Life Network," Carlos laughed as he wiped the baby's mouth and nose with gauze, cracked open a fresh pack of shoelaces to tie off the umbilical cord, and snipped it with scissors he'd sterilized with a couple of alcohol wipes. Gently, he passed the wailing newborn baby to its mother.

Who is this Carlos guy? I thought, as a wailing ambulance pulled up behind us.

Two hours later, the baby had been washed and inspected and was nursing hungrily. Vanessa was laughing and crying into the phone; she'd finally managed to reach Afghanistan. And Carlos and I knew it was time to head back to camp to face the music.

We walked back to the van slowly. I hadn't given two

thoughts to my raw calf all morning; now it was singing for my attention. Tough.

"You were great, Carlos!" I gushed. I couldn't help myself.

He grinned from ear to ear as we got in and he turned his key in the ignition. His eyes danced with excitement and pride. "You were pretty cool-headed yourself."

An image struck me then, like a bolt of lightning. What it might have been like for Carlos and me if his anger and grief hadn't turned him into a mean jerk. If only he'd trusted me with the truth. If only I hadn't jumped to so many conclusions.

In that fantasy world, we could have rocked.

We stopped at a red light. "Carlos?"

"Yeah?"

"You and Brooke were talking—well, *shouting*—pretty loudly last night. I'm sorry about what happened to you, Carlos. To your baby."

Carlos drew in a deep breath and began tapping out a rock anthem on the steering wheel with his thumbs. The light turned green and the van shot forward. I stared out the window, regretting that I'd burst his happy bubble.

But then he pulled into the Tim Horton's parking lot, cut the engine and turned to me. "I thought about it all night long, Rainey. Brooke was right. I need to go home. Get some help. I've been *so* stupid and *so* awful to *so* many people this summer. You especially."

Yourself especially, Carlos, I thought.

He hooked a thumb out the van window. "Want to stop for coffee before I go back to face the firing squad?"

I figured I was already in a heap of trouble, too. "Count me in."

CHAPTER THIRTY-SIX

Over jumbo coffees and a box of Timbits, Carlos talked. And talked. And talked. He told me how he and Kayla had been a couple since grade nine when they'd met at a swim meet. How despite using a condom *every single time* (but one), they'd managed to get pregnant sometime over Christmas vacation. Kayla told Carlos in February that they were expecting, and for a few weeks afterwards, things were okay. His parents were disappointed but supportive. They'd offered to let Carlos and Kayla live in their basement apartment rent free. His mother babysat all his older siblings' kids during the day, so, "What's one more?" she'd said, if it meant Carlos and Kayla could finish school and work part-time. They talked about marrying. "We even decided to name the baby Jessie whether it was a boy or girl," Carlos said.

"Weren't you *scared?*" I asked. I'd be terrified if I got pregnant now, especially after witnessing firsthand what Vanessa went through. My own mother was only seventeen when she found out she was pregnant with me. Look how *that* turned out.

Carlos took a long sip of coffee. "I knew it wouldn't be easy. But I was excited, too, about being somebody's dad."

"What about Kayla's family? How were they with the news?" I stirred sugar into my coffee.

Carlos laughed bitterly. "Kayla waited a long time to tell them; she knew they'd be furious. When they did find out, they tried to brainwash Kayla into thinking that the best thing for her—*for both of us*—would be to have the baby and give it up for adoption." He reached into the Timbit box and extracted a glazed chocolate. "We had terrible fights about it. I told Kayla and her parents that if they didn't want the baby, I'd raise it myself. I could have, you know." Carlos put the doughnut back in the box, like he'd lost his appetite.

"Kayla called me one day and told me her parents were taking her to Florida for the March break. Surprise family wedding, she claimed. But when she came to my house after her 'vacation,' she looked pale, which I thought was strange after spending a week in the sunny south." Carlos plucked the plastic lid off his coffee cup and took a long sip. "Kayla broke down right away and confessed that the wedding trip was a lie. Her parents had taken her out of town to an abortion clinic recommended by some so-called friends of the family."

I didn't get it. "But... *why?*" I asked, wiping sticky Timbit crumbs off my fingers with a paper napkin. "I thought Kayla *wanted* the baby. And weren't her parents pushing for adoption?"

"You're right, on both counts. And Kayla's family is Catholic, too. *Seriously* Catholic. They go to mass and confession all the time. They have shrines and crosses all over their house. Even a fucking—sorry..." Carlos crossed himself. "...Virgin Mary air freshener in their minivan. How could they even *consider* abortion?"

A lump of coconut-covered Timbit stuck in my throat.

Carlos twisted and untwisted his paper napkin. "I found out later that Kayla had been offered a last-minute sports scholarship to a U.S. college. She's a great swimmer. Way better than me. Her parents and girlfriends convinced her that having a baby—even if she put it up for adoption—would wreck her body. That she'd never have a shot at the next Olympics. Kayla decided the only way to settle the matter once and for all would be to get rid of the baby."

"Tough decisions," I mused.

"None of which were mine," Carlos fumed. "I loved her, Rainey. I *trusted* her. If I'd *known* she wanted an abortion, I'd have taken her to court, paid her off, anything to stop her."

"Obviously she knew that..."

"Right. She didn't want the hassle." Carlos finished his coffee and slammed his empty paper cup onto the table. "Kayla pretended we were in it together, then she stabbed me in the back."

Out the window, a man and woman dashed by, pushing toddlers in jogging strollers. Carlos shook his head wistfully. "All spring, my family tried to make me feel better by insisting that in the long run it was all for the best. It got to be I *hated* being at home. I hated to be at school. I couldn't even go to the mall because Kayla worked there."

Piece by piece, the Carlos jigsaw was coming together. "Pineview was your haven," I said.

He nodded. "I had my van. And my swim team kids. And I met you. You didn't know I was a messed-up head case, so you weren't avoiding me like some of the other staff. You just chatted me up at the pop machine like I was a regular guy. You made me feel like my old self."

"Until I wrecked everything by asking you out." I said. "Sorry."

Carlos shook his head. "No, *I'm* sorry, Rainey. I should have said yes. Or at least explained to you why I wasn't ready."

"You needed time."

He crushed his empty paper cup in his fist. "I *needed* to snap out of it. To dig myself out of the hole I was in. Instead, I grabbed a shovel and dug deeper. I guess yesterday I hit bottom."

I had to know. "Was it really just Benadryl you took yesterday?"

"Yup. All I got from the cheap weed my cousin sold me was a headache."

"Izzie said you were drinking rum earlier in the trip."

"Izzie's a shit disturber. It was *candy.*" Carlos reached into his jeans pocket and pulled out a linty roll of Rum and Butter Lifesavers. Half were gone. "Want one?" he asked.

I shook my head sheepishly, then checked my watch and made a motion that we'd best get back to camp.

"Are you sorry about being hired to join WESTEX?" I asked as we climbed back into the van.

"I'm sorry how it all turned out," Carlos replied, digging in his pocket for his keys. "But I needed to learn, the hard way I guess, that I can't just drive away from my problems." Carlos turned the ignition and snickered. "And I learned that I am so absolutely *not* suited for the outdoor life. I like my swimming holes filled with chlorine and my burgers bug free. If I'd even *seen* that bear you and Alain wrestled, I'd have shit myself."

I grinned. "Don't sell yourself short. Look at what happened today with Vanessa. You were amazing!"

"Yeah... well... I don't know what happened. When I left my tent this morning to check out the commotion, all I wanted was to tell the lot of you to shut the hell up. But seeing Vanessa, it was like suddenly everything Brooke said to me last night made sense. These past few months it's like I've had an elastic cord wound around my insides. Every time I saw a baby, or heard a baby cry, the elastic wound tighter, dug deeper. But today... I don't know... What could make you higher than helping to bring a life into the world?"

No wonder Lynda was such a gosh-darn happy person; she brought an average of seventeen lives into the world each week. Then again, sometimes babies died and Lynda would take long drives to the country. Or take showers that lasted for hours. I never knew what to say when she'd come out of the bathroom all pink-faced and pruney, so I'd just eat the batches of cookies that invariably followed these episodes, and stay silent.

Bottom line: on the good days, and even the bad, Lynda loved her job.

I hoped I could say the same about whatever practical/lucrative job I ended up with someday.

"So, what's next for you?" I asked Carlos as he turned from the highway onto the camp road.

"University begins in a few weeks," he replied. "I'm going to find my own apartment. Get back in shape. Hopefully go back to coaching again at Pineview. I've got the long drive home to figure out the details." Carlos paused. "Look, Rainey, can we be friends again when you get back to Toronto?"

I didn't answer. Instead, I reached over and gave Carlos's shoulder a squeeze. He didn't try to knock me out the van door; I took that as a good sign. He reached a hand up and squeezed my shoulder in return. I didn't feel any sparks—of anger or lust. Just an exhausted kind of relief that maybe things might be okay between us from now on.

"You know, Rainey," Carlos said, as we pulled up to the camp check-in window for a wave-through. "I've seen Alain play hockey; my buddy Tom plays for St. Mike's, too. Alain's good. Not Gretzky, but good enough to really have a shot at the NHL. And though it makes me jealous as hell, I know you two artsy-fartsy outdoor enthusiasts are right for each other. Know what I read on a bumper sticker yesterday?"

"What's that?"

"'A Canadian is somebody who knows how to make love in a canoe.'"

CHAPTER THIRTY-SEVEN

Carlos parked and barely had both feet on solid ground when Dan marched over, his face bloated and purple, the vein in his forehead throbbing again.

"Carlos! You were *ordered* last night to stay here and wait for Brooke and me to speak with each other and the school board!"

"We delivered a baby, Dan!" Carlos explained, grinning despite Dan's ire.

Dan glared at me. "And Rainey, your impulsive behavior is one day going to get you into a mess of trouble!"

"Weren't you listening? Vanessa had her baby in my van!"

Dan's fists were clenched at his side. "Delivering babies was not in your job description, Carlos!"

He shrugged. "Just something I had to do. Besides, you fired me, didn't you?"

Brooke came flying down the path from the camp office and wrapped her arms around Carlos and me. "I was just on the phone with the hospital. You were both wonderful!" she exclaimed.

"Carlos was insubordinate!" Dan objected.

Ignoring Dan, Brooke let go of Carlos and smiled up at him. "You're still fired, though, kid. A rental van is being delivered from Hinton after dinner. You're looking at the new WESTEX driver."

Carlos actually laughed. *He could go home!* He glanced over at Dan. "I really am sorry for all the trouble I caused."

Dan collected himself. "We didn't tell the board we suspected drug use," he said begrudgingly. "Just that some unresolved *personal issues* were affecting your job performance. Spend the rest of the summer getting yourself back on track and this termination won't likely affect your eventual admission to a B.Ed. program. I'm an educator myself; I hate to see skills and dreams go to waste."

It was that last bit that I'd write over and over in my journal that night.

Late that afternoon, Lynda called in a panic. "Rainey, I'm so sorry. It was such a nice day that I took Simon over to Centre Island. I should have checked my messages earlier. Is everything okay?"

"Sure."

"But... your message said to call ASAP."

"No worries. Everything's fine now. My friend and I wanted advice is all. We had to... um... deliver a baby this morning."

Dead silence while Lynda tried to figure out whether I was being straight with her—or just sarcastic, as usual. "You're kidding, right?" she asked finally.

Unable to banish the excitement from my voice, I reiterated every great and gory detail.

"Rainey, I am so proud of you!" Lynda gushed when I was through.

"Thanks, Ma," I said. "Guess I'm just a chip off the old block."

I said WHAT?

Another silence. So long that I really wondered if maybe Lynda had passed out from shock.

"Uh... Lynda? You still there?"

"Any more surprises?" she asked softly.

I took a deep breath and let it out slowly. "Well..."

"Oh, Jesus, Rainey. I can tell that something's wrong. Tell me. Please."

Words tumbled out of me before I could snatch them back. "I broke the Flexileg a few days ago. The casing is cracked. I duct-taped it, so it's okay for short distances." *But it pinches like hell.* "And my crutches are holding up fine." *But they aren't much use for hiking long distance.* "So I'm good to go. Like I said before, no worries."

"What *happened?*" Lynda pressed. She'd been there when Greg tried to convince me that it would be better to take my old prosthesis on the WESTEX trip. It was, in fact, her two cents that finally sold Greg on the idea that my comfort should be top priority. Now Greg would be telling Lynda, "I told you so," too.

No turning back now. "I... uh... *clobbered a bear over the head with it.*"

Snort-snort-snort. "Try again, Pinocchio."

"Lynda? *Seriously.* I clobbered a bear over the head with it. Twice."

"What are you telling me, Rainey?"

"What part don't you understand? I *clobbered* a *bear* over the *head.* With my Flexileg. And broke it."

"Shit, Rainey!" Lynda shrieked. "Greg and I thought you'd be safe on that trip! Come home, Rainey. Today. I'll arrange for a ticket."

"Lynda, I'm *fine.* I don't want to come home. I *won't* come home. Besides, the bear's dead now."

Lynda gasped. "You *killed* the bear?"

"Well, no... but I got him to stop attacking my friend. A park warden shot the bear later."

"Your friend who was attacked?" Lynda asked. "He or she has seen a doctor, right?"

"Alain? He's just... *fine.*"

"And can the Flexileg be fixed, do you think?"

"Probably. But I'm not sure if it's insured for 'bear clobbery.' Greg's going to kill me when he finds out. You better start making casseroles for my funeral reception."

"Let *me* explain it to him," Lynda said. "I'm expecting a call today or tomorrow."

"Let him know that the bear wasn't responding to compassionate verbal strategies," I added.

Snort-snort-snort. "Don't worry about Greg, Rainey. You and I both know that he'll be worried—understandably so, wouldn't you say?—but I also know that he'll be glad that you were so brave, and that your friend is safe. It's not like you broke the Flexileg using it to hammer in tent pegs."

"Lynda?"

"Yeah?"

Say it, Rainey. Just say it. Say it, you coward!

"I... uh... miss... your spaghetti and meatballs."

CHAPTER THIRTY-EIGHT

An hour before dinner, I sidled up to Alain. "Hey. Can we take a walk? We need to talk," I said.

Alain's face fell. The area around his stitches was sore looking and shiny with ointment. "I *knew* it."

"Knew what? What's wrong?"

Setting aside his journal, he rose to join me. "That when Carlos snapped out of it, you'd breakup with me and go back to him."

I gaped at Alain, not knowing whether to laugh or slap him.

"You and Carlos did this great thing together today, Rainey."

"You jealous?" I asked, joking.

"Should I be?"

"NO!"

Alain let out a long breath. "Let's walk."

When we told Dan and Brooke that we were going down the road to check the evening's amphitheater schedule, Dan ran his hand through his hair—had it turned gray overnight or was I imagining it?—and apologized for snapping at me when I'd arrived back at camp with Carlos. "It's just... since the bear attack, I've been so..."

"Stressed?" Brooke offered.

"Right, About what would happen if someone got seriously hurt. Or worse."

"I know that, Dan. No hard feelings," I said. "We'll be back in a half-hour to help get dinner started."

Dan laid one of his meaty palms on my shoulder. "You did good today, Rainey. Your mother would be proud."

How would she ever know? "You mean my *stepmother*," I said.

"I mean the one who brought the cake."

"How are you feeling today?" I asked Alain as we set off up the road.

He flexed his shoulders. "I managed some push-ups this morning. I'm not ready to wrestle a bear again anytime soon, but I could probably take on a skunk or squirrel if I had to. How's your leg?"

"Not up to playing World Cup Soccer, but I could probably play a couple of rounds of hopscotch if I had to."

Alain and I walked slowly up the short path that led to the amphitheater. We checked the evening show schedule only to discover there were no Sunday programs. Fine by me.

Alain plunked down on the small stage, resting his shoulders against the plywood backdrop. I settled between his legs and he massaged the crutch-kinks out of my shoulders.

"Did you really want to talk about something," he asked after a while, "or were you just luring me out into the woods so you could have your way with me?"

"You guessed it," I laughed, sitting up and turning to face Alain.

His eyebrows shot up in surprise. "Here? Now? Did you bring the...?"

"Be serious," I laughed. "Doing it on a *stage?*"

He shrugged. "There's no audience—except for the birds and maybe a groundhog or two."

"Forget it, Alain. Not now."

"Soon?"

"Definitely soon. It's just..." I stared into the trees and gathered my words. I spoke quickly. "I'm not one of those wacko, clinic-burning, right-to-lifers, Alain. I'm pro-choice. But *if* I get pregnant, my *choice* will be to keep the kid. I'll raise it myself if I have to, but I won't give it up—or get rid of it. If Greg could raise a kid alone, so can I."

"Who's Greg?"

"My dad. I told you about him."

"Your old man lets you call him Greg?"

"Remember, he's only thirty-six."

Alain did the math and let out a low whistle. "I want children *someday,* Rainey," he said. "But *now?* Still... I'd never ask you to give the baby up or expect you to raise it alone. My dad would expect more from me."

I was beginning to wonder how much of what Alain did was for himself and how much was to live up to his dead father's expectations.

Who are you to talk? I told myself, *struggling to come up with some practical/lucrative career plan for yourself just because think you owe it to Greg for doing his best to give you a decent childhood.*

I'm an artist. And I knew, even then, that no matter what career path I took, I wouldn't be able to sever ties with that part of me any more than I would a baby. Maybe losing a leg and a mother made me just a little bit more possessive than most about what I carried inside me. Colors and textures and shapes and shadows.

I ran my fingers up and down the curly blond hair on Alain's arms just to make them stand on end. I loved that I could do that. Give him goose bumps. "Things are moving fast," I said.

"Too fast?"

"No... it's just... we've come an awfully long way in just a short time, haven't we?" That fight along the banks of the South Saskatchewan River was only a week ago. A week!

Alain laughed and wrapped his arms tight around me. "You saved *my life* two days ago, Rainey. I can joke about it now because everything's okay, but late at night when things are quiet, I'm just blown away by what's happened to me—and *for me*—this week. For the rest of my life I won't be able to look in the mirror without seeing this ugly bear scar on my cheek and thinking nice things about you. Hey, you think now that Carlos is leaving, I can have his tent?"

"Carlos told me that true Canadians have sex in canoes," I giggled.

"Isn't his family from Ecuador?"

I checked my watch and stood up, brushing dust off my butt. "He was talking about *us*."

"Think we have time for a quick trip to the boat launch?" Alain asked as I offered him a hand up.

"We're already late for dinner duty."

"Excuses, excuses."

CHAPTER THIRTY-NINE

As WESTEX said goodbye to Alberta, Carlos said goodbye to WESTEX. The next morning, he started his long trip back to Toronto with a lighter van load and, I hoped, a lighter heart. As much trouble as he'd caused, he'd been a part of our group and the loss of his presence was felt as soon as his ugly green and white oven-on-wheels reversed out of the campsite and disappeared around the bend.

With Brooke at the helm of WESTEX's spanking new, shiny red (air-conditioned!!) rental van, we by-passed Jasper, entering British Columbia through Mount Robson Provincial Park by eight AM. "Did you know that Mount Robson is the highest peak in the Rockies?" Dan asked.

We gained an hour crossing into the Pacific Time Zone, passing through the desert-like Cariboo Region to the turnoff for High Falls Park by early afternoon. Brooke pulled to the side of the road and turned in her seat to address the Six-Pack.

"High Falls Park is the closest thing to *real* wilderness

we'll encounter on this trip," she said solemnly. "The gravel road we're about to travel is long, narrow, winding, and littered with potholes. There will be no 'comfort station' at our campground."

"*No shower hut?*" Izzie groaned. "But... I have to take care of my hair! I'm donating it to cancer kids who need wigs."

"You are not!" Meena said. "You just read a story about some actress who did that in your *Cosmo*." She grabbed the magazine off Izzie's lap and held it up.

"And I was so *inspiiiiired*, I want to do it myself."

"I'll cut your hair off right now and donate it to the forest if you don't put that magazine away and let me finish!" Brooke shouted. "*Most importantly*," she continued when Izzie had shoved her *Cosmo* under the seat, "this park is home to grizzlies." She paused a moment to let that digest. "The park staff are militant about educating the public about the right way to observe bears, and they patrol regularly to ensure proper cooking and garbage practices are maintained. Consequently, there have been no bad encounters. We want to keep it that way."

"Yeah," Dan said. "Because the school board pitched a fit when I reported the bear encounter at Foothills. And now this *thing* with Carlos. They're watching us—watching *me*—very closely. They don't want any more... incidents."

"They don't want any *obituaries*," Brooke explained.

Thirty minutes later, Brooke brought the van to a stop by the side of the gravel road. The Six-Pack had been dozing, our heads bumping in unison against the windows in rhythm with the potholes.

"Wake up, sleepyheads!" she shouted cheerfully.

"Are we there yet?" Homer yawned.

"Hey, check it out," Alain said, gaping out the van's mud-spattered window. He reached into his camera bag for his old black-and-white-film camera.

Across the road, in a grassy field full of blue and pink wild-flowers, stood a falling-down log cabin. A sun-faded, hand-lettered sign was propped in the window: *The Last Chance Gas and Grocery Store.* The rusty gas pump out front probably dated back to the days of Elvis.

"That is *sooooo* not a 7-Eleven," Izzie said.

It was like we'd landed on the set of a Wild West movie. I tried to soak up every weather-ravaged detail so I could sketch it later.

"Follow me," Brooke gestured, herding us in single file to the shop's entrance. As the screen door squeaked open, a back-draft of strong cranberry incense wafted out into the clear mountain air.

"Brooke! Hello!" An old woman in a tattered batik dress smiled brightly. She was missing her two front teeth. Greasy gray hair hung to her waist. A ragged hand-knit cardigan was draped over bony stooped shoulders. I tried to capture every brown liver spot and every blue vein in my imagination. She would make a wonderful painting some day.

I saw a flash and heard the old-fashioned click of Alain's shutter behind me.

"Tara, meet this year's crew!" Brooke exclaimed. She introduced us all. Tara shook everyone's hand. Her skin felt like crumpled tissue paper.

"*JEZUZ! What happened to you?*" Tara remarked, peering closely at Alain's scabs and stitches.

"I got into a bit of a scuffle with a black bear a few days back."

"Lucky the bastard didn't take your whole head off." Tara waved off Alain and turned to Brooke. "Did you tell them about Sally? She had twins this year. Just gorgeous, the color of butterscotch toffee. I've spotted her a few times this summer in the meadow just over the ridge." She pointed back in the direction from which we'd come.

"Sally?" Frank asked.

"An abandoned grizzly cub," Tara explained. "She was raised by locals and reintroduced to the forest when she was two years old. Kind of a local mascot."

"This group has seen enough bears to last one summer," Dan grumbled from the back of the group.

Meena nudged me. "Ick," she whispered, pointing up.

No kidding. Hanging from the saggy rafters were at least a

dozen bearskins, some with heads and claws, some without. Many were just ragged pieces, stitched together quilt-like.

Tara followed out gazes. "I don't support bear hunting," she explained. "Those skins up there I cut from local bears hit out front by trucks and RVs late at night. It's hard work lugging them carcasses into the back room, skinning them, burying the guts, sewing up the pieces, but most of the damn tourists we get here will buy *anything*. I gotta eat, right?"

I peered nervously around at the rest of the Six-Pack. Everyone looked as sick as I felt.

"By the way," Tara smiled. "What can I get you all today?"

"We need bread and hot chocolate mix," Brooke said.

"Bread's there." Tara pointed to a deep freeze. Frank selected two loaves, one white and one brown, both hard as bricks.

"Best before February third?" he read skeptically, passing the bread to Brooke.

"I only sell a few loaves a week," Tara explained. "Frozen lasts longer."

"I'll take a pass on the toast tomorrow morning," Homer whispered to Alain.

"Careful, Homer," he whispered back. "That's a *shotgun* in the umbrella rack by the door."

"And it's loaded!" Tara called out cheerfully.

I watched Frank draw letters on Meena's back with his index finger. W-I-T-C-H.

Izzie and I wandered the store, scanning the food items laid out museum-style on what appeared to be bookshelves. We found a dented can of hot chocolate mix wedged between a jar of instant coffee and a water-stained box of Ritz crackers, and took it up to the counter.

"How much for everything?" Brooke asked Tara.

She shrugged. "Make me an offer."

Brooke laughed and passed her a ten. Tara slipped it into her cardigan pocket. Brooke didn't ask for change, and none was given.

"No gas today?" Tara asked.

"We filled in Clearwater," Dan replied quickly, starting out the door and motioning for the Six-Pack to follow the leader.

Tara waved. "Well, you city folk have a nice day, you hear!"

"Next stop, Jurassic Park?" Homer asked, once we we'd all piled back into the van.

"This trip is just one fucking episode of *Fear Factor* after another," Frank muttered.

CHAPTER FORTY

We arrived at our remote campground an hour later. Requesting that the others set up camp, Dan and Brooke approached Alain and me, and motioned for us to follow them to a deserted campsite across the road.

"Are we in trouble?" I asked as we took seats around a splintery picnic table.

Dan wasted no time on small talk. "Alain, your tent mates have lodged several complaints against you."

Alain blinked. "Really?"

Dan counted out the litany of charges on his fingers. "They say you snore like a rhino, which keeps them awake. You thrash your long limbs around in your sleep, which causes them bodily injury. You have smelly feet and never brush your teeth. You..."

"... fart too much?" Alain added, snickering.

"I *told* you he put them up to it!" Brooke said, whacking Dan on the shoulder.

Dan chuckled. "How much did it cost you?" he asked Alain.

It was a relief to see his sense of humor again.

"Not a cent, so I guess at least some of it must be true."

"You want to move into Carlos's tent, right? That's what this is about?" Brooke asked.

"Yes!" Alain leapt up, eager to set up the tent immediately.

"Not so fast," Dan said. "Brooke wants to talk to you and Rainey about some... issues." He excused himself to go check on the others.

"Are we in trouble?" I asked again.

Brooke drummed her fingers on the picnic table and waited for Alain to sit back down. "It's not easy for me to broach this," she started. "To be honest, it's really none of my business. And I don't want to embarrass either of you. But I have to say that aspects of your relationship are starting to concern me."

What the hell? I thought.

"Relax, this isn't a sex talk," Brooke explained. "Not really. It's just... Dan and I are worried about your safety. We understand that you want to be together. But sneaking off into the woods for privacy is unsafe."

"It's not like we've been..."

Brooke held up a hand to quiet me. "Alain, you were quite seriously injured by the bear. And Rainey, whether you'll admit it or not, I *know* that getting around on crutches and your broken prosthesis has been a struggle."

"Is this because we were late for dinner yesterday?" I asked.

"Partly," Brooke replied. "But *mostly,* it's because even after all that's happened, the two of you snuck off early this morning—*again*—to go skinny-dipping. Don't bother looking so shocked, Rainey. Of course I knew."

"I thought the cold water would be... *medicinal,*" Alain laughed.

"It's NOT *safe!*" Brooke placed her palms flat down on the picnic table and leaned forward, lowering her voice. "Look, I don't want to know if the two of you are sleeping together, and even if you are, you wouldn't be the first WESTEX couple over the years to do it. You *are,* however, the first WESTEX couple to repeatedly, whether on purpose or not, invite danger into the program."

Alain winked at me. "We don't want our first time to be our last."

Brooke winced. "Too much information, Alain. All I'm requesting is that if you feel you absolutely *must* be alone together, don't take off into the woods, especially at night. Or at dawn. I shouldn't have to remind you two of your bear safety." She paused. "Use the tent."

"Ha!" Alain grinned from ear to ear. Threw up his ball cap and caught it on his head.

"Don't misunderstand me," Brooke added quickly. "Dan and I aren't giving you the green light to turn Carlos's tent into a honeymoon suite."

You could have roasted marshmallows in the heat radiating from my cheeks.

"It's just... sex is risky enough without adding to it the possibility of being mauled by a bear. And speaking of bears, *bear* in mind that the tent walls are very thin. Unless it's pouring rain outside, everyone in a five mile radius can hear what's going on inside it."

"So you're saying we should save it for a 'Rainey' day?" Alain asked.

I kicked him under the table. Hard. With the foot I knew would hurt the most.

"Sorry to break it to you, Romeo." Brooke smirked. "The weatherman is calling for record sunshine in B.C. this summer."

After dinner and our team meeting, Dan and Brooke called it a night. The Six-Pack, under strict orders not to leave the campsite except to use the outhouse, gathered around the fire pit.

"Can you believe we've been gone for five weeks already?" Frank remarked after a long silence.

Meena tossed a stick into the flames. "I feel like we've been gone for years."

"Think we'll all stay in touch once school starts?" Homer asked.

Alain and I had already settled this question in Saskatoon. I shot him a little sideways grin. I loved the way his hair was always messy. I loved how he ate peanut butter on everything from toast to eggs to hotdogs. I loved his corny jokes. I loved how he brought the same raw enthusiasm to routine chores, like setting the table or scrubbing pots, as he did to playing volleyball or taking photographs. I even loved those eighteen stitches across his face—because they were his.

But the others? Who wouldn't want to stay in touch with Homer? How could you not love him? He called home every Monday to tell his mother about his WESTEX studies. He sent his family postcards from every town and park we visited. No one deserved to be cut off *less* than Homer.

"My father won't budge," he'd admitted recently. "I can't come home unless WESTEX makes a 'real man' out of me. He won't even come to the phone. He thinks that being gay is a disease you can be cured from—or die from. He probably thinks I *chose* to be gay to punish him for forcing me to take violin lessons."

Alain told Homer that if it didn't work out living with his cousin that he could come and live with him at *his* house.

"What would your friends think?" Homer asked, a bit shocked.

"Who gives a shit?" Alain replied. I remembered how upset he'd been when I'd assumed his friends back home would think less of him for dating a girl with one leg. If anything embarrassed Alain, nobody knew what.

And Frank? Sure, I'd stay in touch. He whimpered about trying new things, but he always tried them anyway. And like Homer, Frank called his mom every week, too, even though everyone could tell from the set of his jaw after those conversations that things were not looking good on the maternal sobriety front.

I would *absolutely* keep in touch with Meena. She was becoming a loyal friend, and her know-it-all tendencies could only be a plus once school started up in September.

But Izzie? Cripes, there were days I couldn't wait until I never had to deal with her word-drawling, hair-flipping ways again. I was sick of her increasingly snotty comments about how Alain and I were "such a *cuuuuute couple.*" And she'd started asking me strange "hypothetical" questions, like, "What would you do if you found out Alain was messing around with someone else behind your *baaaaack?*"

Meena pulled me aside after witnessing one such exchange. "Just ignore her," she said. "Izzie's jealous of you."

I was truly baffled. "Why?"

"Think about it. She's a performer. Izzie's used to the spotlight. You keep upstaging her out here."

"I'm not doing it on purpose!" I protested.

Meena grinned. "I think that bothers her even more."

CHAPTER FORTY-ONE

The following day, WESTEX stopped for an early lunch at a picnic area west of Kamloops.

While the others made sandwiches and vied for what was left of a box of Oreos, I grabbed a juice box from the cooler and wandered over to sit on a boulder near a chain-link barrier erected to prevent curious picnickers from slipping hundreds of feet down a steep rock face into a lake.

All that beautiful scenery and I couldn't enjoy it. My intestines were tied in knots. I had to force myself just to sip the juice.

Footsteps behind me. "I made you a sandwich," Alain said, thrusting it at me and plunking down on the ground across from me, his back against the fence so he wouldn't have to look down. We'd talked one night about his aversion to ledges and lookouts. "I'm not afraid of *heights,*" he insisted. "Or of falling myself. I just don't like looking down and imagining how far Dad fell." He took off his father's Expo hat and twirled it around his index finger. "The shrink tells me I should focus on the fact his heart stopped *before* he fell, that he was already dead, that Dad didn't know he was going to go... SPLAT!"

I inspected the sandwich. Peanut butter and banana. It was "our" sandwich. Some couples had a song. We had a sandwich.

I took a bite. "Our" sandwich tasted like sawdust.

"Want to hear a funny story about peanut butter?" Alain asked, his mouth stuffed full of his own sandwich.

I shrugged.

He swallowed. "The first time I kissed a girl I was eleven. Marie Dumas. We were paired up for a sixth-grade geography project. I thought she was cool because she had a pink streak in her hair. One day, I got up my courage and took her behind a shelf in the library. And kissed her. It was okay. She didn't puke or punch me out. But then, just as I was leaning in to kiss her again, she got this scared look on her face and asked me if I'd eaten a peanut butter sandwich at lunch."

"You eat peanut butter at *every* meal."

"But Marie was seriously allergic. Her whole mouth swelled up. She started gasping for air. The nurse came running with an EpiPen and called an ambulance. I thought I'd killed her."

I took a slurp of juice to wash away the lump of sandwich lodged in my throat. "I thought you said this was a funny story."

"Funny-weird, not funny ha-ha."

"This Marie-chick, did she live?" I asked.

Alain finished his own sandwich in three bites and wiped his sticky fingers on his shorts. "She was okay, but that was the end of that romance. The whole school found out what had happened. I was fourteen before I tried to kiss another girl."

"Alain? Did it occur to you that maybe I don't want to hear about you kissing other girls?"

"Want to talk about what's bothering you, instead?"

"What makes you think—"

"It's your *mother,* isn't it?"

"So, what if it is?"

"So, I still think you should go see her." Alain squeezed my hand. "Tomorrow we have to pass right through Squamish on our way to sightsee in Vancouver. If *I* were you, I couldn't *wait* to see my mother."

If he were really me, he'd know I couldn't wait for this leg of the trip to be over.

A few minutes later, Alain left to make himself more sandwiches. Only then did I notice Dan standing nearby watching a VIA train snake its way through the mountain valley below us. He'd lectured us at breakfast about the role of Chinese immigrants in the construction of the Canadian Pacific Railway. Homer told us his great-great grandfather on his mother's side had been killed in a nitro explosion in the Fraser Canyon.

Now, Dan wandered over to me. "I overheard you talking to Alain, Rainey. I didn't mean to eavesdrop, and I know it hasn't been my habit to interfere with the interpersonal—"

"Cripes, not another sex lecture," I interrupted.

"No, no, no." Dan blushed. "It's about your... mother."

My eyebrows shot up. "You know my *mother?*"

Dan frowned. "Of course not. But from what I overheard, she's in Squamish. I just thought I could offer you the perspective of someone who's been there."

"Been where? To Squamish?"

"Rainey, I'm adopted."

"I'm *not* adopted," I replied.

"Okay, but my impression is that your mother is someone you, a) haven't seen for a very long time, *and* b) are apprehensive about meeting."

"My life is already complicated enough, you know?"

"I do." Dan nodded.

I scooted over on the boulder. Dan plunked himself down heavily beside me. "When I was eighteen, in a fit of impulse, I put my name on a registry to find my birth mother. I'd always wondered about her, but when I didn't get any response after six months, I put it out of my mind, finished university, and got on with my life."

"Good move."

"Except that fifteen years later, I got a call from the registry. My mother had contacted them and wanted to meet me. By then, I was teaching full-time. I'd recently buried both my adoptive parents. I was building a house. I, too, didn't know what point there was in complicating my life."

"Did you meet her anyway?" I asked.

"Yup." Dan picked dirt out of his nails. "She was *polite*. We had lunch. Talked about our lives and why she gave me up for adoption."

"Why did she?"

"She was too young. Not enough support. Felt I had a better chance with a mature couple. The usual."

"Do you still see each other?"

Dan shook his head. "That was over five years ago. We still exchange cards on holidays, but... well... it made me appreciate the years I had with my adoptive parents all the more. It's love, not blood, that makes a family, Rainey."

"Yes! Finally someone understands that it's a *good* thing that I've decided not to call my mother."

"That's *not* what I said."

"What did you accomplish by meeting your mother, Dan, if all you got for your efforts is a lousy card at Christmas?"

"Two things," he replied calmly. "I get to put the time and energy I used to spend wondering about her towards other things. And, I realized that the success in seeing my mother wasn't so much about the outcome of that meeting as it was about my getting over my fear of meeting her."

"Dan? I'm not *afraid* to meet my mother."

"Well... in that case..." Grunting, he rose to his feet.

"I'm *terrified*," I whispered.

Dan howled with laughter. "You fought a goddamn *bear*, Rainey! How much more frightening could your mother be?"

"You never know."

CHAPTER FORTY-TWO

Next up: a roller-coaster ride south along Highway 99 through the Coast Mountains.

"Now you know what it feels like to hug a mountain," Dan remarked when Brooke stopped for gas at the bottom of yet another hairpin turn. The Six-Pack piled out to stretch. Standing there, on the side of a snow-peaked mountain, with the sun warming my face and the wind ruffling my hair, I tried to stifle the urge to just spend the next three days right there with no company but my sketchbook and watercolor pencils. I could almost understand why someone would leave behind their family and an ordinary Ontario life and run west.

Almost.

A half-hour past Whistler, Brooke turned left off the highway.

Margaret Lake was like no other campground we'd seen so far. Each campsite was carved into a stand of red cedars taller than most Toronto office towers. Massive deadfall, hundreds of years old, carpeted the forest floor. Giant ferns and thick moss gave the woods a beautiful, eerie, jungle-like feel.

"Which way to the beach?" Frank asked, scanning the trees worriedly. He had a new fear, thanks to a B.C. wildlife brochure Dan had picked up at the campground office: cougars. Did he think he could out-swim them?

Now that we'd lost Carlos, Brooke and Dan had amended our "no swimming without a lifeguard" rule. They'd agreed to a "buddy system," on the condition that "the buddies swim at an official beach, during daylight hours, *wearing appropriate swimming attire.*"

After a quick dip, it was my turn at dinner prep. Charred hotdogs and rubbery macaroni and cheese.

"The greatest thing about camping is how you get so hungry that you'll eat anything," Homer said, digging in cheerfully.

"Ketchup is like duct tape," Dan said, as he upended the bottle onto his plate. "A fix-all."

"I should just stick to making juice and handing out napkins," I apologized. Maybe in the fall, I'd let Lynda teach me how to cook. But why? I didn't need her to teach me how to deliver babies, did I?

Alain shoveled in his food like it was a five-star lobster dinner. But he'd eat pinecones—dipped in peanut butter, of course—if that was all that was available.

"Oh, *puuuuuke.*" Izzie rolled her eyes skyward and pushed her plate away.

Later, around a roaring campfire, Dan reviewed the history of the B.C. lower mainland. He spun lofty tales about Captain George Vancouver, Governor General James Douglas, and a nineteenth-century saloon owner named John "Gassy Jack" Deighton.

"He must have eaten some of Rainey's cooking," Frank said. "I'm feeling kind of gassy, too."

"Gastown," the area that developed around the saloon, Dan explained, became the town of Granville, then the City of Vancouver in 1886 with the coming of the Canadian Pacific Railway. "Tomorrow we'll cycle the seawall around Stanley Park," Dan said. "Lord Stanley, the Governor General of Canada from 1888 to 1893, dedicated the park for *'the use and enjoyment of people of all colors, creeds, and customs for all time.'*"

"The Stanley Cup is named after him, too," Alain added, tossing his ball cap high up into the air and catching it with his head mere milliseconds before it went sailing into the fire.

"Three goddamn cheers for Lord Stanley," Izzie sulked. She'd been in a terrible mood all day. I hoped it was just PMS. Or indigestion.

No sleep that night. Stress, the sheer proximity of Sara, and Dan's talk with me earlier in the day had me as wired up as the Christmas light display at Toronto City Hall. It was barely five in the morning when I unzipped the tent and, on crutches, made my way to the deserted shower station. I stood under the hot shower for a long time, wishing the water could wash away my fears and uncertainty along with the layers of sand, sweat, and campfire soot.

I left the hut a half-hour later, resolved to do something that Greg, a "Man with a Plan," would never approve of: play it by ear. If, later that morning, we drove through Squamish and I was hit with a sudden urge to go see Sara, then I'd go for it, and accept the consequences, good or bad. If the rebel butterflies storming my digestive system persisted, I'd take that as a sign that meeting my mother wasn't meant to be, and accept those consequences also.

"*AHHHHHHHHH!*" I was grabbed from behind. Alain.

A dog barked. Then another. And another.

"Great," I mumbled. "We just woke up the whole camp-ground. Should I add stalking to your lists of talents?"

"Don't be grouchy," he said, sniffing my clean hair and nuzzling my neck. "Kiss me, instead."

Moments later, Izzie stomped up the path. "The two of you certainly never seem too busy to draw attention to yourselves!" she snarled.

"Did she ever wake up on the wrong side of the air mattress," Alain whispered to me.

"We were just goofing around." I explained to Izzie. "Isn't that why we're all here?"

Wrong thing to say. Izzie flipped out as only Izzie could.

(Okay, okay, I did a pretty good flip-out myself from time to time.) *"You know what this trip is for me!"* she yelled.

More dogs howled in the distance.

"A *briiiiibe!* My parents know a guy on the WESTEX selection committee. My acceptance was fixed! My parents said that if I came on this trip, and stuck it out, they'd buy me a car in September. Anything to keep their *wiiiiild* child out of their hair for the summer."

To my utter disbelief, Izzie threw herself crying at Alain. He shot me puzzled grimaces over his shoulder.

After almost a minute, she kissed Alain's cheek and stepped away. Then, with a sly glance in my direction, she whipped her hair over her shoulder, flung her towel around her neck like a feather boa, and flounced into the shower station.

Whatever, I thought. Izzie's a drama queen, and I've got enough on my mind already.

CHAPTER FORTY-THREE

Passing through Squamish on our way to Vancouver that morning, the butterflies in my stomach flapped around like bats on speed. I hunkered down in my seat. Kept my eyes trained on the professional climbers scaling the Stawamus "Chief," a massive rock face south of town, and on the sketchbook in my lap. If I was going to see my mother at all, I wanted to see her first. But I had no idea what she looked like now. I could feel Dan shooting me curious glances. Alain kept nudging me. I ignored both of them.

I don't think anyone was happier to reach Vancouver than me. On rented bicycles, we made our way along the seawall at Stanley Park, stopping frequently to read plaques, examine the sculptures, and watch the sailboats. The taped-up Flexileg gave me no troubles during the low-impact bike ride, and I sucked it up and tuned out the relentless *pinch, pinch, pinch* during a tour of the aquarium, where we gaped at the huge belly of a pregnant Beluga whale. It made me wonder how Vanessa was doing. And how *Carlos* was doing. He'd be halfway home by now.

Mid-afternoon, Brooke drove us to the heart of downtown and found parking near the Pan Pacific Hotel. Dan said we could split up however we wanted—as long as no one went off alone. He ordered us to synchronize our watches and be back by nine PM sharp.

Homer wanted to check out Chinatown and Meena agreed to go with him. Alain talked Frank into going with him to the B.C. Sports Hall of Fame. I would have been happy to blow off Dan's buddy rule and tour the art gallery alone, but Izzie grabbed my arm, insisting that we *needed* to explore the shops on Robson Street. I reluctantly agreed, hoping that spending some time alone with Izzie might iron out the tension between us.

For the better part of two hours, I trailed Izzie through one trendy shop after another, watching her blow her spending money on the same shirts and jeans she could have bought on Queen Street in Toronto. All I bought were souvenir Olympic T-shirts for Lynda and Greg, and a ceramic dog bowl with mountains and sailboats painted around the rim for Simon.

"Are you and Alain *sleeeeeeping* together?" Izzie asked when we stopped for a 7UP.

I ignored the question. Like it was any of her goddamned business. I'd been practicing compassionate verbal strategies with her for the past two hours and it was time for a break.

Frank, Izzie, Alain, and I met up for dinner at a deli in the old Gastown area. When the diners beside us stared rudely at

Alain's stitched-up face, he just grinned at them, asking, "Is there lettuce stuck in my teeth?" Alain was like a duck; he just let life's irrelevancies roll off his back. Beside him, I felt like a sea sponge, absorbing toxins and all.

After we ate, I excused myself to use the washroom. I was gone five minutes, tops, but when I came back to the table, no one was talking. Alain looked annoyed. Izzie looked smug. Frank looked bewildered.

"What's going on?" I wanted to know.

Alain checked the time on his cell phone and pushed himself up from the table. "We need to get going," he said.

On the sidewalk, Frank declared a sudden need to hit a cash machine. He motioned for Izzie to go with him.

Izzie shook her head. "No, thanks, but I'll just *haaaaang* out with—"

Frank grabbed her arm. "WESTEX policy. No going off alone."

Alain shot him a look of gratitude.

"You owe me, man," Frank mouthed over his shoulder, as he and Izzie started up the street.

"What was that all about?" I asked.

"I just want to be alone with you for a few minutes," Alain replied. His lips were smiling, but his eyes told me something was wrong. So much for the duck theory. And he kept swiping at his ear with the palm of his hand.

"Alain? What's wrong with your ear?" Did he have some

exotic, antibiotic-resistant bear infection?

"Let it go, Rainey. You don't want to know."

"Yeah, Alain, I *do*."

He sighed. "Izzie stuck her tongue in my ear."

"She *what!*"

"You heard me. If it matters to you, I told her to piss off."

"That's all?"

"What do you *want* me to do, Rainey? Cut my ear off like that Picasso guy did."

"It was Van Gogh who cut his ear off."

Alain grabbed my shoulders and kissed me hard, tongue and all, right there by the steam clock on Cordova. "I love you, Rainey. The thing with Izzie? Seriously, just let it go."

Let it go how far?

CHAPTER FORTY-FOUR

The following afternoon, after an early day trip "exploring the hype," as Brooke called it, of Whistler Resort, Dan suggested we all return to Margaret Lake Park and hike the five-kilometer trail through the dense rainforest surrounding the campground. Since the bear incident, Dan declared all major hikes full-group activities. "Didn't you know," he'd ask, "that there's safety in numbers?"

Refusing to be left behind with Brooke, who'd opted out to take her turn at dinner prep, I slapped an extra cotton sleeve over my stump and double-checked that Dan had his trusty roll of duct tape in his pack. I wasn't going to give up the chance to tromp through an old-growth rainforest even if it did mean an evening on crutches. Not if it gave Izzie any more opportunities to stick her forked tongue in Alain's ear when my back was turned. Or me another chance to avoid Sara.

Two hours into our hike, as we neared the end of the trail, Dan, still convinced that noise would keep the wildlife away, began another round of his favorite old camp song, "Alice the

Camel." Moments later Izzie did the "*BOOM, BOOM, BOOM*" thing with her hips so hard that she lost her footing and tripped off the narrow dirt path into a huge clump of ferns.

I was about to laugh at her pratfall when she scrunched up her face and wailed, "*I HUUUUURT MY ANKLE!*"

I'd have sworn that Izzie had fallen on her butt, not her leg, but Dan rushed to examine the ankle in question. There was no obvious redness or swelling.

"Can you walk on it?" he asked, helping Izzie to her feet.

She tried a few steps. "No," she sniffled. "It hurts! *Alaaaaain,* will you piggyback me back to camp?"

"Faker," Meena whispered to me. "She fell on purpose."

She might be hurt, I thought. One of the compassionate verbal strategies Greg was always harping about involved giving people the benefit of the doubt.

"Are you sure you're okay with her?" Dan asked Alain. "Don't strain yourself. I could call the park office and get a carry-out, or Homer and I could..."

Izzie had already climbed aboard. "It shouldn't be too much further, anyway," Alain said.

"Oh, what big muscles you have," Izzie commented, running her hands all over Alain's chest.

"I'm going to strangle her," I snarled to Meena after Izzie and Alain disappeared up the trail.

Fuck compassion. (Sorry, Greg.)

When the rest of us traipsed onto the campsite a while later, Brooke was examining Izzie's still-not-swollen ankle. Alain had gone to take a shower.

While the rest of us sprawled around the picnic table, Dan explained to Brooke his version of what had happened on the trail. Brooke frowned at Izzie. "I'm taking you into Squamish to see a doctor."

"Not necessary," Izzie said. "Maybe if I just sit and rest a while, I'll be okay."

"Injuries require doctor visits. WESTEX policy."

"You can take my crutches, Izzie," I offered, smiling sweetly. *Please, take them before I smash you over the head with them, you dumb bitch,* I thought.

"Won't you need them?" Izzie noticed I'd removed my prosthesis and had set it against a log. "Maybe Alain could come with me to the doctor and—"

Instead of replying, I hopped up off the picnic bench and did a perfect handstand. After balancing a few seconds, I walked a good ten feet on my hands before hand-springing myself over onto my right foot. I glared at Izzie. "I'll be just fine."

"*Shooooow*-off," Izzie pouted.

Brooke hustled Izzie into the van. "Better get you to the clinic before gangrene sets in."

They returned to camp two hours later.

"Izzie's fine," Brooke announced, making a beeline to the cooler to scrounge some dinner leftovers.

Izzie claimed she wasn't hungry and slunk off to bed without a word to any of us, her shoulders slumped and her head down, momentarily defeated—at what game I had yet to figure out. Her Oscar-winning limp had disappeared. The rest of us played poker with M&Ms until the campfire burned down.

CHAPTER FORTY-FIVE

For the third night in a row, I shot to attention each time a car crunched along the gravel road near our campsite. I was terrified that Sara's curiosity would make her break her promise to Greg. That she'd come looking for me. Try to orchestrate a "happy reunion" scene.

Then, after each car passed without slowing, I would worry about why Sara *hadn't* broken her promise. If it were me, wouldn't I do *anything* for a chance to see my kid?

What to do?

What to do?

What to do???

It was already Wednesday night. WESTEX was leaving the Squamish area first thing Friday morning.

Tomorrow it would be now or never.

In the morning, a persistent drizzle dampened everything, including our spirits. The Six-Pack spent the day at picnic tables under tarps, scribbling in our journals and working on individual projects. I'd hoped to polish off a sketch of Margaret Lake at sunset, but ended up ripping the page out of my sketchbook and feeding it to the fire after more than an hour of fighting a losing battle with the light-dark contrasts.

Fingers of guilt poked at me all day. But I just wasn't ready to see Sara. Dan suggested quietly over lunch that contacting my mother wasn't the sort of experience I'd ever be "ready" for; that like playing "hide and seek," it was a "ready or not, here I come" situation. I gave him a look that made him stick his nose back in his lunch where it belonged.

Shortly after dinner, Alain was going through his nightly ritual of cleaning his cameras when Izzie approached, toting his cell phone. "I was in the van hunting for my new Vogue when it rang," she said. "It's finished charging."

Alain put his cameras aside and reached for the phone.

"It's some chick named Jennifer." Izzie smirked. "Said she was your... *giiiiirlfriend?*"

I figured it must be a wrong number, but Alain burst out laughing. "Really?" He tossed his cap up, caught it on his head, and then grabbed for the phone.

Izzie sashayed over to me. "He certainly does spread himself thin," she said.

Over by the van, Brooke called out, "I'm going into Squamish to pick up a few supplies. Anyone want to come for the ride?"

No takers.

Alain cooed into the phone. "Hey, Princess! How's it going?"

What the hell, I thought.

"I miss you, too," he continued, like he didn't have a care in the world. Like he didn't even care that I was standing less than ten feet away, hearing every word.

"Brooke! Wait! I'll go with you!" I called out, jamming my leg into my prosthesis; I was too angry to feel the pinch. I grabbed my day pack, and made fast strides to the van.

A cackle from Izzie. *"Trouuuuuble in Paaaaaradise!"*

"Rainey!" Alain yelled. "Wait! I'll come with—"

"Don't keep Princess Jennifer waiting!" I shouted back over my shoulder.

"Just give me a sec. I'll—"

I climbed into the van, slamming the door closed on anything else that two-timing scumbag might have to say.

"Did I miss something?" Brooke asked as we turned onto the highway.

"Everything's fine," I fumed.

She frowned. "I should mind my own business, but you shouldn't worry about Izzie. She's got a short attention span."

"This isn't about Izzie. It's about *JENNIFER!*" I shouted.

"Who the hell is Jennifer?"

Ignoring Brooke's question, I stared out the window at the drizzle. The forest lining both sides of the highway, usually so fresh and green, looked gray and menacing. What if the past six weeks had all just been a strange dream? One where I'd wake up in my attic room with Simon snuggled beside me, Lynda making French toast with blueberries in the kitchen, my Pinecrest day camp job almost done for the season, and Carlos still playing the pseudo-romantic lead in the farce that was my life.

Welcome to Squamish, the sign up ahead proclaimed.

I shoved my hand deep into my day pack, extracting the scrap of paper that had been folded and unfolded and refolded so many times that summer it was soft as flannel. "Brooke? Take a left and drive down Cleveland Street?" I pointed.

She nodded and made the turn, seeming not at all surprised or confused by my request. Dan must have tipped her off. Blabbermouth.

Thirty seconds later, there it was. *Sunflower Books and Crafts.* Open until nine, the sign in the window said.

"Stop the van," I whispered, my right hand squeezing the door handle. "I want to..." *Throw up?* "... get out."

Brooke pulled over to the curb. "I'll do the errands, then swing back around for you. Will an hour be enough?"

I nodded. No point overstaying my welcome—or whatever I was in for.

I opened the van door and almost fell out onto the street; that's how bad my knees were shaking.

"Good luck, Rainey," Brooke called out the open van window,

then gunned it up the street, probably so I wouldn't have time to change my mind and beg her to let me back in.

I was *going* to see my mother.

Ready or not.

CHAPTER FORTY-SIX

The shop door jingle-jangled as it opened, sending me almost clear through the ceiling, such were my jitters. I took several deep breaths and cased the joint.

Sara's tiny shop was lined with floor-to-ceiling bookshelves haphazardly stacked with used paperbacks and picture books. Stained-glass ornaments were stuck with small plastic suction cups to the windows. Old wood tables displayed hand-crafted items: beaded and silver jewelry, beeswax candles, cakes of brightly colored soap. The heady scent of fresh pine incense mingled with the stink of old floor wax and leather furniture. If I'd been a tourist, it might have been nice to browse awhile.

But I wasn't. I was there on gut-wrenching family business.

Across the shop, a teenage guy, my age or slightly younger, perched on a stool beside the cash desk, thumbing away at a Gameboy like his life depended on it. His straggly beige hair hung in his face. His toes curled around the tips of his muddy flip-flops.

I ahemed. He glanced up, raked hair out of his eyes, and sneezed. "I think there's a sale on jewelry today," he said, nodding toward the display.

"No, I was just—"

He sneezed again. "If you're looking for Olympic postcards, we're sold out until the next delivery."

"No... I... uh..."

The guy peered through the dusty late afternoon light at me. Gave me the once-over. His eyes locked on mine for several uncomfortable seconds. "Rainey?"

I just stood there—stunned. "Uh... yeah."

He tossed his game aside and bounded off his stool toward me. "You came!"

I stepped back reflexively, my weak knees sending me tripping backwards over my heels. I landed on my butt on the floor.

"Shit. Sorry. Here," he said, thrusting a hand down to grab mine. "I didn't mean to scare you like that."

I struggled to my feet and brushed off my pants. I didn't know whether to be embarrassed or furious. Who the hell was this guy who looked like he wanted to hug me?

Oh. My. God.

That hair. That nose. That height.

Whenever I let myself be curious about Sara, I always stopped myself short of wondering if somewhere out there I had any half-siblings; it was too painful. I'd begged Greg for a little brother when I was younger, asked for one each Christmas. I was in third grade before Greg explained that it wasn't simply a matter of picking one out at Wal-Mart.

But wait. The arch of this mystery guy's eyebrows, his lips, the way he stood with his hands in his shorts pockets while rolling back onto his heels, and the clincher—a faded vintage *Beam Me Up, Scotty* T-shirt. This was Greg's kid. My brother. No *half* about it.

"I'm Evan," he said, extending his hand. He had Greg's knuckles. "Evan" was Greg's middle name.

I wanted to say something, I really did. But I couldn't stop gaping. Evan even had the same narrow gap between his two front teeth that I'd had before my stint with braces in junior high.

My knees were still so shaky the Flexileg was creaking against the hardwood floor boards. Stupidly, I'd left my crutches at camp when I'd stormed off. Not that I wanted this brother-guy thinking I needed them, anyway.

Evan dragged another stool out from behind the counter. "Here. Sit down."

I sat.

He pulled his own stool up beside mine. "In case you were wondering, I was sixteen two weeks ago."

I did the math. Sara would have been roughly two months pregnant when she left Mollglen.

"You didn't know about me, did you?" Evan asked, sneezing again.

"Isn't it obvious?"

He shrugged. "Weird, eh? I didn't know about you, either. Until last fall."

"Who told you?" I choked out.

"Nobody. I saw the magazine advertisement for your..." He pointed. "... the leg-thing. What do you call it?"

"A prosthesis."

"Right. Anyway, I saw the ad at the walk-in clinic down the street. I'd gashed my arm skateboarding. Mom took me to get stitches and a tetanus booster. We were flipping through some magazines in the waiting room. I pointed out your photo to Mom. Not because of *you*; I just liked your in-line skates. I've been saving up to get a better pair for ages. Mom glanced over at the magazine and practically had a coronary right there in the clinic."

"Where *is* she?" I asked, glancing around furtively.

"Who?"

"Sara. Sara Jenkins. Your... *our*... mother."

"Mom? She calls herself Joanna now. Joanna Mancini."

"Isn't that... *Italian?*"

Evan shrugged. "Don't ask me. She changed her name before I was even born. Maybe it's because she likes pasta. Well, mac and cheese, anyway."

"Where were you born?" I asked.

"Vancouver. East side. The Skids. You may not believe it, but living above a dusty little store in Squamish is five-star accommodation by comparison. We moved around a lot just to get this far."

So many questions circled my brain—like a swarm of buzzards. Why would Sara/Joanna raise a child in poverty when she didn't need to?

"Don't be too hard on her, Rainey," Evan said. (I guess my sneer betrayed my thoughts.) "She'll never win any 'Mother of the Year' awards, but she's okay. I always had a roof over my head, and food and clothes and toys."

"So... where is she?" I repeated.

Evan stuck his thumb over his shoulder towards a doorway to a back room. "Out for a smoke. Mom only smokes when she's stressed, and she's smoked about ten packs this week knowing you'd be nearby, wondering if you'd call. I don't know if she was expecting you to just drop by like this."

"I wasn't planning to." In fact, I was starting to wonder if it wasn't too late to run for my life.

"Well, I'm glad you did," Evan said. Nothing in his eerily familiar eyes suggested he was lying. "I thought about cycling out to wherever you were camping and shaking you out of the bush myself. I always wanted a sibling. That, or a boa constrictor," he laughed.

Glad he was taking this all so lightly.

He sneezed again. "But Mom wouldn't tell me which park you were staying at. She said that it was your decision to call or not. That forcing contact after all these years would ruin everything... whatever *that* was supposed to mean. Mom's not big on explanations."

I knew that already. "Does she make you work here?" I asked, glancing around.

He shuddered. "Me? Nah. I'm allergic to all the soap and candles. I work days at the Dairy Queen. I only came down tonight because the upstairs air conditioner is on the blink. Hey, you want a drink? We've got pop upstairs. The fridge works okay."

"No, thanks." My only thirst was for knowledge. "Does my... our... father know about you?" He'd kept Sara's whereabouts a secret from me for months. Who knew what else he was keeping from me.

Evan chewed his lip. "I doubt it. You should know... Mom always told me my father died of meningitis before I was born."

"CRAP!" I yelled, jumping off my stool in anger. I thrust a finger at Evan's chest, poking Captain Kirk in the eye. "Our father is, as we speak, in Japan on a business trip!"

Evan held his hands up defensively. "I know who my father is *now*. Gregory Evan Williamson, computer wizard. Mom spilled the whole can of beans when I wouldn't let up about her freaking at your magazine ad. You should have seen the crazy way she ripped the page out at the clinic and carried it around with her for days, staring at it like it was a winning lottery ticket. After about a week of that, I threatened to e-mail the magazine and find out for myself who you were." He grinned. "*And* where you bought the great blades."

Something struck me—like a bowling ball. I poked Evan's T-shirt again. "You browse *Star Trek* Web sites, right?"

"Doesn't everyone?"

I let that go and perched back on my stool. "What are your favorites?"

"Hmm... *Trekmania* ... *Trekuniverse*... *KirkLivesHere*..."

Bingo. "You ever post messages or chat online with *KirkLivesHere's* Webmaster?"

"Captain G? Sure. He *rocks* at trivia. I've got the last five years of his newsletters printed out. He knows where to find the best action figures and—"

My heart thumped in my ears. "He's your father."

My brother's eyeballs popped out. "Are you for real!" he gasped. "No shit?"

I nodded. "No shit."

"Holy. Fucking. Cow."

At the back of the shop, a screen door creaked open, then slammed shut.

My mother's flip-floppy footsteps carried her into the shop through an arched doorway. She tossed her lighter in a drawer, and busied herself with a pile of catalogues on the counter. Giving Evan and me barely a glance, she said distractedly, "I've asked you a million times, Evan, not to socialize with your girlfriends in the store." Grabbing up a pile of paperwork, she disappeared once again into the back room.

"Leaving again so soon, Sara?" I called out.

Well... *that* got her attention. My mother materialized again in the doorway, her face about three shades paler than it had been ten seconds earlier.

"Rainey?"

So, that's what I'll look like when I'm thirty-five, I thought. Same shaggy hair lightly littered with strands of gray. Fine lines around my eyes and mouth. Arms still strong and well-defined. Despite her smoking habit, Sara looked and carried herself like an athlete. Maybe she skis, I thought. Or climbs The Chief, that big rock face. Maybe I'd ask her, I thought, but not now.

Now, I was pissed.

Sara/Joanna rushed over and gripped my shoulders. *"Oh my God, Rainey? You came! You're so tall. So grown up!"*

"Did you think I'd still be in Pampers?"

Sara/Joanna smiled. "Of course not. You were seventeen on June twenty-sixth. I always think about you on your birthdays."

"Too bad I'm not telepathic," I hissed.

She backed off like I'd slapped her. "Please don't be angry," she said.

But I was. Without warning, seventeen years of worry and resentment blew out my mouth like a geyser. "Angry? Why should I be angry?" I spat back. "Certainly not because you left my father and me without a trace; it happens. Or because I have a brother I've never laid eyes on before tonight; that happens, too. But how could you *not* tell Greg he had another kid? How could you let Evan grow up believing his father was *dead?* Look at him... *Joanna.*" I poked Evan's chest again. "How could you let him wear that dorky *Star Trek* T-shirt and not let him know that his father has one, too?"

Evan frowned. "It's not dorky. I paid forty bucks for it on eBay."

I pulled open my wallet and extracted my favorite photo of Greg, taken at a Halloween party a few years back. He was dressed in the authentic-looking Captain Kirk uniform he'd had custom made by a designer he'd built a computer program for. I tossed the picture to Evan. "Keep it. I have an enlargement at home."

I next extracted a picture of Grandma and Grandpa Jenkins at their thirty-fifth anniversary party and slapped it down on the counter near Sara/Joanna. *"How could you let your own parents think you were dead?"* I sounded belligerent and self-righteous but I couldn't stop myself.

My mother's eyes filled with tears. I didn't care. What did I come for if not for explanations? "Greg will want to know about Evan. He'll want to meet him. *In person,*" I added.

"What if Evan doesn't want to meet Greg?" Sara/Joanna asked.

Evan's jaw hit the floor. "But I do! Absolutely! You *know* that, Mom! I've wanted to meet my father ever since you told me he wasn't dead after all. But you kept saying that he wouldn't want to get to know me. That he'd just assume you wanted to hit him up for back child support or—"

"How could you say such a thing!" I screamed at my mother.

Sara/Joanna rubbed her eyes wearily and walked to the shop door. Turned the OPEN sign to CLOSED. "Come upstairs with me, Rainey. We'll talk."

"Evan, you come, too." I gestured.

My mother extracted a tissue from her pocket and wiped sweat from her forehead. "You met Evan ten minutes ago and already you're the bossy big sister?"

"Why not? He's family," I said. "What I need to know is who the hell are *you*, Joanna Mancini?"

CHAPTER FORTY-SEVEN

Sara/Joanna herded Evan and me through the shop's cluttered back room and up the stairs.

"You can make it up okay, can't you, Rainey?" Sara/Joanna asked. Hard to miss the not-subtle *creak* of the broken Flexileg with each step.

"I'm fine," I replied, thinking if I ever *did* get a tattoo, it would say, I'M FINE, in fancy script right across my forehead.

"You're sure?"

My prosthesis would have to split in two and send me tripping headfirst down the stairs before I'd give my mother the opportunity to think she'd given birth to Wimpy Gimpy Girl.

Sara/Joanna and Evan lived in an apartment about half the size of my attic room back home. The heat brought back memories of the Carlos-mobile. My mother walked over to a small window and propped it open with a brick to let in some breeze.

"Can I see?" Evan asked, pointing to my Flexileg. We'd settled on a worn plaid sofa and my pant leg rode up exposing my spring-loaded ankle.

"Sure." I slid it off and handed it over, silently thankful for the chance to give my sweaty stump a breather.

Sara/Joanna, from her perch on a moose-print upholstered armchair, blinked back fresh tears as she noticed my empty pant leg droop down over my stump.

Get over it, I thought. Don't you *dare* feel sorry for me. Or, was it that she only felt sorry for herself for bringing me into the world?

Evan launched into a million techno-geek questions about the mechanics of the Flexileg, which I was happy to answer. Then he asked, "Why've you got it taped up like an old hockey stick?"

I quickly told Evan about my bear-bashing in Alberta. When I was finished, he let out a low whistle. Sara/Joanna sat through my story, picking clear polish off her ragged nails, glancing up at me from time to time, her eyebrows raised, her eyes flashing concern? Curiosity? Contempt? Or were those just my own emotions reflected in her face?

"I had no idea you were so..." Sara/Joanna paused, trying to come up with a word. It was like all the "handicapped daughter" assumptions she might have made about me over the years were wrong. It was like... *wow, my deformed daughter not only has a mean swing, she even managed to find herself a boyfriend.*

At least for a while. Until Princess Jennifer called, I thought.

But I couldn't think about all that now.

I took a deep breath and leaned back against the couch, hugging a throw pillow to my chest as if to protect my heart from whatever emotional dagger Sara/Joanna might throw next. "Are you sorry now that Evan saw the Flexileg advertisement?" I asked her.

She shook her head. "No, no, no, Rainey. I've always wondered about you."

Yeah, but did you miss me? That's what I wondered.

Evan lay my Flexileg down on the couch between us, and padded to the fridge. He brought back three 7UPS and tossed one to each of us. Sara/Joanna popped hers immediately and guzzled like she'd just spent a week in the desert.

She was still chugging when I cut to the chase. "Did you leave Mollglen because my leg grossed you out?"

Sara/Joanna choked. *"Oh, God, Rainey, no!"* She set the can down on the wooden crate that served as a coffee table. "Your father didn't let you think that all these years, did he?" She patted all her pockets, probably looking for the cigarettes she'd left on the table in her shop.

"What was I supposed to think?"

"Rainey, you have to understand; Greg and I just weren't meant to be together."

"I *could* understand if you and Greg had split up," I said. "But why did you just *disappear?* Grandma and Grandpa didn't even know where you were, if you were dead, or kidnapped, or—"

Sara/Joanna sighed. "It wasn't that simple, Rainey. When I left I was young. And undereducated. And confused. And *pregnant* for the second time. I felt so desperate, Rainey. Restless. I knew I had to leave... to get out of Mollglen... before... I..."

"Killed yourself?" Evan suggested, stifling a burp.

I couldn't tell from his expression whether he was joking or not, but maybe he had a point. One of the conference lectures that Lynda practiced on Greg and me last spring was about postpartum depression. Many women got mild cases of "baby blues," Lynda said, in the months after giving birth. But some women developed something called "postpartum psychosis." Some of *those* mothers threw themselves off bridges. Or drowned their children in the tub. Or set fire to the nursery.

Had Sara/Joanna's leaving actually been an act of kindness? Her way of saving me from some whacked-out plan of hers to commit murder-suicide?

But she tittered at Evans words. "Oh, no. Nothing like that. Nothing so... dramatic."

So much for *that* theory. "Then, before what?" I asked, impatient now.

"Before I ruined my life."

"Greg and I ruined your life?"

I waited for her to deny it, but no. If I'd had any hopes of this mother-daughter reunion ending well, they'd just been dashed. "It's a long story, Rainey," she sighed.

I clutched the pillow tighter. "I've waited a long time—and come a long way—to hear it."

Sara/Joanna had always been a restless kid. "Loudmouthed and mischievous," she admitted. "The class clown in elementary school. The class misfit by ninth grade."

Grandpa Jenkins had moved his family to Mollglen from Ottawa when Sara was expelled from her private school for chronic class cutting and general disruptiveness. "I was just so BORED with everything!" Joanna/Sara exclaimed, throwing her arms up. "The structure, the expectations, the limits..."

I'd taken the Abnormal Psych elective last semester. Did Joanna/Sara have ADHD? Was she bi-polar? Obsessive-compulsive? Cripes, I hoped not. Mental illness was sometimes genetic. *I have enough to make me crazy without worrying that I might actually BE crazy,* I thought.

Sara/Joanna continued. "My parents blamed my behavior on the bad influence of the so-called 'wild kids' I used to run with in the city. They thought starting over in a lazy little town like Mollglen would be incentive for me to stop jerking around. They wanted me to *focus*. To *graduate*. To establish a *career*. To meet a nice *man*. To *settle down*. To *start a family*. In that order."

"Guess that deck got shuffled," I said, frowning. I didn't know what bothered me more: that Joanna/Sara was slamming my grandparents, or that she might be right about them. I thought about all the birthday cakes my grandparents bought me over the years. The vanilla ones with pink frosting instead of the chocolate I liked better. Or the "appropriate" Barbie bike when I'd asked for the "cool" boy's BMX. Or the hardbound set of "teen classics" I received for Christmas the year I'd asked for a subscription to *Seventeen*.

And what about the way Greg tried to persuade me to pursue a lucrative/practical career, when all I wanted to do was mix colors and play with light and shadow and explore brush strokes and paint textures? Or the way he lectured me about those damn compassionate verbal strategies when all I wanted was to tell the jerks in my life to piss off?

No wonder my father and my maternal grandparents always got along so well.

Still... it was no excuse for Sara/Joanna to just... leave me. I was only six months old!

Sara/Joanna sniffed. "Rainey, I didn't get pregnant on purpose."

"But you *did* get pregnant."

"And I was *glad*. It was a great excuse to move out of my parents' house. God, they used to put plastic runners on the carpet and insist that the bathroom towels line up largest to smallest across the rod..."

I almost laughed. "Yeah, that was... weird."

"I expected that having a baby would be a fun project. An adventure..."

I grabbed up my 7UP, snapped the top, and drank until bubbles filled my throat and I thought I'd drown. Finally, I swallowed and said, "You should have just bought a puppy."

I waited for Sara/Joanna to tell me that I was wrong. But she just stared down at her chapped hands. And nodded.

"I better go," I said, slamming my pop down on the table hard enough to make leftover 7UP slosh out the top. I swiped at the spill with my sleeve, shoved on my Flexileg, and rose to leave.

"Please don't," Evan said, picking a loose piece of foam from his flip-flops. "Not now. Not like this. I don't want this to be the last time I ever see you."

I glanced over at Sara/Joanna, who had thrown her arms up over her head in exasperation—or defense; I didn't know which. *Women who don't shave their pits shouldn't wear tank tops,* I thought.

"You're more like me that you'd ever know, Rainey," she said.

I lowered myself back onto the couch. "I am not."

"How will you know if you don't hear her out," Evan said.

Whose side was he on, anyway?

CHAPTER FORTY-EIGHT

"It's like this, Rainey. Even before you were born, Greg wanted—and my parents expected—us to get married."

"Well, you were pregnant. You'd moved into Greg's *house*."

"I was seventeen."

"In some countries girls are married for years by that—"

"Evan, that's not helpful," Sara/Joanna said. "Anyway, Rainey, I kept stalling Greg and my parents about marriage, telling them I wanted to lose all my baby weight before getting married. So I'd look good in a dress. I even picked horrible fights with Greg, hoping that he'd breakup with me. But he was just so damn... *nice*. And mature. Nineteen going on thirty-five. So full of practical career plans. But me? I was too confused to shower regularly; forget planning a wedding or looking for a job."

I laughed incredulously. "You weren't too *confused* to get pregnant again." Had she and Greg never heard of birth control? Did she not feel guilty about sleeping with a guy she obviously didn't love? There were words for girls like her—slut, skank, whore—but who liked to think they applied to her own mother?

She giggled. "Greg was so... hot. Besides, I didn't know it could happen again so soon."

"And you just figured the best thing was to just... go?"

Sara/Joanna nodded without hesitation. "I knew that if I told Greg and my parents I was pregnant again that within weeks I'd be an old married lady. Destined to life as a minivan-driving, casserole-making, small-town soccer mom before I was twenty. It was *too* much pressure. I just couldn't—"

"—take it anymore," I replied. After all those years I knew what the "it" in Sara/Joanna's departure note meant. *It* was my grandparents' desire for her to lead a responsible and respectable life. *It* was my father's multi-tasking parental competence over-shadowing Sara's immaturity. "He loved you!" I yelled.

"He loved *everything*," Sara/Joanna replied. "Me, my parents, his work, his stupid—sorry, Evan—sci-fi movies and comic books. And *you*, Rainey. *You* most of all. And he was *busy*, Rainey, accepting every freelance cyber-job he could get his hands on. Carrying a full load of online university courses. Taking time off work to go to all your orthopedic appointments; he'd have lists of questions for the doctors all typed up in advance. He used to brag about how he could type with one hand and give you a bottle with the other."

"But..."

She held a hand up. "Let me finish. My parents watched

Greg doing the lion's share of caring for you and got on my back about how I needed to *step up,* be a better mother. And Rainey, I *did* try. I'd rock you at night so Greg could sleep, humming lullabies while you squirmed and cried for your daddy, all the while driving myself nuts wondering if your leg was my fault. Wondering if I should have eaten more vegetables when I was pregnant. Feeling so guilty that I'd failed you and Greg. And so damn restless. And *jealous*—of *you.* Imagine, being jealous of a little crippled baby."

"I'M NOT CRIPPLED!"

It was like she hadn't heard me. "Evan was my second chance to be a good mother."

"So you just took off with him!" I spat.

Sara/Joanna nodded. "I cleaned out the cash from the coffee can and hitchhiked to Vancouver. Closed my eyes, pointed to a random name in the phone book at the bus station, and never called myself Sara Jenkins again. An agency helped me find a place to live, a job, and pre-natal care. Now, *that* was an adventure. You fought a bear, Rainey? Try fighting the social service system some time."

I wanted to strangle her. I sat on my clenched fists, wanting to pick up my Flexileg and bash her with it, too. *I knew it was a mistake to come here!* I thought.

Sara/Joanna seemed oblivious to my fury. She reached out and ruffled Evan's hair. "Your brother hasn't had all the opportunities and privileges you've had, but he turned out okay."

"At least he had his *mother*," I hissed.

Sara/Joanna reached for a tissue and blew her nose. Good, I'd hurt her. Or maybe her on-again/off-again crocodile tears were—like Izzie's—just a fine acting job.

I took a deep breath and willed myself to calm down. "Okay, you got what you wanted, Joanna. Freedom. Adventure. Whatever," I said. "So why, then, did you want to meet me? Why *now?*" I had a nagging feeling that it wasn't just about satisfying her curiosity. She *wanted* something from me. Surely not forgiveness, since I don't think it ever occurred to her that leaving Greg and me, and worrying her parents, was wrong. Cutting ties with people who cared about her was simply the price of getting what she wanted for herself.

Selfish bitch.

"Maybe that magazine was a sign that it was time for me to..." Sara/Joanna struggled to find the word she wanted. "... to *reach out* to you."

"Great timing," Evan said, his eyes shooting darts at his mother and his mouth twisting in a pout. "Now that you're moving to Whitehorse? What chance do we have to stay in touch with anyone up there?"

"Evan, now's not the time to—"

"Tell her, Mom," Evan prompted. "How you're taking off. Again."

Sara/Joanna wrung her hands. "I'm not... *taking off*."

"Her partner lives in the Yukon," Evan explained. "They met last April at a craft show in Vancouver. Bessie runs a—"

"Bessie?"

"Mom's bi." He said it like it was no big deal, which I guess in the grand scheme of things it wasn't. Seemed appropriate even—surely Joanna/Sara wouldn't want to be limited to just one sexual preference.

"Bessie runs a bed-and-breakfast in Whitehorse," Evan continued. "Mom's joining her up there in January when the lease on this shop expires."

What Sara/Joanna wants, Sara/Joanna gets, right? Then again, would Greg have followed *Lynda* to the Yukon? Stupid question. He'd have followed her to the moon—and no doubt dragged me along for the ride, too.

"I'm not going with her," Evan said.

"You are so!" Sara/Joanna shouted.

"No, I'm not!" Evan used the exasperated tone of someone who's had the same argument many times before. "I'm sixteen! I love you, Mom, and I want you to be happy, but you just said it yourself: I'm not a baby anymore. I've got a future in technology and I can't get the education or experience I need in *Whitehorse!* If you think true love—or whatever—is calling you North, then fine, go... but let me live my life, too! It's not like I'd be living in the streets; you know that I was offered a scholarship to Mount Grenken School."

Joanna smirked. "You told me last year that boarding school was for geeks."

"I'll *never* get into CTI if you drag me with you up to the fucking *North Pole!*" Evan yelled.

"Don't swear! And Whitehorse is *not* the North Pole!" Sara/Joanna's nose flared when she was angry. Just like mine.

I'd had no idea what that mother and son argument had to do with me until Evan mentioned CTI. And then I was floored.

Everything–*finally*–made sense.

"You want to go to the Canadian Technology Institute?" I asked Evan.

"It's got the best video game development program in Canada." He took a long breath that caught somewhere in his throat. "Oh, shit... Captain G told me about it."

"Don't swear! Who's Captain G?" Sara/Joanna asked.

"Just... someone I talk to online."

"Not a pedophile, I hope. I wish that goddamn computers had never been invented."

"Don't swear!" Evan sneered at Sara/Joanna. "It's the career that I want."

"Well... like that Rolling Stones song, you can't always get what you wa-ant," She sang.

"*Like you would know!*" Evan shot back at her.

I ahemed. "Would you prefer, Joanna, that Evan just cleaned

out the coffee can one day and was never heard from again?"

Truth hurts. My mother covered her face with her hands. After a few silent seconds, she lowered her hands and spoke. "Rainey, you have every right to be upset with me. I know I must have hurt you and Greg and my parents very much."

You might know, but you're not sorry, I thought. "Why weren't you just honest with everyone?" I asked.

"I thought the truth would hurt you more, Rainey."

"Bullshit!"

I guess the no-swearing rule didn't apply to me because Sara/Joanna said nothing as she reached to take a fresh tissue from the box on the side table. She blew her nose loudly, like a *Canada Goose,* I thought cruelly.

"I was *so* young, Rainey. I made ten truckloads of mistakes and bad decisions, but please believe me when I say I *never* regretted having you or Evan."

Of course she didn't. I'll give her that. If Sara/Joanna hadn't *wanted* us, she would have aborted us without a second thought.

I sat back against the couch. I thought of Vanessa's breathing exercises to deal with labor pains and wondered if they'd help for other types of stress. Remarkably, after just a few seconds of deep inhaling and slow exhaling, I felt my anger begin to drain like dirty bathwater.

I studied the lines of my brother's face, an intersecting mess of hurt and confusion and hope. *He* was why Sara/Joanna had called Greg and expressed interest in seeing me, I'd determined.

My mother wanted to see how I'd turned out.

She wanted to see if Greg was still a good father.

Because she wanted to let Evan "live his life," but she didn't want him stuck at some geeky boarding school. Seeing the Flexileg ad the previous November reminded her that she had... options.

Maybe there was something to all Greg's mumbo jumbo about everything happening for a reason, after all. If not for WESTEX, Greg might never have told me about Sara/Joanna's call. And if not for Jennifer's call to Alain earlier in the evening, I'd have been willing to let the opportunity to meet my mother—and in doing so, my *brother*—pass me by.

I hugged my knees up to my chest and gave my mother what she wanted. And what my brother *needed*.

"Uh... Joanna," I started, "why doesn't Evan move to Toronto when you go north? Our house is huge. You *know* that Greg will be thrilled to learn that *one* of his offspring inherited his techo-genes." I turned to Evan. "My high school has a School of Technology program. And when you graduate, CTI is only a few hours' drive away—halfway between Toronto and the town where I grew up. The town where *you* would have grown up, too, if..." I leaned forward suddenly, my eyes nailing Sara/Joanna to the back of her moose-print chair. *"But you knew that, didn't you?"*

Evan's jaw fell to his chest. "You *did?*" he asked his mother.

She nodded slowly. "Rainey, I appreciate your enthusiasm, but I've been thinking it over and—"

"Thinking what over?" Evan asked.

"—I can't imagine what Greg's wife would think about all this."

"Lynda? She's great!" I said, playing her up, partly to piss off Sara/Joanna and partly because... *it was true?* Turning to Evan, I started counting on my fingers. "Lynda's a doctor. A great cook. She has a goofy Golden Retriever named Simon. And... you know her, too. Lynda is... *alienbaby.*"

Evan sucked in his breath and let it out in short gasps. "I... posted back and forth with her... like... three days ago. About the final... episode... of *The Next Generation.*"

Sara/Joanna's eyes ping-ponged between Evan and me, confused.

"Oh..." I added, to Evan, "in person, Lynda's six-one. And gorgeous."

If I was trying to make Sara/Joanna jealous, I'd failed. "Greg's never lost his thing for tall women," she laughed. "Look at *you,* Rainey. As tall as me." Then she gazed at Evan wistfully. "*If* I let you go, and if Greg and this Lynda woman agree to have you, I'd miss you so much."

Well, at least she loves one of her kids, I thought.

"I'd be okay," Evan said, looking dazed. "I'd call every week.

Visit every summer. It's not like I'd... like we'd never... see each other again."

I got up to peer out the window. Brooke was parked across the street, waiting. It was time for me to go.

I still didn't know how I felt about Sara/Joanna. I thought about Homer and how, despite the scorn of his family, he'd stayed true to himself *and* open to the possibility his parents might accept him again one day. I thought about my father and how naïve he'd been, and how lonely he must have been when Sara left without even saying goodbye. I thought about Grandma and Grandpa Jenkins, who'd always been there for me—even if some of their gifts had sucked. I thought about Evan and me; we wouldn't have even been born if not for our mother's impulsive "adventures" and our father's seeming disregard for condoms.

Sara/Joanna wasn't perfect. She was eccentric and selfish—and she smoked. I doubted she'd ever understand the extent to which her "adventures" impacted those around her. Or how her unexplained absence from my life had made me so distrustful of others. Or how she'd left me baffled by Lynda, who'd often come home from a trip to the mall with cookbooks and travel brochures—plans for the future—like she really believed that techno-geek Greg and his hot-headed daughter were worthy of her time and homemade muffins and... compassion.

Over the years, Sara had *never* given me a birthday gift. Or sent Christmas wishes. Or even provided Greg with an address I could send all those stupid school Mother's Day crafts to.

But I didn't hate her. Today she'd given me something I wanted: a brother. And something I needed: the truth. Two things I could work with.

And, like it or not, I'd inherited her not-bad looks and artistic tendencies.

"So," I asked her, doing a full turn. "Did I pass inspection?"

Sara/Joanna jumped to her feet. "Ah, Rainey, you're magnificent! A little temperamental, but I'm sure Greg would say that you get that from me."

Evan rose, too, and hugged me like he didn't want to ever let go. *Don't worry, little brother,* I thought, *you and I will have plenty of time to get acquainted.* "I'll get in touch with you as soon as I get home and have a chance to talk with Greg and Lynda," I said in his ear, whispering, "It'll help that you've already met each other out there in cyberland."

I gave my mother a more awkward hug. I knew we'd never get back the lost years, but maybe she and I might one day be able to find a small place in each other's lives.

Or not.

On our way through the shop to the front door, my compassionate verbal strategies kicked in and I told Sara/Joanna that her store was awesome. She beamed, admitting that she'd hand-crafted most of the jewelry and pottery herself. She picked out a pair of dangly silver earrings for me that she said were her favorites.

Quickly, I pulled my sketchbook from my pack, ripped out the moose watercolor I'd finished back at Algonquin Park, and passed it to my mother. She hadn't asked about my interests or aspirations during our visit—to be fair, I hadn't given her much of a chance to—but maybe it was time she knew that her daughter was an artist, too.

"Rainey, let's try not to lose each other again," Sara/Joanna said.

You try first, I thought, and waved goodbye.

CHAPTER FORTY-NINE

At some point during my time with the Mancinis, the day's drizzle turned to downpour.

When I dashed across the road to the van, Brooke was dozing in the driver's seat, her *James Taylor's Greatest Hits* CD blaring.

She turned the sound down as I opened the door and slid into the passenger seat. "Want to stop for coffee?"

I shook my head and cranked the music back up. It had been a "Fire and Rain" sort of day.

Halfway back to Margaret Lake Park, the dark skies opened wide. Wind rocked the van like a horror-movie cradle. Ice balls battered the windshield. Lightning shredded the sky.

Not again, I thought, remembering the storm that had set in motion so many "adventures" in Alberta.

Brooke pulled to the shoulder to wait it out.

"Hope everything's okay back at camp," I said. The tents had rain flys but they weren't exactly typhoon proof.

Brooke sighed. "Actually... Dan called me awhile back all in a dither; he's not cut out to play referee."

"Meaning?" I wasn't sure if I wanted to know or not.

Brooke switched off the ignition and turned to me. "Meaning all hell broke loose shortly after we left. Apparently, Izzie and your tarnished Prince Charming had an earsplitting argument that carried on for so long that a patrolling camp warden had to break it up."

"About?" I bit my lip and tried not to let Brooke see how much that information cheered me.

She shrugged. "You'd know better than me, Rainey."

"How's Meena with the weather?" I asked.

"Dan said she'll be okay. Frank kicked Homer out of their tent and dragged Meena inside with him."

"Where I'm sure more is sparking than the weather," I giggled.

Brooke waved her hand at me. "Enough about everyone else. How are you?"

"Fine... in an overwhelmed sort of way."

"You want to talk about it?"

"Nope," I said. But after a few seconds of silence, words started spilling from my lips anyway. "I always thought my family tree was this small sickly shrub, but, well... I think it's starting to... to bud."

Brooke laid a hand on my arm. "You know, Rainey, the most important thing about the WESTEX trip isn't so much about how far we travel. It's about who we come to be along the way."

The thunderstorm moved on, but it was still pouring rain when Brooke and I pulled into our dark campsite a little after ten PM.

"Guess everyone's called it a night," I said. I'd had enough excitement for one day, too. The events and revelations of the past few hours whirled around in my head like breadcrumbs in a high-speed blender.

Brooke frowned, gesturing towards the picnic tables. "Not everyone."

There, in the beam of the van headlights, in the downpour, sat Alain.

"Rainey, I need to speak with Dan," Brooke said, cutting the engine and lights, opening the van door, and grabbing her flashlight off the dashboard in one smooth sequence. "Do me a favor? Get that lovesick puppy of yours out of the rain before he catches pneumonia." She slammed her door closed and set off down the dark path to Dan's tent at the edge of the woods.

I climbed down out of the van, took my flashlight from my day pack, and approached the picnic table. "Hey," I said.

Alain didn't move. Droplets of rain were dripping off the ends of his hair and nose. He didn't speak for what seemed like a full minute. Finally, he glared up at me, putting a hand over his eyes to shut out the glare of my flashlight. "You ran away. Again," he said, his teeth chattering.

I switched the light off and set it on the table. I didn't want Alain to see my hurt expression. "I needed time away from Izzie and her snide comments. It burns me that she found out about your other girlfriend before I did. Actually, it burns me that you have another girlfriend *at all,* because it means you're a liar. It *also* burns me that you were chatting up this Jennifer person, calling her 'princess' and 'gorgeous' right in front of me like some insensitive prick." I crossed my arms over my chest.

Alain stared ahead, shaking his head like he thought I was the biggest loser on the planet.

"So I went with Brooke into town."

"Exactly!" Alain pushed himself up from the table suddenly. "You ran away! Again!"

"I went to see my mother, Alain! *And* my brother. My sixteen-year-old *brother,* who I didn't even know existed. Look, Alain, could we finish this inside? We're getting drenched." Without waiting for a reply, I trooped off in the direction of his tent, flash-light trained on the wet ground so I wouldn't slip or skid into a mud puddle.

Alain trudged up the path after me. When we'd both crawled inside his tent, I zipped the door flap closed and rooted around in the dark until I found some dry towels. While I rubbed at my dripping hair, Alain silently stripped off his drenched clothes and wrapped his naked, shivering body in his sleeping bag.

Something came over me then, a fit of jealousy, of nerves,

I'll never know. I chucked my own wet clothes and my Flexileg, and with something I hoped approached *passion,* launched myself at Alain full force.

He pushed me away. "No way! Not now!"

"You're worth fighting for!" I hissed, trying to kiss him again. In the dark, my mouth missed his and I ended up with a mouthful of his wet hair.

"Get off me!" Alain pushed me away again. His words spilled out at me fast and choppy as a flash flood. "Rainey, listen to me! You don't have to 'fight for me.' *There's nobody else. Jennifer* is my eleven-year-old next-door neighbor, for Christ's sake. The *sister* of my friend JP who is looking after the house for me this summer. She has *Down's Syndrome.* She's learning to use the phone at summer school, and called to say hi because she has a little crush on me, even made me a big mushy bon voyage card when I left for WESTEX. But she's *hardly* someone you should be jealous of. Case closed. I wanted to explain, but you took off in such a hurry."

Whoa... did I feel stupid. "Alain... I was..."

"Wrong? No shit."

"But Izzie said..."

"Izzie? She's just a troublemaker. Sure, she's been putting the moves on me; you knew that, already. But it's you she's getting the rise out of. I had it out with her tonight. I made her cry. You're worth fighting for, too, goddamn it. *Don't you know that?*"

I took a few deep breaths before speaking again. "I know I make too many assumptions. I know I need to stop thinking the worst every time I don't understand something. I'm really, truly sorry, Alain, for calling you a liar. I hope..." I found his hand in the dark, but he yanked it away.

"You also called me an insensitive prick."

"I'm sorry for that, too. You have no idea."

"Sorry enough to stop *doing* it every goddamned time we have a fight?"

Maybe Alain's hockey shrink dealt with teens like me, too. Ones who were so busy jumping to conclusions that the truth sitting right in front of them sometimes seemed blurry. "Alain, I'll do anything to make you believe me. I'll... eat dirt. I'll..."

Alain sighed. "Look, Rainey, I understand how it must have sounded. But believe me, I'm just not the chick magnet you seem to think I am." He laughed darkly. "With all these stitches, I'm not even cute anymore."

I didn't know what to say. I felt such... shame. I was so used to being the indignant one. Now I'd fallen so far off my high horse, it was like I'd had the wind knocked out of me.

"Rainey?" Alain's voice was softer now. Maybe I hadn't killed us this time, after all. "What happened with your mother? And you have a *brother? Really?*"

The pounding of rain on Alain's tent fly was so loud we could barely hear each other talk, let alone hear anything that

was going on outside the tent—or in anyone else's tent. I tried to make a joke. "Why do you want to hear all this now? Don't you want to take advantage of the bad weather?"

"Your *life* interests me, Rainey, not just your body."

So I crawled under the blanket with him and, in the complete darkness, told Alain the sordid story of Greg and Sara, a fairy tale gone amok if ever there was one. In the end, Alain said that if things didn't work out for Evan living with Greg and Lynda and me, he'd be welcome in his house.

"You starting a fraternity?" I asked.

"I'm used to a noisy, crowded house full of guys. And maybe I don't want to be alone. Maybe I'm still afraid of monsters under my bed."

"Any girls allowed *chez Alain?*" I asked.

"Not unless you plan to move in."

"Fat chance. Greg had his own house, too, when he was your age. Look what happened to him."

Alain was quiet so long, I thought maybe he'd fallen asleep.

But no. "You happened to him," he whispered in my ear.

It rained the rest of the night.

CH_APTER FIFTY

My hopes for a sneaky six AM retreat to the girls' tent were
dashed when I stuck my head out Alain's tent flap and spotted
Brooke making her own disheveled exit from Dan's tent.

She glanced over at me, waved sheepishly, and began walking
briskly toward the path to the outhouse.

"Morning, Brooke!" I laughed.

Brooke stopped and examined her fingernails. "Dan and I
were just... playing *Trivial Pursuit*. I take it everything's okay
with you and Alain?"

I nodded.

"Good," she said, and disappeared up the path.

I heard another zipper, this time from the direction of Homer
and Frank's tent.

Meena's head popped out the flap, then back in like an embarrassed turtle when she saw me. A few minutes later, her whole body
emerged, dressed in one of Frank's ratty Old Navy sweatshirts.

"We were playing chess," Meena explained.

"She's a slow learner." Frank appeared behind Meena and slipped his arm around her waist.

"Where's Homer?" I asked.

"Here," he called, making a quick exit from the she-tent, the one he'd had no choice but to share with Izzie. "Where were you, Rainey? Izzie's been stewing all night. Says she *neeeeeeds* to talk to you."

"I was... um..."

"HE SHOOTS, HE SCORES!" Alain shouted, crawling out, messy head first, from the tent, wearing only his blue and white Leafs boxers.

"I'll go talk to Izzie now," I told Homer.

Together, Izzie and I walked slowly to the shower station.

"I'm *sooooo sooooorry*, Rainey," she said, kicking at pebbles on the dusty camp road.

"I was a total bitch, trying to steal Alain away from you. I didn't really want him for myself, you know—all those stitches of his are a serious fashion faux pas. It's just... I found out last week that my parents are getting divorced."

What the hell did her parents' divorce have to do with Alain?

Izzie laughed sharply. "It's not that I *caaaaaare* about the divorce. My parents hate each other."

"You've sure been upset about *something,* lately."

"It's like this. Dad's been offered a job in New Mexico; he's going to take it. Mom's moving to Brampton to be closer to my sisters and the grandkids. Neither of them *waaaaants* me to live with them."

"What'll you do?" I asked, swatting at a mosquito buzzing my head.

Izzie wrung her hands like she was starring in some Shakespearean tragedy. "My parents enrolled me in Jacoby's Girl's Academy for senior year. I'll have to live in a *dooooorm*! I'll have a *cuuuuurfew*! There are no *booooys*!"

"At least they aren't sending you to Hogwarts."

I don't even know if Izzie heard me. "My friends at Kingsway High will desert me; they'll call me a *priiiiivate* school snob."

"Your real friends will stick by you," I lied. Sure they would. Like Jemma had stuck by me.

"And I'll have to wear an ugly plaid uniform! My *liiiiife* is over!"

Something clicked. "Now I get it, Izzie. You were hoping Alain would hook up with you and let you move into his house for the school year."

Izzie stopped by the side of the road to pick a daisy. She began plucking off the petals one by one. "Is that *craaaaazy?* Then again, don't answer that. Alain's obviously *immuuuuune* to my come-ons. He told me last night—well, he screamed—that he was 'head over heels in love.' With *youuuuu*, Rainey. No guy's ever told *meeeeee* that he loved me." Izzie sighed. "Not even Sammy."

WESTEX was on the B.C. ferry to Nanaimo by nine-thirty. Wind had blown the early morning fog from the Strait of Georgia, giving us a spectacular view of the Gulf Islands. The Six-Pack visited the gift shop, fed quarters to the vending machines and arcade games, and hung over the railings on the outdoor decks, hoping for a glimpse of the orcas and dolphins our guidebooks had assured us were down there somewhere.

"The drop doesn't bother you?" I asked Alain.

"Water's different. I can dive," he replied, and for a second, he got this devilish look on his face that suggested he just might.

Twenty minutes before we were due to reach port, Izzie, flushed with excitement, returned to the deck from a trip to the washroom. "Be very quiet and follow me," she whispered to us all.

With the five of us trailing, Izzie turned a bend, stopped, and put a finger to her lips. She pointed to a stairwell leading up to the highest deck. A sign indicated, "STAFF ONLY."

"We're not allowed up there," Frank whispered back.

"Look *uuuuunder* the staircase."

Alain was the first to burst out laughing. His cackling spread among the Six-Pack like wildfire.

Dan and Brooke were making out. Kissing up a storm. Tonsil hockey worthy of a Stanley Cup.

Alain tossed his hat up in the air and caught it on his head, and the *entire* Six-Pack broke into a chorus of *The Love Boat* theme song.

Brooke regained her composure quickly. "Just practicing some advanced CPR techniques," she said, brushing wrinkles from the front of her T-shirt.

Dan, his face covered in blotchy red patches of humiliation, nodded. "Practice makes perfect," he choked out, which set the Six-Pack hooting again.

Homer gestured for us all to move on. "I don't want to be around when they start in on the Heimlich maneuver."

During an early fast-food lunch in Nanaimo, Dan swallowed his embarrassment in one gulp—along with the Big Mac on his tray—in order to thrill us with the history of Vancouver Island, after which Brooke passed around itineraries.

"Well, folks, this is it," she said. "Seven short days left before we turn and start back home. This week, we'll visit the Royal B.C. Museum in Victoria, bike the Marine Scenic Drive, hike the Juan de Fuca Trail, explore the—"

"Uh, excuse me? Will we have any free time?" Frank asked. He wasn't nearly as interested in exploring the Pacific Coast as he was in exploring Meena.

"*NO!*" Dan and Brooke shouted simultaneously.

Frank's face fell like an avalanche.

Brooke rolled her eyes. "We were just kidding. There will be the usual amount of free time."

"Good," I smirked, dipping a fry in ketchup. "Because there's nothing like having time for a good game of *Trivial Pursuit*."

"Huh?" Dan set his milkshake down mid-slurp.

Brooke threw a McNugget at my head. "Don't be a wise-ass," she said.

CHAPTER FIFTY-ONE

We took the Trans-Canada south from Nanaimo to Victoria, then headed northwest up the other side of Vancouver Island, past Sooke to French Beach Provincial Park on the Juan de Fuca Strait.

Now old pros at setting up camp, we completed our chores and were relaxing on the rocky beach—a long swath of multi-colored pebbles, ocean vegetation left behind by the last tide, and massive driftwood stumps—by three PM.

After a quick dip in the frigid ocean waves, I stretched out on my towel in the wind and sun. And there, on the western-most edge of Canada, I promptly fell asleep.

Much later, a familiar laugh roused me. *Snort-snort-snort.*

Startled, I opened my eyes. Lynda—*Lynda?*—was perched twenty feet away on a long driftwood log beside Alain. A cookie tin sat between them. The remainder of the Six-Pack, it seemed, had vacated.

Lynda was using the antiseptic wipes, scissors, and tweezers that she always carried around in her purse to remove Alain's stitches. Lynda snipped and pulled. Alain winced and stuffed a cookie in his mouth. Lynda would wait for him to finish chewing, then the cycle would begin again.

"Hey! Save some of those cookies for me!" I called.

A ray of sunshine lit up Lynda's face. "Hey! Sleeping Beauty!"

Flabbergasted at her presence, I scooted gracelessly across the sand like a three-legged spider. I hiked myself up onto the log on Lynda's other side. "What are you *doing* here?" I asked, wondering if I was having some sort of sun-induced hallucination.

"Maintenance strike at U of T. My conference was canceled last minute. I'd already booked the time off at the hospital, so decided to take a vacation."

"To spy on me?"

"No. To *Japan*. To surprise your father. To see a few sights. He and I will fly home together at the end of next week."

"So what are you doing *here?*"

Lynda sighed. "I knew ahead of time that my overseas flight would include a fifteen-hour stopover in Vancouver, so I checked the copy of your itinerary that Greg left with me and figured out a way to surprise you, too. I rented a car at the airport in Vancouver, drove onto the ferry, and well... here I am! I can't stay long, but I... I don't know... I *missed* you, Rainey. Don't be upset. I brought *lots* of cookies."

And God, the look on Lynda's face. She really *had* missed me. And it had only been six weeks since I'd seen her. Six days since we spoke on the phone.

Sara had been gone seventeen years without missing me. Without ever getting on a plane, renting a car, taking a ferry, or anything else, just to *surprise* me.

Alain cut in. "The doc here said my stitches were ready to come out and saved me a trip to a walk-in clinic. And good news! Apparently, in a year or so, the scars will fade enough so that my face won't look so much like a chewed-up baseball mitt."

"One more to go." Lynda snipped, yanked.

Alain winced, grabbed another cookie.

"Here." Lynda thrust the tin at his chest. "Take the rest back to camp with you. Rainey and I will be along shortly."

Alain bent down and kissed Lynda's cheek. "Thanks, Doc." Then he nibbled my earlobe. "See ya later, alligator."

"Is he always like that?" Lynda asked, watching Alain lope off down the beach.

"Pretty much."

"I like him. He's funny, and he could charm the spots off a leopard. But he's intense, too, isn't he? There's this incredible depth in his eyes. He's probably a lot more mature than he acts."

So she sees it, too, I thought.

"And, wow... those pecs. You're being careful, right?" Lynda asked, the same way she might ask if I'd like more potatoes at dinner.

I was aghast. "How did you... ? Cripes, did Alain—"

Snort-snort-snort. "Relax. It was just a hunch."

I frowned at Lynda. "You made sure I'd be... careful."

"Greg wasn't too pleased about me slipping those condoms into your care package," she admitted.

I dug my foot into the sand. "Doesn't Greg realize that using condoms when he was my age would have saved him a lot of trouble? Trouble named *Rainey?*"

"He wanted a child, Rainey. He wanted a family."

"Get real. What teenage guy right out of high school wants a barfy, poopy, one-legged baby to deal with?"

Well... maybe Carlos.

"He'd just lost his mother. He had no other living relatives," Lynda said. "Greg never thought of you as anything but a gift."

"He *told* you that?"

"On our first date."

"And you agreed to a second?"

Lynda nodded. "Probably for that very reason. Well... that and the fact he's hotter than a jalapeno. Anyhow... you and Alain are still making time for your schoolwork, right?"

"I'm not a freaking nymphomaniac!"

"Alain's your first?"

"Yeah," I said. "So?"

Lynda gazed out across the strait towards the Olympic Mountains in Washington state. *Oh, no, here comes a lecture,* I thought.

She turned to me. *Snort-snort-snort.* "My first time? Back seat
of a Honda Civic. After a Bryan Adams concert. I was fifteen.
Freddy Sampson. He was popular and athletic, and all the other
girls warned me that he was a scumbag, but did I care? He dumped
me a week after the concert. Sure, I got over him, but by the time
I met my first true love, at nineteen, I wished I'd waited."

"So you disapprove." *Did I care?* "You think I should have
waited for my 'first true love.'"

Snort-snort-snort. "What if you've *already* met him?"

Okay, so maybe she didn't necessarily disapprove. *But what
if Alain is my first true love, but I'm not his?* Sara had been
Greg's first true love and... well... you know.

"Can I ask you a question, Lynda?"

"Of course."

"What happened with you and your first true love? Why did
you breakup? He wasn't a hockey player, was he?"

Snort-snort-snort. "He was a musician. A cellist. And Chris
and I *didn't* breakup." Lynda took a deep breath. "We got married.
But he died of leukemia four years later. We never had a chance
to start a family."

"I... I'm... "

Lynda rested her hand on mine. I didn't pull mine away.
"Don't say you're sorry, Rainey; it was part of what brought
Greg and me together. We both knew what it was like to lose
someone we loved. We both knew what it was like to try to

move on. To open up again to... opportunity."

To *love*. I had questioned many things about Lynda over the course of her relationship with my father, but I had never questioned her love for my father. It oozed from her pores and smelled like cinnamon rolls fresh from the oven. "Lynda? I met her yesterday. Sara."

Lynda beamed. "You did it! I'm so glad!"

I stared at her pale, freckled hand resting on my tanned one. "Can I tell you something, Lynda?"

"Of course, Rainey."

"It's major. You have to *promise* me that you'll wait until I get home before you discuss it with Greg. It's something I have to tell him myself. In person. But I want you there when I do it. He'll need you. *And* a stiff drink, most likely. It's going to freak him out."

"More than when I told him about your little bear adventure?"

"How bad was it?"

"Pretty bad... but everything's okay now. Nothing like a little overseas phone sex to—"

I recoiled. "Eeeeew, Lynda. Too much information. Anyway, this is worse. Or maybe *not* so bad. Depending on how... It's about Sara. And Evan."

Lynda's forehead crinkled with confusion. "Evan?"

"Evan's my brother. Greg's other kid."

As the tide rolled in, and the sun sank lower over the Pacific, I told Lynda everything I knew so far about Sara/Joanna and Evan. "So... how would you feel about having another teenager in the house in January?" I concluded.

"That's quite some West Coast souvenir you'd be toting home, Rainey. You know there's room for a half-dozen kids in the house. But it would require many discussions first. Between Greg and me. Between Greg and Sara. And does Evan even want to come to Toronto? Sara's not just looking for a place to dump Evan so she can take off to the Yukon unencumbered, is she?

I shook my head vehemently. "Evan is *dead* set against moving to Whitehorse. He wants to get to know me, and he knows that Greg has excellent connections in the tech world." I paused and fished around in the zippered pocket of my shorts for the folded up sticky note Evan had pressed into my hand when I left, containing his cell phone number and e-mail address. "Evan's... *earstoyouspock,*" I read to Lynda. That would win her over.

"He's what?"

"Not what, *who. Earstoyouspock.* Evan is a Trekkie, too. He's been visiting Greg's Web site for years. He told me he was just on-line chatting to you, to *alienbaby,* a few days ago, about..."

"*The Next Generation!*" Lynda gasped. "That was... wow, talk about 'the next generation.'"

"And Captain G's the one who told Evan about the game design program at CTI."

Lynda whistled through her teeth. "And Captain G's still in Japan, oblivious to it all."

"I miss him," I said, gazing out over the Pacific as if it were possible to actually see him all the way across that big ocean in Japan. "It's been such a long summer."

"I miss him, too," Lynda said, wistfully. "Especially now that I'm bulging with... news of my own. "

"What news?"

Lynda flashed me a sly smile. "It's one of the reasons I'm off to surprise your dad in Japan. I was thinking of waiting until you were all back home to say anything, but... oh, what the hell." Lynda took my hand. Placed my palm on her stomach.

"*You're going to have a baby!*" I screeched.

Lynda gulped. "I'm going to have... *two* babies!" she screeched back.

"Twin Vulcan babies! Greg will be so... excited!"

"The poor guy left for Japan thinking he only had one kid. He'll come back and find out he has *four!*"

She reached into a shopping bag. "I brought another surprise for you, Rainey. Just a hunch that it was something you could use." She pulled out my old mid-grade prosthesis, the one I'd *insisted* I could do without that summer—insisted my Flexileg and crutches would be enough. It didn't afford me the same range of motion as the Flexileg. It had developed a chronic squeak after Simon used it as a chew toy. The ankle joint had developed a bad habit of locking and tripping me up when I least expected it. But I knew the casing was undamaged and would fit over my stump; I hadn't grown since I was fourteen. I pulled off the broken Flexileg and slipped it on. It was like putting on fuzzy slippers after a week in too-tight dress shoes.

"Thanks, Lynda!"

"It's just until you get back to Toronto and can get the Flexileg fixed. I got you an appointment at the prosthetic clinic the second week of September."

"But... can Greg afford... maybe I need to take a semester off school and find a practical/lucrative job just to foot the bill."

Snort-snort-snort. "Foot the bill... that's a joke, right? Greg told me where to find the insurance policy. It covers *everything.*"

"Everything?"

"Greg knows you better than you might think he does, Rainey. He told me what you did to Derek when you were seven."

"I should have hit him harder."

"You've moved on nicely, Rainey."

"Lynda?" I hesitated. "I've got... kind of... an embarrassing question."

Snort-snort-snort. "I'm an OB/GYN. There are no embarrassing questions. And once you get home, I'll see if Carol can see you at the clinic." Dr. Carol Walters shared an office with Lynda at the Parkdale Youth Clinic. Lynda worked there on Tuesday afternoons, dispensing birth control advice and pre-natal care to teens referred by schools and family doctors. "She'll put you on oral contraceptives, give you an hour-long lecture on why you must absolutely still use condoms every single time, and send you home with enough pamphlets to start your own consulting service."

How did Lynda do it? How did she always know what I needed, even when I didn't know what I needed half the time? "Couldn't you just write me a prescription?" I asked.

Lynda shook her head. "You'll need blood work and a physical."

"Yuck."

"You're playing with the big kids now, Rainey."

Alain told me once that the greatest asset a photographer could have wasn't a great camera; it was the ability to know and capture "moments." No one took a picture, but I'll never forget the smell of the sea, the wind in our hair, the long shadow created on the sand when I stood up, bringing Lynda with me, and hugging her hard. Golden dog hair clung to the shoulder of her sweater and her hair smelled like blueberry muffins. She reminded me of... home.

"I love you," I whispered in her ear.

I used to assume that anyone as competent and confident as Lynda couldn't be anything but cool and collected in any situation. But maybe, like me, she only pretended to suck it up.

"I love you, too, Rainey," she cried into my hair.

Minutes later, we took one more long look across the strait and gathered up our belongings.

"This place is beautiful," Lynda sighed.

"An artist's paradise," I agreed wistfully.

"Will you paint a mural in the babies' room next winter?" she asked as we walked up the road to the campsite. "Anything you want. After all, you're going to be the famous artist of the family, aren't you?"

There was that million-dollar question again. But, for the first time all summer, the answer seemed obvious. "I'd love to!" I replied. Anyone with Lynda's brand of confidence in me deserved the moon, or, at least, way better than the crap I'd been giving her for the past year. "And... maybe... I could paint a mural in your office, too? Maybe some of your patients would see it and want one, too?"

"What a fabulous business idea!" Lynda exclaimed. "What a wonderful way to start your professional painting career!"

Business? Professional? "You make it sound like I'm headed for art school next fall," I sighed.

"*Aren't you?* OCAD is so close to home. I'd hate it if you up and left for university just when we were starting to get to know each other."

"But... Greg..."

Lynda stopped in her tracks and turned to me. She rested her firm, confident, baby-delivering hands on my shoulders and looked me in the eyes. "He wants you to be happy."

I sighed. "Then what are all his lectures about?" I deepened my voice to imitate Greg. *"Art is a nice hobby, Rainey, but make sure you don't paint yourself into a corner."*

Snort-snort-snort. "To provoke you to get out there in the art world and prove him wrong."

"He told you that?"

"No."

"Then how do you know it's true."

Lynda shrugged. "It's up to you to *make* it true."

"Will you stay for dinner?" Dan asked Lynda when we arrived back at camp.

"He probably wants you to *make* dinner," I warned her.

"I'd *love* to!" Well... that was Lynda for you. Only she could take a mega-can of brown beans, two iffy green peppers, a package of frozen hot dogs, and a jumble of miscellaneous spices, and come up with something that had everyone lined up for seconds.

When the last bean was gone, Lynda pulled three extra tins of cookies from the trunk of her rented car.

Alain draped an arm around her shoulders. "In September, don't be surprised if I show up on your doorstop every morning like a stray dog begging for scraps."

"I'll do better than feed you," Lynda said. "I'll *teach* you how to cook for yourself. Rainey pretends she has a learning disability when it comes to the culinary arts, but you seem to have more of an 'appetite' for that sort of knowledge."

Lynda had taken it in stride when I told her Alain had his own house. "That'll be a huge responsibility," was all she said. "Let him know he's welcome at our place anytime."

"Even overnight?" I joked—sort of.

"Just make sure he doesn't break his neck on the fire escape."

CHAPTER FIFTY-TWO

The next morning, we set out north along the coast for the final physical challenge of our journey: a leisurely (ha!) four-day, forty-seven kilometer hike along the Juan de Fuca Marine Trail.

Caution signs were posted everywhere; this was black bear and cougar territory. Dan had gone to an outfitters the previous day and gotten "bear bells" for all of us that fastened to our packs with velcro loops.

"You're packing a gun, now, too, I hope," Frank said, not convinced that a one-inch metal ball, noisy as it was, would save him from the jaws of a hungry carnivore.

"We sound like Santa's sleigh," Homer exclaimed when we first set out, prompting us to spend over an hour marching through the forest belting out every Christmas carol we knew.

Except for early morning fog as thick as a McDonald's shake, and night temperatures that dipped into bone-numbing single digits, we were blessed with good weather. Traipsing through rainforests around gigantic firs and cedars, wading in tide pools along the shore, crossing suspension bridges (Alain with his eyes forced shut and me guiding him across like a faithful guide dog), and huddling around campfires on the beach each night, listening to Dan tell stories of the West Coast Aboriginals, the Six-Pack regained the camaraderie that had eroded over the past weeks as alliances formed and personal battles raged.

As for me, my dusty, squeaky, temperamental old prosthesis had given me back the spring in my step—literally.

After four long days in the wild, we found ourselves at an Esso station in the city of Victoria first thing the next morning.

Brooke filled the van with gas. Dan filled us with facts.

He stated what we'd all known since third grade: that Victoria had been named in honor of Queen Victoria of England, and was the capital of British Columbia.

He stated what we'd already observed for ourselves: that a great deal of Vancouver Island's old-growth rain forest had been decimated by clear-cutting in the past century.

And he stated the wild and wacky: that in her day, the artist and writer Emily Carr was reviled as an eccentric old biddy who preferred the company of dogs to humans.

Without WESTEX—and maybe Alain—*and* Lynda—that may have been me in a few years.

Brooke parked on Dallas Road across from Beacon Hill Park so we could pose around the Trans-Canada "Mile 0" sign at the foot of Douglas Street like billions of tacky tourists before us. Then, with rented bicycles beneath us, the eight of us set off northeast along the Marine Scenic Drive as far as Mount Douglas Park, where we had lunch and played Frisbee before retracing our steps—or tread marks, as it were—back downtown, where Dan made us drag our sore butts up Douglas Street to the Royal B.C. Museum.

"Are you trying to *kill* us, Dan?" Izzie moaned, after our short guided tour.

Dan beamed. "Exercise keeps us all out of trouble."

"But it's free time now," Brooke said. "All we ask is that you gather back at Beacon Hill Park at seven, so we can arrive back at camp before dark."

Growing nostalgic now that our days together were numbered, the Six-Pack stuck together and pressed on to see more sights, despite our fatigue. We visited Emily Carr's house, had an early dinner at Market Square, and rode around town in a double-decker bus.

As seven PM approached, we began wondering out loud where Brooke and Dan had disappeared to. We hadn't crossed paths with them all afternoon.

"The Empress Hotel?" Meena suggested.

Homer shook his head. "They weren't dressed up enough to go to such a fancy place."

Izzie giggled. "They're probably at the Holiday Inn, not dressed at all."

When we met up at the designated time and place, nobody asked Brooke and Dan where they'd been. They didn't ask where the Six-Pack had been. In fact, nobody said much of anything until Dan stopped in front of a tree. "It's a Garry Oak," he explained. "The largest and oldest brand of deciduous tree in western Canada."

"Looks like a gigantic spear of broccoli," Alain said, tossing his Expos cap up in the air and...

His eyes grew wide with surprise. Alain's hat was up in the tree, stuck on a branch at least forty feet above ground. "It must have got swept away in the wind," he said.

Except there was no wind. Not even a breeze.

"You threw it up there on purpose, you *doooooofus*," Izzie remarked.

Had he?

Alain just stood there, gaping up to where his dad's cap was lodged in the tree. It was up too high to reach it with a stick. Too high, even, to shake it down like fruit from an apple tree.

"Just leave it up there, Alain," Dan said. "It's time to head back to camp."

"I'm not leaving here without it," Alain said, in the same tone of voice he'd used at the Hinton Hospital when he'd refused to let Dan and Brooke call his mother.

"The fire department isn't going to come and rescue a hat from a tree," Frank said.

"Just a minute. I'm thinking."

"Maybe we could scout around for a pole of some sort?" Homer said helpfully.

Alain shook his head and inhaled sharply. Then, "I'm going up."

Without another moment's hesitation, Alain, as deftly as a squirrel, climbed the tree, shimmied out on the thick limb where the cap was lodged, grabbed it, and put it on.

And that was all it took. Or maybe Alain had been tossing his Dad's cap up, practicing mentally for *that* day, *that* tree, all summer.

Now, just as deftly, he swung down hand-over-hand, like Tarzan, to a branch closer to the ground. Hanging by one arm, he began screeching like a monkey.

Monkey see, monkey do. Two minutes later, the entire Six-Pack was up in the tree, striking precarious primate poses.

"Group shot!" Dan held out Alain's camera. "Say cheese!"

"*SEX!*" we all yelled.

"Doesn't this remind you of a scene from *The Sound of Music?*" Izzie remarked.

Homer laughed. "All we're missing are those hideous green outfits made of curtains."

That got us all belting out, "The Hills Are Alive..." which attracted a lot of tourist attention, *and* that of a humorless park attendant who told us to "get out of the tree before I call the cops."

"Ready to go home, everyone?" Brooke asked the Six-Pack later that evening, as we gathered around the picnic table for our nightly team meeting. It was our last night at French Beach, our last night at the western edge of Canada. Tomorrow, we'd begin our ten-day trek east through Kelowna, Calgary, Drumheller, and Moose Jaw, back to Toronto. To home.

Dan ahemed. "Did you know... that Thomas Wolfe said, *'You can't go home again'*?"

"Suits me," Frank said.

"All that means," Brooke explained, "is that when you leave the so-called family nest for a time, you change. Your family changes, too. When you go back, things may be better or worse, but they'll never be the way you left them."

"How do you know when you're ready to leave the nest for good?" Meena asked.

"You get *pushed* out," Frank said. Convinced that his mother—who'd been off and even *under* the wagon all summer—wasn't going to dry out anytime soon, Frank had called home the previous day to say that he'd only be back long enough to collect his stuff. He was going to room with Alain for a while. I suspected that Frank's mother had called Frank a lot of things he chose not to repeat to the rest of us. I also suspected that that one act had taken more courage than anything else Frank had accomplished that summer.

Izzie, Homer, and Alain nodded in agreement. Their reasons for being "pushed" out of the family nest were different, but

E P I L O G U E

The night before we arrived back at Toronto, the Six-Pack sat around a final campfire at Sturgeon Bay Provincial Park on the east shores of Lake Huron, contemplating the flames and our futures. Far from excited to be within a stone's throw of home, we were pensive, wondering if WESTEX had just been a good time, or if the skills and knowledge we'd gained about Canada and ourselves those past eight weeks would serve us well in the challenging months ahead.

Alain was leaving in two days for his week-long visit to New Brunswick. He'd invited me to go with him, but my family dynamic was about to change forever, and I needed to be with Greg and Lynda, at least until the initial dust settled.

"I'll miss you while you're gone," I said.

"As tempting as it might be," Alain laughed, "don't moon over me too much."

"You won't miss *me?*" I asked.

"Nope," he joked. "I'll be too busy practicing my bagpipes to their situations were similar. They were all now pretty much on their own.

"Maybe it's easier that way than having to decide for yourself when you're ready for independence," I mused.

"I'll *never* be ready," Meena concluded.

"Then I'll have to kidnap you," Frank told her.

"Can I kidnap *you* from your nest, too?" Alain whispered in my ear. He got a noseful of my unruly hair and sneezed.

I shook my head. WESTEX had taught him and the others how to live without their families. But, strangely, it had brought me closer to mine. It might be several years before I could—before I'd even *want* to—leave home. "But maybe you could kidnap me from my tent tonight," I suggested.

Alain got up from the table and began bouncing around in circles, hooting, and shaking his arms at the clear night sky.

"What is that crazy boy up to now?" I heard Dan ask Brooke.

"It's a rain dance!" Alain called to him over his shoulder.

"Now why would—"

"Why don't you go join him, Dan?" Brooke laughed.

Seconds later, Dan, Brooke, Alain, and the rest of the Six-Pack were jumping and laughing around the picnic table. No longer about rain, the dance had become a simple celebration to mark the turning point of a complicated summer.

give you a second thought."

Truthfully, I'd be busy, too. I had to talk to Greg. I'd invited Lynda to go with me to see a watercolor exhibition at the AGO. I planned to visit Dr. Walters at the youth clinic. And I'd be stopping by Pineview to pick up my fall work schedule.

"Think you'll run into Carlos?" Alain frowned.

"I hope so." If Carlos was back at Pineview, it meant that he was doing okay, that he was back on track.

A long pause.

"Alain, don't even—"

"Fooled you," he said, nuzzling my neck. "Say 'hi' to the asshole for me."

I knew better than to think things would always be so easy between Alain and me. And I knew, even if he didn't, that there existed a possibility that once he returned to the family farm he wouldn't come back. That he'd see that his family needed him more than his hockey team or I did.

I also knew better than to *assume* that Lynda would have healthy, happy Vulcan twins, and that Evan would move to Toronto, and that the Williamson family tree would grow tall and strong. As families spliced, and branches thickened, there were bound to be knots and gnarls and lightning strikes and bugs along with the blossoms.

"What's the first thing you want to do when you get back to Toronto?" Homer asked. "Me? I'm going to keep practicing my J-stroke. In my cousin's bathtub."

"Speaking of bathtubs, I'm already fantasizing about a long, hot bubble bath," Meena sighed.

Frank grinned. "What time should I be there?"

Meena scowled. "Don't even think about it! Wait until some night my parents go out."

Izzie rolled her eyes. "I have to go shopping—for—grrrrrrrr!—regulation navy *kneeeeehighs*. But, hey! All is not lost!" she added, tossing her hair. "I read in my new *Vogue* that *plaaaaaid* skirts are making a comeback this fall."

Alain tossed his Expos cap in the air and caught it on his head. "I'll be making a mad dash to my darkroom to develop my 'Nutcase Tara' photos."

"What about you, Rainey?" Meena asked. "What are you planning to do?"

Something else Greg was always saying, some old quote: *The journey of a thousand miles begins with a single step.* I'd traveled over twelve thousand kilometers that "Wild West" summer, but the trip of my life was just beginning.

I took a deep breath and grinned around the group. "I'm going to paint."